Hero could

Craggy with l... smile to lighte... which no long... without express... He had given no sign of recognition and neither did she. The man she remembered so vividly did not resemble this creature in the slightest. How could she have been so mistaken? wondered Hero despairingly. Her childish dream had no part to play in the real world of a young woman past her prime with no valid hope of marrying except for purely worldly reasons.

Dear Reader

Sarah Westleigh has enjoyed a varied life. Working as a local government officer in London, she qualified as a chartered quantity surveyor. She assisted her husband in his chartered accountancy practice, at the same time managing an employment agency. Moving to Devon, she finally found time to write, publishing short stories and articles, before discovering historical novels.

Recent titles by the same author:

CHEVALIER'S PAWN
A LADY OF INDEPENDENT MEANS
ESCAPE TO DESTINY
A MOST EXCEPTIONAL QUEST
HERITAGE OF LOVE
LOYAL HEARTS
SET FREE MY HEART
THE INHERITED BRIDE

FELON'S
FANCY

Sarah Westleigh

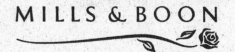

MILLS & BOON, the Rose Device and LEGACY OF LOVE are trademarks of the publisher.
Harlequin Mills & Boon Limited,
Eton House, 18–24 Paradise Road, Richmond, Surrey TW9 1SR
This edition published by arrangement with
Harlequin Enterprises B.V.

© Sarah Westleigh 1995

ISBN 0 263 79410 5

Set in 10 on 12 pt Linotron Times
04-9512-79228

Typeset in Great Britain by CentraCet, Cambridge
Printed and bound in Great Britain by
BPC Paperbacks Ltd

CHAPTER ONE

THE Honourable Hero Langage stared at her sire in blank astonishment.

'Wed?' she cried, her utter disbelief echoing around the library, the threadbare carpet and few books gracing the shelves powerless to absorb and soften the outrage in her voice. 'You wish me to wed, Papa?'

Baron Polhembury glowered across the desk, intent upon subduing his daughter into obedience. 'That is my command, miss.'

'Why now?' Hero demanded abruptly. 'Since Mama died and I left the schoolroom you have refused to introduce me into any society where I might meet an acceptable suitor, for it served your purpose to keep me here at Polhembury Hall as your housekeeper. Why now?' she repeated, and added indignantly, 'And to a creature I have never met? Whose reputation is of the lowest kind?'

'Would you rather see me ruined?' blustered her father in return. 'What would become of you then, miss, a lady no longer of tender years cast adrift upon the world? Without a penny piece to your name?'

'And whose fault is it,' raged Hero, shivering at the thought but determined to fight for her future happiness, 'that I am almost three and twenty and still unwed? Or that you are threatened with ruin for debt?'

'Mine, daughter, I freely acknowledge my guilt, but now I am making amends,' declared the baron grandly,

thrusting aside the past with a wave of his hand. 'I
have found a gentleman of considerable rank and
substantial means willing, nay, demanding to wed you!
In return for your hand he will settle my debts, thus
setting both matters of which you complain to rights.'
The baron heaved his considerable bulk to his feet,
put his fists on the desk and leant repressively towards
her. 'I will brook no more arguments, miss. You will
wed the Earl of Calverstock,' he ordered heavily.

'But I can never come to love such a man!'

The cry came from her heart. For an instant Hero
was back in the village, seeing the hard, harsh features
of the man she had met so suddenly in the doorway of
the grocer's, the collision between them making her
drop her basket. He had given an apologetic smile as
he stood back, which had softened the lines of his face
and held so much charm that Hero's heart had lurched
and confusion had brought colour to her cheeks.

'My apologies, ma'am! How infernally careless of
me!' he'd murmured, making an impeccable bow.

Although a gentleman of means and taste by the cut
of his blue superfine jacket, he had wasted no more
time on pleasantries but set about gathering up her
scattered fruit and putting the plums back in her
basket. His grey eyes had twinkled down at her as he
had handed it back. She had been able to see the
admiration in them, won despite the old faded blue
dimity gown she wore and the rather shapeless chip
bonnet upon her head, and the knowledge had brought
a deeper blush to her cheeks.

'Thank you, sir,' she had managed to utter, dipping
a small curtsy of appreciation.

Instinctively, she had known he was a man she could

come to respect, admire, even love. She had never met his like before and, incarcerated in Polhembury, was unlikely to do so again.

'Love?' scorned her father, breaking ruthlessly across her thoughts, which had, since that afternoon a few days ago, possessed a distressing tendency to stray in the stranger's direction whenever not otherwise occupied. 'What has love to say to anything? It is high time you put all that foolish schoolroom nonsense behind you, miss! Ladies of your rank wed for duty, for fortune and position, not for love. You have been reading too many of those rubbishy novels you borrow from the vicar's wife.'

'Miss Austen is not considered rubbishy,' muttered Hero, not because she felt the need to defend her reading but because she must keep arguing with her father or submit.

Lord Polhembury glanced down briefly at a letter lying open on his desk. Hero noted the crest embossed at the head of the page, the bold decisive writing beneath and the self-confident signature.

'His lordship is coming here tomorrow,' Lord Polhembury informed her curtly. 'You will provide hospitality and present yourself in your most attractive gown.'

'The old green velvet riding habit? 'Tis too hot for this weather,' said Hero, scornful in her turn. 'I will wear my yellow sprigged muslin if I must. Matty can iron it up for me. But I do not promise to accept the gentleman's offer.'

'You will have no choice,' her father informed her, his heavy features grim. 'Be about your business, child.'

She was no longer a child, thought Hero rebelliously

as she mounted the stairs to find the sanctuary of her room. There had been something ominous in her father's tone as he'd told her she had no choice which worried her considerably. What plan had he hatched with this ex-convict who had inherited an earldom and an immense fortune to go with it? She would put nothing past *him*, or her father either.

She could not, would not submit. She would run away rather.

As the idea came to her a slow smile lit up Hero's anxious face, bringing a gleam to eyes which she had long ago decided matched the colour of the hazelnuts growing in the hedgerows despite the darker patterns etched into the light golden-brown iris. Her determined chin set firmly. It would be difficult, but she could do it.

Matty, knocking sixty now and crippled with rheumatism, was too old to go with her, though. Could she travel alone? And how? She had no money of her own to pay coach fares and the month's meagre housekeeping allowance was already spent. Otherwise she might take the stage to London, if she could manage to make her way to Exeter. Her late mother's sister lived in Dorset Square and there had been talk of Hero's staying with her Aunt Augusta for her come-out, but talk was all it had been. Her father had had no intention of depriving Polhembury Hall of her valuable services. Not until now. He must be desperate to have his debts repaid.

Well, he would have to manage in the future, whether she wed or ran away. Even if she had to walk, she determined, she would get to London somehow. Perhaps Bessy Foster, the youthful maid of all work, would go with her. Hero no sooner thought of that solution than she discarded it. Bessy had no education and little sense. When Hero's plums had scattered on the ground all she had been able to do was first shriek and then cry out embarrassingly, 'Oh, Miss Hero! After all that risk us went to to pick they, too!' while the gentleman had immediately responded by grovelling around retrieving them. Grovelling extremely elegantly, she remembered with a pang. Though his hands had been strong, had looked no stranger to hard work, unusual in a gentleman, they had handled the ripe plums with exquisite care.

But Bessy would be nothing more than a hindrance on the journey. The young maid had lost what little wit she had once possessed after her brother was caught stealing produce from the gardener's store and been transported for seven years for the offence. Hero had pleaded with her father not to prosecute the lad— he was young, worried sick because his father had been stricken down and his family near starving, unable to survive on his pittance of a wage. But Lord Polhembury had ignored her entreaties.

'Let Ben Foster off?' he'd snorted. 'You are too soft-hearted, Hero. 'Twould only encourage others to become criminals. We'd be stripped bare in no time!'

Ben had been sent to the penal colony of New South Wales on the other side of the world. Bessy's father had died and her mother and the younger children been reduced to paupers. Hero had taken them food whenever she could and eventually the older children had found employment in the village. Then, a year or so ago, their fortunes had improved considerably when Mrs Foster had been offered a position as housekeeper to a widow living in Gloucestershire. How she had come by the appointment was as much a mystery to her as it was to Hero, but she had gone, and had taken all her children with her except Bessy, who had asked to stay. The cook, Mrs Blackler, was kind to the girl, who adored Miss Hero. Besides, she knew where she was at the Hall, she didn't want to leave for somewhere strange, even to be with her mother.

Lord Polhembury had been reluctant to keep Bessy on after Ben was convicted but in this Hero's arguments had prevailed. The girl was not responsible for her brother's crime, they had no reason to suspect her honesty and her labour was cheap.

But none of this helped to solve her own immediate problem. Mrs Blackler, Matty and Bessy were the only servants still resident at the Hall apart from a boot boy who acted inadequately as footman, answering the door and running messages. Many of the rooms in the house were disused, the furniture languishing under dust covers. The heavy housework was done by women from the village, who came in daily. They could not be called upon to accompany her. A groom and boy lived over the stables and a gardener and his wife occupied a cottage on the estate, for the baron would not consider giving up his horses whatever other economies he might demand, and the services of a competent gardener were imperative to keep the kitchen provided with vegetables. But she could not call upon any of them for help, either.

Young ladies were not supposed to travel alone, but Hero reckoned she was old enough to take care of herself and strong-minded enough to disregard what people might say. In any case they would soon forget, provided her aunt received her kindly.

That, of course, could not be guaranteed. She could not even remember what Aunt Augusta looked like, not having seen her since her mother's death. She vaguely remembered a rather formidable lady, not at all like Hero's mother, who had been kind and loving.

But she would cross that bridge when she came to it. Definitely, she refused to remain at Polhembury Hall to be forced into a marriage for the convenience of her father and on the inexplicable whim of the unknown Lord Calverstock.

'You can't, Miss Hero,' said Matty worriedly some time later. 'It wouldn't be right for a young lady like you to travel all that way alone.'

She had come to help Hero change for dinner and found her busy packing her things into a bag ready to leave that very night. Now Matty stood twisting gnarled fingers together in distress.

Hero spread her hands in a helpless gesture. 'I must, Matty, don't you see? Papa is threatening to force me to marry a man I don't even know.'

'You might not find him so bad, my chick,' ventured Matty reasonably.

'A convict?' retorted Hero, frowning at the elderly woman who had been nurse, maid and friend for as long as Hero could remember. 'A man who has inherited a fortune and appears set upon squandering it on gambling and high-flyers?'

'You shouldn't talk like that, Miss Hero,' reproved Matty. 'And 'tis all gossip anyway.'

'I'll wager 'tis true enough,' said Hero, not to be deflected from her opinion.

'Ben Foster is a convict,' reminded Matty. 'He was a decent enough lad. Maybe some of the others must be, too. What was this lord's crime?'

'I don't know,' admitted Hero, thrusting slippers and a nightgown into the bag with unnecessary energy. 'But he was no Ben Foster, he was the grandson of an earl. It must have been something bad for him to end up on a convict ship.'

Matty hesitated. Then she spoke with unusual decision. 'If you must go, then I'll come with you. I'd never forgive myself if anything happened to you, my chick. I promised your blessed mother to look after you, and I will!'

'Oh, Matty!' Impulsively, Hero took the old woman into her arms and drew her close. 'I would never have managed without you! But I can't ask you to make such a long, uncomfortable journey, I really can't, it would be too great a sacrifice. Papa wouldn't have you back, you know, if I couldn't keep you with me. But once I'm settled, I'll send for you if I can, I promise!'

'You're not asking me, I'm telling you, Miss Hero! I'll come with you. But must you go tonight? Why not wait and see what this Lord Calverstock is like? That can't hurt, can it? Then, if you won't have him but your papa still insists on the match, we'll leave tomorrow night. How about that?'

'I don't know.' Hero felt uneasy about that arrangement yet couldn't really fault Matty's reasoning. In the end she nodded. 'All right. As you say, it can't do any harm to wait and meet the man. Truth to tell, I'm curious to see what he's like!'

Matty beamed. 'I'll press your yellow muslin, then, shall I, chick?'

'Yes, all right. But I shall not unpack my bag. For I believe that in the end I shall be forced to seek sanctuary with my aunt in Dorset Square.'

'Is that where you were going?' Matty looked relieved to discover that her mistress had not intended to entirely discard her family, but nevertheless pursed her lips doubtfully. 'She has daughters of her own, I believe, but whether they are wed or not I do not know. You are a beauty, Miss Hero. If they are not already settled...'

Hero chuckled. 'You are prejudiced, Matty! I am far from beautiful! My hair is brown not golden, my eyes hazel and ordinary, not large and blue! And besides, I am practically at my last prayers.'

'But your eyes glow, Miss Hero, and your hair is thick and wavy and when it is just washed, as it is now, it shines like polished mahogany. Don't you put yourself down. You're beautiful all right, even if it isn't in the fair, simpering way folks seem to think is fashionable these days. And you're not too old to wed, that's certain. Otherwise the earl wouldn't be asking for your hand, now, would he?'

Matty was used to speaking her mind and often did it forcefully. But she'd never before been so outspoken about her appearance. Perhaps she did have some semblance of looks, thought Hero, who had never suffered from vanity but rather the reverse. And she did have a reasonable sort of figure, she supposed, tall but not too tall, well-covered without being exactly plump, and it went in and out in all the right places. The yellow sprigged muslin suited her colouring and the tight band beneath her generous bosom allowed the skirt to fall gracefully about her hips and legs. The fashion was out of date, of course, for waists were lower now. But still, with its lowish neckline and tiny puffed sleeves it was just right for summer and it did make her look her best.

Just as her father had ordered, she thought ruefully, and almost determined to wear something else. But in the end she decided to comply with his wishes for the moment. Rebellion could come after her meeting with the earl. She did not relish the prospect of being examined like a prize pig going to market, but two could play at that game. She wondered how his lord-ship would react to her critical scrutiny of him.

His lordship was due to arrive in the afternoon, after the light nuncheon Hero normally had served at two.

Having partaken of very little, she repaired to her room to change. The day was hot and airless and windows were open throughout the used part of the house.

'I swear, I am glad I am not a gentleman,' Hero declared, going to the casement and drawing a deep breath. 'How they manage not to dissolve from the heat inside their coats I shall never comprehend!'

''Tis a different story in the winter,' remarked Matty as Hero returned to sit before her mirror to have her hair dressed. 'They are warm while the ladies shiver in their muslins.'

Hero laughed. 'Right as usual, Matty, though we can always carry a shawl!' She sobered as she watched the maid pile her abundant hair on top of her head and secure it in a becoming topknot with a few curls arranged to frame her face. Matty's gnarled hands could still work wonders, thought Hero affectionately.

Her hairstyle was out of date too, she knew, short hair being all the rage at present, but she had been reluctant to part with the luxuriant growth when she came out of the schoolroom, and still was.

'He won't like my complexion,' she stated critically. 'I have been too much in the sun. Perhaps he will not take to me and then I shall be free of this odious business.'

In sudden frustration she turned to Matty, who gave a 'tsk' of warning. 'Be still, Miss Hero, or you'll spoil your hair!'

'Much I care,' declared Hero forcefully. 'I could do without this charade!' Her voice rose in her indignation. 'How could Papa do this to me? Expect me to wed with a *convict*!'

'He is an earl, my love,' Matty pointed out placatingly.

'Faugh! By some unfortunate quirk of fate! He is the son of a common woman and is an ex-convict to boot! What can Papa be thinking of?'

''Tis not like you to be high in the instep, my chick,' muttered Matty reprovingly. 'No doubt his mama was a gentlewoman, if not one of high degree.'

Hero sighed and went on more moderately, 'I expect you are right, Matty. I am being excessively rude to a woman I do not know—if she is still alive.' She glanced at the clock ticking on her mantelpiece. 'He should be arriving soon. Since I am Papa's hostess, I should go down to the morning-room ready to receive him. No doubt he will think it strange to be entertained there, but the drawing-room is under covers and the notice was too short to bring it back into use.'

'Then you'd better put your gown on,' said Matty dourly. 'Come here, Miss Hero, and stand still. There!'

Matty fastened the last hook, straightened the ribbon streamers flowing from the bow beneath Hero's breasts and stood back. 'You'll do, my chick. He'll be a fool if he doesn't want you for a wife.'

'It seems he does,' muttered Hero. 'Unseen. I wonder what possessed him to pick on me?'

'You will inherit the estate when your father dies,' suggested Matty.

'But he has land enough and the estate is not worth anything now!'

'Maybe it could be.'

'It'd need a lot of money spending on it first.'

'He has more than enough by all accounts.'

'True.' Hero twirled in front of the cheval mirror, hardly aware of the reflection of herself in it, her mind obsessed with what seemed to be an insoluble puzzle. Why had the Earl of Calverstock demanded her hand in marriage? There must be plenty of doting mamas in London who would overlook his deficiencies in order to secure a title for their darlings.

Braced for the coming interview, one hand on the worn handrail, Hero descended the curved oak staircase, one of the beauties of Polhembury Hall which she kept lovingly polished around the threadbare carpet running down the centre of the treads, and made her way to the morning-room, which she used as a sitting-room.

As she approached the door, which was open a crack, she heard voices. Her stomach muscles tightened. Her father's accents were unmistakable and the chilly tones now addressing him must belong to the earl. A quick glance at the hall table, graced by a top hat and riding crop, confirmed her suspicion. He had already arrived.

'I think you will agree that the sum of ten thousand pounds which will be required to clear your debts is an excessively generous payment to make for the hand of your daughter, my lord. You will oblige me by including the horses in your stable in the settlement. Despite my generosity you will not have the means to keep them without incurring more debt, I collect.'

'But——' blustered the baron, but before he could say more the earl interrupted.

'You may keep a hack, of course, for you will need one to see to your estate, which is in a sad state of neglect. Since it is your only source of income, you will doubtless feel obliged to bring it back into productivity. The only alternative to the course I have proposed is incarceration in a sponging-house prior to being thrown into a debtors' prison. The choice is yours.'

Hero stood rigid in the doorway, the shiver shaking her nothing to do with the breeze from the window issuing through it as a draught. The cooling air would have been welcome. But much as she herself had often wished to set her father down, to hear this upstart treating him with barely concealed contempt made her furious. Her papa was in a financial hole caused in no small part, she was convinced, by the man now dunning him. She drew a deep breath and prepared to fling the door back and confront this cold-blooded felon who had bargained so cruelly for her hand.

Even as she did so, she knew that she would have to

save her father, undeserving as he was, painful as it would be. Ten thousand pounds! He had gambled a fortune and lost. She was his only remaining asset, for the run-down estate was not worth half that sum.

Head high, indignation ousting all thought of nervousness, Hero pushed the door wide and stepped into the room.

Her father stood by the empty fireplace, his protest at having his horses taken from him frozen on his lips. Hero scarcely glanced at him. Her eyes focused immediately on the tall stranger standing with his back to the open window, his features in shadow.

The shock almost made her faint, but she was not given to the vapours. Even without a clear look at features imprinted on her mind, she knew it was he. The blue coat was the same, as were the buff pantaloons and the gleaming boots, which must have been dusted off if he had been riding, which it seemed he had.

'Hero!' exclaimed her father, attempting to regain his composure and at the same time project his authority over her. 'There you are, miss! His lordship has already arrived, as you may see. Your lordship,' he turned to the silent man at the window and performed the introduction, his voice hoarse. 'This is my only daughter, Hero. Hero, Lord Calverstock, the man I have decided you shall marry.'

The gentleman moved. He took a step forward and bowed. 'Madam,' he intoned, his voice tight.

Hero could see his face now. Craggy with lines of harsh experience. No smile to lighten and transform it. Grey eyes which no longer laughed but regarded her without expression.

Hero wanted to spit into those chips of ice but breeding won. She inclined her head, made her curtsy and murmured, 'My lord,' her voice as devoid of warmth as his eyes.

He had given no sign of recognition and neither did she. The man she remembered so vividly did not resemble this creature in the slightest. How could she have been so mistaken? wondered Hero despairingly. Even the slight, unlikely hope of meeting him again somewhere, that one faint vision of possible felicity, had been ruthlessly exposed for what it was: the childish dream of an adolescent which had no part to play in the real world of a young woman past her prime with no valid hope of marrying except for purely worldly reasons.

'I trust everything is now satisfactory to you, my lord?' blustered Lord Polhembury, giving his daughter a repressive stare. 'The matter is settled?'

'Provided Miss Langage is agreeable. Have you any objection to the match, madam?'

His voice held an undercurrent of anger Hero could not understand. It made her own hackles rise and she wanted to hurl her defiance in his face but knew she could not. Her rebellion had been short-lived, she thought wretchedly. How she wished she had run away last night, as planned. Yet she could not have remained away, knowing what it was costing her father. She would rather suffer at this man's hands than see her father thrown into a debtors' prison.

Hero lifted her chin and met his eyes, her own full of contempt. 'None, my lord,' she said.

'Good! Capital!' Baron Polhembury's manner became effusive and as a knock at the door echoed into the room he exclaimed, 'That will be the admirable Reverend Cudlip! You have the licence, my lord?'

Calverstock nodded and reached into his breast pocket to produce an official-looking document.

The boot boy announced the vicar. As greetings were exchanged and introductions made Hero realised that she was to be left no time to change her mind. In a few moments, for good or ill, she would be wed.

The preliminaries were short. The vicar, knowing nothing of the tensions in the room, took the proffered special licence and prepared to proceed with the ceremony.

'We shall need witnesses,' he observed, peering through his spectacles first at one and then at the other of those about to be joined in holy matrimony. They were standing stiffly yards apart but he apparently saw nothing strange in this, nor did he sense anything amiss.

His wife would have been immediately aware of her own mutinous discomfort, thought Hero. She and Mrs Cudlip had become friends over the years, for Hero had found the kindly young matron a congenial companion on her visits to the poor and sick in the neighbourhood and she knew her as well as anyone apart from Matty, who probably knew her better than she knew herself. What must Mrs Cudlip be thinking now, presuming she knew the nature of her husband's mission to Polhembury Hall? And Matty. She must be wondering what was going on.

The thoughts flashed through her head as her betrothed's voice answered calmly, 'My man will do for one. He is in the kitchen with Lord Polhembury's cook. She can act as the other. They may also witness your signature to the marriage settlement, my lord. My lawyers witnessed my signature,' went on Calverstock relentlessly, indicating a document already spread upon a nearby table, no doubt the subject of their earlier discussion. 'I shall require yours before the marriage ceremony proceeds.'

Hero opened her mouth to suggest they call Matty instead of Mrs Blackler but closed it again without saying anything. Matty would wonder, be uneasy for her chick, who could do without waves of sympathy flowing over her at the moment. Later she could cry her heart out in the security of Matty's motherly arms.

Her father sent the boot boy to fetch the witnesses but the entire indoor staff, who had been gathered in the kitchen wondering what their betters were up to, presented themselves to ask that they be allowed to witness Miss Hero's wedding. A strange man, grave yet pleasant-looking, presumably the earl's servant, followed them in.

Matty looked anxiously at Hero, who returned a reassuring smile, wondering how long she could hold back the tears which threatened at sight of her maid. In one way she had been right not to want Matty near, yet her presence was a comfort.

The elderly maid then turned her attention to the earl and an expression of relief washed over her lined face. She did not know the half of it, Hero thought bitterly. All Matty saw was a strikingly elegant gentleman of some thirty years whom any girl might be happy to wed at first glance. Bessy had stared blankly at Calverstock with no sign of recognition in her eyes, thank heaven.

After only a slight hestiation her father signed the

marriage settlement. Hero wondered what terms Calverstock had laid down, what provision had been made for her should she become a widow. But really, what did anything matter except that she was about to wed this cold-blooded devil who had her father in his power?

The ceremony proceeded. Hero made her responses in a firm, cold voice, as did her bridegroom, whose given names she discovered to be Drew Wystan. His family name she already knew. Drew Wystan Challoner, fifth earl of Calverstock, became her husband in a matter of minutes.

'You may kiss the bride,' said the Reverend Cudlip benignly the moment he had pronounced the blessing.

Calverstock obliged, doing what was expected of him with no sign of emotion. His hard lips touched hers in a brief salute which lasted no more than a second but it sent such a *frisson* of distaste shivering down Hero's spine that she almost gasped. Heat rose in her cheeks and her vision was momentarily impaired as she saw everything as if through a dark, eddying mist.

'A drink!' her father cried and Hero could sense the relief beneath his false cheerfulnes. 'We must have drinks to toast the happy couple! Mrs Blackler, you may pour ale in the kitchen!'

Mrs Blackler bobbed her thanks and addressed Hero. 'We all wishes you happy, Miss Hero. We'm sorry to lose 'ee, that we be, but we be that glad 'ee've found a good man at last.'

'Thank you, Mrs Blackler,' choked Hero, appreciating the sentiment while doubting its accuracy.

Matty, taking advantage of her long service and

special position, came over and kissed Hero before addressing Calverstock.

'I'll be coming with my lady,' she announced firmly. 'I hope you make her happy, my lord. She deserves the best.'

Calverstock did not react with anger to what could have been considered an impertinence but eyed Matty gravely before inclining his head in acknowledgement of her concern. 'Much will depend upon Lady Calverstock herself,' he said. 'Her eventual happiness lies in her own hands.'

Matty gazed at him steadily and then nodded, as though satisfied. 'I'll go and pack her ladyship's things,' she said.

'No need for undue urgency,' murmured Calverstock with a faint shrug. 'My wife will remain here tonight. Have her things ready by morning. I will be here with the carriage at six.' He turned to Hero, who stood by listening to the conversation unable to believe it was taking place. Matty must have gone light in the attic to be taken in so! 'We will travel to my London house tomorrow,' he told her. 'I trust you have no objection, ma'am?'

'None,' returned Hero faintly, her main emotion other than astonishment at the conversation which had just taken place one of immense relief.

He obviously did not intend to claim his marital rights that night.

Their servants left to partake of ale in the kitchen. A glass of sherry was placed in her hand by the earl's inscrutable man, who then served her father, the vicar and Calverstock himself. A toast was drunk. Hero barely allowed the liquid to touch her lips.

Calverstock was chatting quite amiably with the vicar, whose fawning manner Hero had never noticed before. His living was in the gift of her father and she knew Cudlip would do anything to please him, but he had no need to curry favour with the earl. Except, she supposed bitterly, that he might hope to be well paid for conducting the wedding at such short notice. But, dear lord, they were actually laughing together over some stupid joke of the vicar's as though nothing in the world were wrong!

The stifling room had become overpoweringly hot. Hero moved towards the open window, seeking air and solitude in which to recover her composure. She became aware that the earl had come to join her.

'It will be a long journey tomorrow,' he informed her formally, as though he had never laughed in his life, 'for I do not wish to make more than one overnight stop. Have your maid pack a small bag with the things you will need at the inn.'

Hero nodded, the merest acknowledgement of his words.

'Then I will take my leave, ma'am. I engage to be here at six tomorrow.'

Realising he would receive no further word from his bride, Calverstock turned to her father.

'I will take the horses now, Polhembury. Two hunters and a useful road horse, as agreed.'

'You drive a hard bargain, Calverstock,' muttered the baron with renewed hostility. 'They are all prime cattle, and you leave me with but a broken-down hack. But,' he waved a petulant hand, 'they are yours. Do with them what you will. Good day to you, my lord.'

Hero noted bitterly that the loss of his precious

horses seemed to distress her father rather more than the prospect of losing her.

Calverstock addressed the entire company with a supremely elegant bow and left, his man following closely upon his heels. If the earl noticed the vicar's bemused expression he made no sign.

'I must be on my way too,' murmured that gentleman, at last perceiving that all might not be quite well. 'I wish you happy, Lady Calverstock. Mrs Cudlip sends her felicitations and trusts she will have the pleasure of seeing you when next you visit Polhembury.'

'I do so regret that I shall be unable to bid her goodbye. I should account it prodigiously kind of you if you would return this book to her?' Hero had just remembered the collection of Lord Byron's verses she had been reading only yesterday. It seemed an age ago, when she had been a different person. She picked up the volume from the table on which it lay and handed it to the vicar. 'Tell her I shall write.'

Alone with her father at last, Hero turned to him with a resigned, helpless gesture which was yet full of outraged hurt.

'You see what a fine mess you have landed me in, Papa? What possessed you to play with Calverstock and allow him to fleece you of money you did not have?'

'I did not, daughter. Oh, yes, I play deep when I visit London but have the sense never to engage in a ruinous contest with a single opponent. I own to several large debts of honour and had run up the usual tradesmen's bills, my tailor and so on. And it costs a great deal to keep this place going,' he added self-righteously.

'We have been living in penury for years,' snapped Hero. 'You cannot blame the bills here for your journey up the River Tick!'

Polhembury glared back. 'The horses——'

'Were an extravagance,' cut in Hero fiercely. 'How many times have I pleaded with you to sell them? You could not afford to keep such a stable.'

'Well, they are gone now, so I collect that you will be satisfied at last, miss!'

'Madam,' bit back Hero, 'by your own contrivance, Papa!'

'But I owed no one person enough to put me at *point non plus* and it was deuced unlikely that all those to whom I had lost at the gaming tables would decide to call in my debts at the same time,' growled her father. 'I'd have managed if Calverstock had not bought 'em all up, gambling and otherwise. The total staggered even me,' the baron confessed in a more conciliatory tone.

'Calverstock did that?' breathed Hero, her fury rising not against her father now but against her husband. 'And asked for my hand in repayment? Why?'

'I know that no more than you do,' said her father heavily. 'He demanded the money knowing I could not pay and said that if you would wed him he'd save me from a debtors' prison by cancelling my vowels and settling my tradesmen's accounts. God knows why he wanted you but, devil take it, Hero, I'm confoundedly glad he did, for you're no great catch!'

CHAPTER TWO

'I HAVE no objection to travelling to London with His Lordship,' Hero declared later, alone in her room with her maid. 'It is where I intended to go to escape him.'

'But you're wed now, my chick. You can't go running away from your husband,' protested Matty.

'I shall if he drives me to it.'

Matty sucked at her nonexistent front teeth. 'I can see no reason why he should. He seems a nice enough gentleman to me.'

'Matty!' cried Hero in exasperation. 'Don't tell me you have not seen what he has done to my father! Why should he treat me any better?'

'Because you're his wife,' said Matty stubbornly, 'and I do not think he is indifferent to you. If he treats you badly it'll be because you ask for it, Miss Hero— my lady,' she corrected herself quickly.

'He has bamboozled you,' snorted Hero, hiding the tightening of her nerves at Matty's remark and wondering what had induced her maid to make it. For Matty did not know that she and Calverstock had met before, that on that occasion she had sensed his interest to be as great as her own despite the brevity of their encounter. 'Did you not see the way he regarded me?' she demanded, her heart crying out to know what had happened to change his attitude so. 'As though I were beneath contempt!'

'The way you were acting you were,' said Matty

roundly. 'All right, my chick.' She held up a placatory
hand as Hero turned on her indignantly. 'I'm not
saying you did not have reason according to what you
have told me. But the sooner you find out why he did
what he did and stop driving yourself into a frenzy, the
better.'

Hero was not ready to hear such sound advice. 'I
am not in a frenzy!' she denied hotly. 'But after what
he has done to my father and the way he treated me,
can you wonder that I have taken him in dislike? To
him I was no more than a sack of coals to be bargained
over! And if you are going to vex me so by taking his
side then, perhaps it would be preferable for you to
remain here.'

'You don't mean that, Miss Hero,' cried Matty,
immediately contrite for taking her mistress to task
when the child was so upset. 'I was just trying to make
you see it would be wise to make the best of the
situation, that's all. After all, he is a fine, upstanding-
looking gentleman despite his past. His family is an
old and respected one. But of course I'm on your side,
my chick.' She gave her gappy smile. 'Here, let me
brush your hair. That will soothe both of us.'

Under Matty's ministrations Hero began to relax.
She was, as she had said, quite willing to accept her
new husband's escort to London; she had never been
there and would enjoy seeing the capital. What gave
her unease and a certain *frisson* of fearful excitement
was what might happen when they reached the inn
where they were to lie overnight. He had not pressed
his claims on her immediately. Would he be so for-
bearing tomorrow? And the night after, in his London
residence? He had regarded her with disdain but there

had been something in his expression which echoed the admiration she had seen in his eyes in the village. Only, admiration had changed to a cool, rather derisive assessment of her charms. The scrutiny had proved every bit as offensive as she had anticipated but she had been too shocked, too overcome by the treatment meted out to her father, to answer him in similar coin.

Now, as she sightlessly contemplated her own reflection as Matty stroked the brush through her crackling waves, she acknowledged that she had had no need to examine his face or figure. Both were indelibly imprinted on her mind. And even at his most chillingly austere, despite the detestation in which she now held him, his hard features and commanding presence had the power to excite her in the most extraordinary way.

Long after she was tucked up in bed Hero could hear Matty rustling about packing the few things she intended to take with her. Most of her clothes were too old and worn to be much use but she must have something to change into. In London, perhaps, she would be able to ride again, so she had told Matty to pack the green velvet habit, unused since her much-loved mare had been sold, together with the carriage horses and the carriage itself, since the baron considered them unnecessary to his own pleasures.

He had kept the two fine hunters Calverstock had now claimed in order both to hunt and to race them; the road horse to journey to local friends and acquaintances, and the hack for the groom to ride. None was trained to a lady's side-saddle. Hence, unless she could beg a lift or cared to ride on the carrier's cart, for the past few years Hero had been unable to travel further than she could walk.

But now, she supposed, she would have a carriage at her disposal and no doubt a dress allowance. The prospect held a certain charm. She would, she decided, as the maid at length pinched out the last candle and retired to her own room, take Matty's advice, make the most of her new circumstances and use her allowance to help her father if she could. And ignore her husband as far as possible.

On this comforting note she finally slept, to be awakened, it seemed, mere moments later.

"Tis time you were up if you are not to keep his lordship waiting,' Matty told her as she set a cup of chocolate on the table by the bed.

'What time is it?' yawned Hero, gathering her wits as fast as she could. His lordship! Her stomach turned a somersault and she was suddenly wide awake. Of course, today she began the journey to London with her new husband.

'Gone five, my chick. I've got your hot water here.'

Hero was up, dressed and ready to leave when she heard the sound of a carriage approaching the door. Six of the clock precisely, she thought with irritation. His lordship was prompt, if nothing else. Had he been tardy she would have been equally provoked, she acknowledged wryly. In her present mood nothing the wretched creature did was likely to please her.

She rose from the breakfast table, having swallowed no more than a mouthful of bread and butter, which had almost choked her, and went through into the hall.

'I must say goodbye to Papa,' she declared as the boot boy sped to answer the door.

'He should have been down to see you off,' muttered Matty, who looked lined and tired beyond her years

that morning. Hero felt a pang of guilt. Matty could
not have had above three or four hours' sleep.

'You know he seldom rises before ten unless he is
hunting,' she retorted, hiding her deep disappointment
that her father had made no effort to see her off. News
of her departure had reached the outside staff and
everyone except her father had gathered in the hall.

'I'll go up and fetch him,' muttered the groom, Ned
Tribble, who, when occasion demanded, acted as the
baron's man. Her father's valet proper had left a year
or so before and he had never replaced him.

'No,' said Hero. 'I'll go.' She had not yet greeted
her husband, who, a sidelong glance told her, stood in
the doorway blocking the light from outside. The sun
had risen to silhouette his figure against its brightness:
tall, straight and menacing in its dark immovability.
She made a slight inclination of her head in his
direction and addressed him formally. 'If you will
excuse me, my lord, I must bid my father farewell.'

She did not wait for his answer but mounted the
stairs to hurry to her father's room. Receiving no reply
to her knock, she opened the door and went in.

Baron Polhembury lay on his bed, fully clothed,
snoring. An empty brandy bottle on the floor near his
limp, drooping hand betrayed the cause of his
insensibility.

Tears rose to Hero's eyes. Perhaps he did care after
all and had been unable to face the prospect of her
leaving. Or, more likely, she acknowledged cynically,
blinking back the signs of her ridiculously sentimental
distress, he simply wanted to forget all his troubles.
They would surely multiply without her to see to the
running of the household. He would be far less

comfortable, be unable to ride as he wished, to visit his cronies whenever he liked. Much as he irritated her and had abused his power over her, she discovered that she did still hold him in some affection. As she lifted his flaccid hand and placed it on his chest she determined to send Tribble up to put him to bed.

As she took her leave of Mrs Blackler and Bessy she instructed them to look after the master well in her absence. 'I'll see he's fed, never you fear, Miss Hero,' promised the cook comfortably.

Ned Tribble stood a little apart, dressed in his best, Hero noted. As she moved towards him she detected a certain unease in his manner.

'Goodbye, Ned,' she said and added softly, so that Calverstock should not hear, 'Go up and see to the baron, will you? He needs your help to get to bed.'

Tribble's discomfort grew. 'I'm sorry, miss...my lady, but I can't do that. Popping up to fetch him was one thing, but serving him's another, if you'll forgive the presumption, my lady. You see, I'm to travel to Ashworthy with Lord Calverstock's head groom to help deliver the horses there. I work for the earl now, my lady. Lord Polhembury won't need more than the boy to look after the hack and there was no proper job for me here any longer, so I accepted his lordship's offer of employment.'

Hero looked at the man in disbelief. Then she turned to her husband, who had entered the house in her absence upstairs and now stood waiting, none too patiently, she observed.

'You are ready, ma'am?' he enquired icily.

'No,' denied Hero furiously. 'I am not! Not only do you steal *me* from my father but Ned Tribble, too! He was groom and valet to Lord Polhembury. How will he manage without Tribble's services?'

'Well enough, I imagine,' returned Calverstock with an indifferent shrug. 'He no longer needs a groom and valeting was never intended to be part of Tribble's duties. His love is of horses. He will be happier serving in my stables.' He turned to Tribble. 'Once the horses are safely delivered to Gloucestershire, you will proceed to London by mail coach, as we arranged.' As Tribble touched his forelock in acknowledgment of the order, Calverstock addressed Hero again. 'My head groom, Cuthbert, is of more use to me supervising the stables at Ashworthy than in London. I needed another experienced groom and Tribble will suit me perfectly.'

'And you do not care what becomes of my father!' accused Hero angrily.

Calverstock bowed, his expression unreadable. 'As you say, ma'am. Shall we proceed?'

He gestured towards the door. Hero controlled her temper, knowing the staff stood gawping. It would do no good to slap that infuriating face, although she longed to do so. For the moment she was helpless. She was his wife, his chattel, sworn to obey him. And her father was not ill, not incapable. He could pick up the pieces of his life, find a new valet, set the estate to rights, if he wanted to. She just doubted whether, left to himself, her thoughtless, selfish, profligate father would have the determination to succeed. Even with her to chivvy him he had fallen further into idleness and debt.

Instead of giving vent to her feelings in the way she truly wanted, Hero tossed her head, sending the yellow ribbons on her best bonnet dancing. She wore the sprigged muslin again, since it was the only decent dress she possessed and would be cool in the heat of the day. At the moment she had it covered with a pelisse, for the early-morning chill still lingered in the air.

'Come, Matty,' she said, stalking past Calverstock without another glance, twitching her skirt aside as she did so to ensure that it should not touch his immaculately booted leg.

Their meagre luggage was already strapped on the back of the carriage with Calverstock's trunk and his man's bag. The step had been lowered. The earl's man opened the crested door and helped her in, his face still impassive though she detected a hint of disapproval in the downward curve of his mouth. No doubt, like most valets, he resented the intrusion of a wife into his master's life. Her presence was scarcely her fault, thought Hero, and he would have to adjust.

Tribble had joined a man she presumed to be Cuthbert, since the latter was leading a string of horses, one a fine bay gelding, two more obviously for the servants to ride and three she recognised as her father's. To have his own riding horses with him, Calverstock must have been staying somewhere in the neighbourhood, she deduced. Somewhere where he had been able to house his carriage and stable her father's horses as well as his own. But why take Papa's yesterday when today would have done? Simply to rub in the fact of his possession, she imagined. Indignation threatened to overcome her again as she settled into the comfortable, padded interior of the earl's coach and watched the two grooms take cheerful though respectful leave of him.

Matty followed her into the vehicle and silently took her seat beside her. To Hero's surprise and relief Calverstock did not enter the coach to seat himself opposite but climbed up on the box. His man, having closed the door and raised the step, got up beside him. The whip cracked and she heard the earl give the horses the office to start. Presumably he intended to act as gentleman coachman and drive the four post horses himself.

As the carriage moved forward Hero clutched at a strap, hoping Calverstock could manage the four-in-hand. She peered backwards through the window. Cuthbert and Tribble had mounted up ready for their journey. Behind them stood the old house, familiar and beloved in its neglected greyness of stone and slate, the only home she had ever known. A lump formed in her throat as she saw Mrs Blackler and Bessy standing on the step waving and realised that Matty was returning the farewell salute, tears wending a convoluted course down her wrinkled cheeks. Matty had lived at Polhembury Hall for longer than she, for she had come with Lord Polhembury's bride, been nurse to the Polhembury heir, the brother Hero had never known, who had died soon after her own birth. Matty had been the one to whom Hero had run with all her troubles for as long as she could remember. At her mother's death she had been scarce fourteen and had wept out her grief in Matty's arms. Matty's pain must be almost as great as her own, she realised. As the building disappeared round a bend in the overgrown, weed-studded drive she reached out to take Matty's knotted hand in hers.

'It is a wrench,' she said softly, 'but truly, we have both lived there for far too long. We must consider this an adventure.'

'I'm glad to hear you say so, my chick.' Matty sniffed and patted Hero's hand with her free one, then broke away to clutch at the nearest support as the earl wheeled the team out of the gates with such expertise that Hero, clinging to the strap and swaying with the vehicle, began to relax. He did know what he was doing.

During the miles into Exeter, where she guessed he would change the horses, Hero watched the high-banked hedges speed past. Now and again she glimpsed a panorama of the lush, hilly countryside through a gap but more often than not the view was blocked. She could not help wondering when she would next see the familiar scenery. London seemed a world away and Gloucestershire distant enough, with the whole of Somerset to traverse before one reached it.

Despite her brave words to Matty a pang struck through her. She was leaving everything she knew and loved. If only her husband was a man she could admire! Then she might not have felt apprehension, might have eagerly anticipated exploring his establishments and estates instead of already feeling heartily homesick.

Matty was not one to speak much unless encouraged and dozed quietly in her corner, making up for her lost sleep. At least the carriage was well-sprung, thought Hero, glancing at her maid affectionately. Perhaps the journey would prove less trying for Matty than she'd feared. If the elderly woman could sleep for most of the time she would scarcely notice the miles being eaten up under the horses' hooves.

As she had predicted, the horses were changed at the Half Moon in Exeter. Calverstock had sent a groom ahead to arrange for fresh teams to be waiting at post stables along the way. She declined the opportunity to descend and stretch her legs, though she did remove her pelisse, wishing the coach were an open one, for the day promised to become uncomfortably warm for travelling. Matty stirred as ostlers bustled about the coach, hooves clattered on cobbles and the carriage swayed as the new horses were put to.

'We shall swelter in here,' Hero grumbled as they set off after the next brief halt to change the horses. 'I wish his lordship had provided a barouche or a landau.'

'We'd only get smothered in dust,' Matty pointed out. 'I've always heard it said that an open carriage is no good for travelling long distances. If you are too hot we could lower the windows, though, lord knows, that would let in enough dust.'

'Perhaps just a little would be all right,' Hero suggested. 'We can always shut them again. But this is the main London road and doesn't seem quite so dusty as the lanes.'

'Do you know where his lordship intends to spend the night?' asked Matty as she resumed her seat after pushing down the glass in the windows.

Hero shook her head. 'Somewhere like Salisbury, I should think. He is driving the horses hard and wasting no time at the post houses. If we alight to stretch our legs we are off again before we've had a chance to so much as solicit a drink from the waiter!'

'It's all stop and go,' grumbled Matty. 'Besides changing the horses every hour or so there are all the toll gates and barriers to stop us in between. I'd forgotten what it was like to make such a long journey.'

'I never have, so it is all new to me. Still,' Hero remembered, 'it used to take Papa a week to travel to London. Now we shall do it in two days.'

'Aye, the roads and the coaches have improved, there's no disputing that. I remember when I came to Polhembury Hall with your mama. Bumping and lurching all over the place we were, no springs and terrible lumps and ruts all over the road. Couldn't put the horses to more than a walk in those days.'

'But his lordship is able to keep his at a fast trot all the time. It doesn't get dark until late and he will not stop early, I collect.'

Matty sighed and settled back into her corner. 'I hope he will stop for a nuncheon.'

'I could not eat a thing.'

'You haven't eaten more than a morsel since yesterday morning,' chided Matty. 'You'll be making yourself ill, my chick. That won't do you or anyone else any good.'

When they stopped in Axminster in the late morning, she declined his lordship's invitation to join him for refreshment in the inn.

'I will partake of a drink out here and walk a while,' she declared. 'The fresh air will do me more good than sitting in a stuffy inn parlour.'

'I cannot allow my wife to starve herself into a decline,' said Calverstock coolly. 'You will come inside, eat a small meal, relieve your thirst and refresh yourself, ma'am. The next decent inn is some thirty miles distant and we shall not reach it until mid-afternoon.' He held out his hand to help her alight. 'Come; my man, Benbow, is ordering our repast.'

It was a command Hero could not dispute. The inn yard was full of people and she had no wish to make a spectacle of herself. But she ignored the outstretched hand and prepared to descend from the carriage with dignified independence.

Had her skirt not been so unfashionably tight and the cobbles been better laid, all would have been well. As it was Hero's ankle turned on an uneven stone and her skirt prevented her from regaining her balance. She stumbled and would have fallen but for the two strong hands that grasped her and set her on her feet again as though she were a child.

'Did you hurt yourself?'

There was a definite trace of concern in his voice but Hero was too mortified to notice it. 'No!' she snapped, wrenched herself free from a touch which seemed to scorch her bare arms and marched ahead into the inn.

An obsequious landlord showed them into a private parlour. His wife, on Benbow's instructions, was load-ing the table with cold meat pies, cold chicken, cheese, bread, butter and some fruit tartlets. A flagon of wine and another of lemonade soon followed. Having seen their master and mistress served, Benbow and Matty retired to a corner of the parlour to consume the victuals provided for them.

Hero's initial reluctance to enter the inn had been lost in the interest the incident afforded. She had never passed inside the portals of a hostelry before and she was enthralled by the experience despite the stench of stale beer and the noise coming from the taproom. And truth to tell she was hungry as well as thirsty and privacy to attend to her personal needs would be most welcome. Were it not for the disagreeable presence of her husband she would have enjoyed the novelty immensely.

'You are not finding the journey too uncomfortable, I trust?' enquired Calverstock politely as they began to eat.

'The carriage is most comfortable, as I am certain you are aware, my lord. I did not feel in need of refreshment, apart from a drink.'

'So you said.' He smiled slightly, seeing the relish with which Hero bit into a slice of fresh white bread liberally spread with butter. 'We will lie in Salisbury overnight and be on the road again by seven tomorrow. We may take nuncheon at Basingstoke and should reach my residence in Kensington by seven in the evening.'

Hero inclined her head. 'Thank you for informing me, my lord.'

After that they ate in silence. Hero consumed both chicken and cheese with the new bread spread lavishly with butter and washed it all down with lemonade. Calverstock chose pie followed by cheese and drank deeply of the red wine.

'Would you like coffee?' he asked at length, breaking a silence which had become oppressive.

Hero nodded. 'Yes, please.'

Benbow left to order the drink and while it was being brought Hero excused herself and took Matty to the room set aside for the convenience of ladies. She returned to the coach feeling comfortable and replete.

Somewhere between Axminster and Dorchester, warned by a blast from the guard's horn, Calverstock was compelled to slow down to allow the Exeter mail coach to pass in the opposite direction without hindrance. Hero, her interest aroused, watched the fine-looking vehicle flash past, just managing to glimpse the royal crest in its door. She almost envied the two outside passengers their enjoyment of the fresh air and remarked on how exciting it must be to travel in that way.

'Uncomfortable,' said Matty sourly, speaking from bitter experience. 'And dusty. Especially if you've been up there since last evening.'

'I didn't think of that,' confessed Hero.

They stopped briefly at Dorchester, this time merely for a drink. Hero found herself dozing alongside Matty as Calverstock tooled the carriage across Salisbury Plain. Without hills to tire the horses he made excellent time, lingering at the post stables only to change the team, though late in the afternoon he extended the enforced wait while they again partook of refreshment.

By the time they reached Salisbury that evening Hero was almost too tired to eat. Calverstock sent·her straight up to her room with Matty, promising that a tray would follow in half an hour.

Hero wanted to thank him for his consideration but as she looked up into that hard countenance, despite the lines of tiredness she detected about his eyes, brought on no doubt by the strain of driving so far and so fast, the words died upon her lips. Instead, she acknowledged her approval of the arrangement with a curt nod.

'We will breakfast in the parlour before we leave,' he informed her. 'I have ordered it served at six-thirty of the clock. I depend upon you to be ready on time. You will be roused with a cup of chocolate at six. We leave at seven.'

'I shall be ready,' said Hero grimly, uncertain whether to be relieved or offended at his evident reluctance to sample the pleasures of the marriage bed. For her own part, she had no desire so to do, she told herself firmly as she followed mine host's ample wife up the narrow stairs to the room she was to share with Matty.

The next day followed a similar pattern to the one before. Calverstock stopped for refreshment at Basingstoke and Bagshot and crossed to the north bank of the busy, sluggishly flowing Thames at Staines. Hero was glad to stretch her aching limbs on its banks at Brentford and accepted a cup of coffee at the inn before mounting the step into the coach ready to cover the last stages into London.

If her own limbs were so cramped, what agonies must Matty be suffering? Yet the elderly woman had made no complaint as she struggled down from the carriage, assisted by a Calverstock bent on charming her into the sort of devotion offered him by Benbow.

But Hero was really too tired to resent his wiles as she should. The countryside passed by in a blur until the coach reached Kensington on the western outskirts of London. The traffic was heavier here but Calverstock threaded his equipage through the midst of carts, horses, donkeys and pedestrians with assurance and expertise until, having passed an inn called the Halfway House, he suddenly swung through gates already standing open and sped along a sweeping drive to pull up before an imposing mansion. Calverstock House, she soon learned, had been built in Kensington Gore, one of the residences erected there at the end of the previous century, and commanded views over Hyde Park.

Benbow sprang to the horses' heads as the coach drew to a halt beneath the portico, the great double doors opened, footmen hurried down the steps and grooms came running through an archway leading to the stables. Before she knew it Hero was being escorted up to the entrance by her new husband, leaving the bustle of busy footmen and grooms behind. Benbow followed, bringing Matty with him.

Calverstock must have sent word ahead. The staff had gathered in the vast, vaulted hall to greet their returning master and new mistress. The butler stepped forward to greet them.

'Welcome home, my lord,' he murmured with a respectful bow.

'Thank you, Grindley.' A firm hand in the small of her back propelled Hero forward. 'This is my wife, the new Lady Calverstock.'

How could the butler contrive to look both well-fed and complacent yet at the same time austere? wondered Hero, eyeing his expressionless face with some misgiving.

'Good evening, Grindley,' she murmured.

His expression did not change yet a spark of curiosity lit eyes which were by no means hostile. 'Welcome

to Calverstock House, my lady. It will be my pleasure
to serve your ladyship to the best of my ability.'

Hero's lowered spirits raised a little at this but
quickly sank down again as she was confronted by an
intimidating woman of mature years, dressed in black
from cap to toe, who must be the housekeeper. She
curtsied stiffly with a rattle of keys, a bunch of which
hung from her waist by a chain. Her badge of office,
thought Hero wryly, flaunted like a challenge. But
perhaps she was being over-fanciful.

'My dear,' said Calverstock, holding Hero's elbow
in a vice-like grip which belied the pleasant mildness
of his voice, 'this is Mrs Deacon, my housekeeper. I
am sure you will do all in your power to make her
ladyship feel at home here in Calverstock House, Mrs
Deacon.'

As her eyes left Hero to rest upon her employer,
Mrs Deacon's rather grim features relaxed into a smile
that softened the set line of her mouth.

'Indeed, my lord. The mistress will not lack for
guidance from me.'

'Capital,' said Lord Calverstock inanely, smiling at
the woman in a way that Hero could have sworn
brought a blush to her sallow cheeks. She supposed
Mrs Deacon to be another of his conquests.

Beside the housekeeper stood a small, foreign-look-
ing man wearing a chef's hat, introduced as Monsieur
Vodin. His lordship employed a French cook, then. He
looked the most friendly of the upper servants, bowing
with a flourish and offering her a wide smile of welcome that showed all his yellowed teeth.

'I shall cook like ze dream for you, madame,' he

promised, kissing the tips of his fingers at her in an expansive gesture of intent.

The minions were dismissed. Calverstock instructed Mrs Deacon to take Matty up to the chamber her ladyship would be using so that she could unpack her ladyship's things. Their luggage had already been carried up the superbly carved, winding mahogany stairway by a procession of footmen who had disappeared from view. Hero's threatened headache now held her head in a vice every bit as strong as that with which her husband continued to grip her elbow. He turned to Grindley.

'Have supper brought to the small drawing-room,' he instructed. 'A tray of tea for her ladyship, brandy for me. Come, my dear.'

The grip on her elbow tightened as Calverstock urged Hero towards the staircase. Her feet sank into the luxurious softness of thick pile and for an instant she longed to be treading the threadbare carpet at Polhembury. But a new awareness was growing upon her. An awareness of wealth such as she had never known. She would be a fool to let her grudge against her husband, the provider of all this luxury, spoil her enjoyment of it.

They reached the next floor and Calverstock guided her towards a pair of open doors. The stairs went on up and Hero imagined the bedrooms would be above. He was not taking her there, she decided with relief.

'The main drawing-room,' he announced softly as they entered the huge mirrored and gilded apartment. 'We will use the smaller room leading from it. When I entertain it becomes the card-room.'

It was still light. The open windows overlooked a

long garden in which sweeping, sloping lawns, surrounded by shrubs and flower beds, led the eye out
over the southern landscape. Away to the left, behind
the stables, lay a walled garden. Immediately beneath
the window a terrace led down to a small flower garden
laid out with paths and seats. The pungent, flowery
perfumes of evening wafted on the air to invade the
room, obscuring the odour of the stables, which Hero
felt certain would obtrude at certain times. Not that
she objected to the clean smell of hay and horse dung.
It would remind her of home.

Drew had released her elbow as soon as they
entered the smaller room. She stood by the window,
inhaled a refreshing breath and turned to her husband.

'This is a most pleasant room,' she acknowledged,
'but I would prefer to seek my own.'

'All in good time,' he returned easily. 'Give Matty a
chance to make things ready for you. We shall share
the master suite.' As he saw the sudden tightening of
her features his voice hardened. 'One of the bedrooms
is mine, and so is the dressing-room. You will have the
use of the other bedroom and the boudoir. I shall
expect to visit you to consummate our union later
tonight.'

The words had been spoken in brisk, unemotional
tones. Hero swallowed. 'I am very tired.' Surely he
would not press his attentions upon her immediately?

He bowed. 'As am I. But supper followed by a hot
bath will revive us, I am certain. And I have no wish
to delay matters further. This marriage will be a true
one, madam, despite its inauspicious beginning.'

CHAPTER THREE

HERO consumed little of the cold dishes Grindley brought to them, all too conscious of the silent man in the chair opposite, who ate with obvious appetite. But she had to admit that two cups of tea did much to remove her headache and later, having excused herself to her formally polite husband, luxuriating in the comparative privacy of her splendid bedroom, she found that the warm bath eased the aches from her limbs.

She sent Matty away to find her own bed as soon as she could, insisting on brushing her own hair.

'You are even more weary than I, Matty. You must be stiff as a board. Call a footman and I will instruct him to order you a bath. You need one every bit as much as I do.'

The young footman looked only slightly put out at this strange request. Matty left her mistress with a chuckle. 'They won't like waiting on a maid, my chick.'

'But they will do it or I'll know the reason why. You are my personal maid, Matty, a lady's maid. You must demand respect from the other servants. Only Mrs Deacon can claim to be above you.'

With Matty gone, Hero brushed desultorily at her hair, despising the shaking of her hands. But how could she expect to be anything else but nervous? He had said he would come to consummate their union and there was no way, short of feigning illness, that she could escape the consequences of her agreement to wed him, however reluctantly it had been given. And pretending to be ill would only serve to delay the inevitable.

The throbbing in her head threatened to return as a dull ache behind her eyes. Anticipation stretched her nerves, clenched her muscles into knots. She had thought that stroking the brush through her hair might relax her but if anything the mild activity was having the opposite effect.

Disgusted with herself, she threw down the brush and sprang up, her slippered feet silent on the deep-piled rug that almost covered the floor as she paced around the room. Paced round the great tester bed with its mahogany canopy, deep feather mattress, snowy linen and lavish silken cover and curtains.

She thought about climing in and trying to go to sleep before her husband came but discarded that idea almost as soon as it occurred to her. She was far too strung up; she'd never be able to lie still, let alone manage to fall asleep.

Why had this happened to her? Why could God not have sent along a rich, kindly gentleman whom she would have been happy, if not delighted, to wed, who would have rescued the baron from his debts because he loved her?

For the hundredth time her eyes strayed to the door through which Calverstock would come. The door which communicated with his dressing-room. On first coming up she had investigated, wondering whether to assert her own preference by locking him out, only to discover that although there was a lock there was no key to turn in it. Just as there was no means by which to fasten the door between the dressing-room, with its many dark oak cupboards, its shaving chair and mirror, and Calverstock's bedroom. All the rooms in the master suite intercommunicated; there was nothing to bar either of them from invading the other's privacy.

Having strained her ears to make sure Benbow was not about, she had peeped in, ready with an excuse should she be wrong and find him there going silently about his business. Someone had been up to light the candles, which added a soft flickering, shadowy glow to the otherwise austere apartment, but to her relief there was no one there. Curious, she had stepped inside, careful to make no sound on the bare, polished boards. His bed was as large as hers and looked as comfortable but whereas her room was decorated in palest pastel spring yellows and greens, with white lace and patterned damask at the windows and a silken bedcover to echo the theme, his was done out in deeper, more sober hues, plain or striped greys and blues, the dark oak of the furniture boldly obtrusive, not softened by drapes like the mahogany in hers. A splash of white marble round the empty fireplace and a pale cream rug by the side of his bed were the only signs of lightness, of softness. A room fit for a man who had no room for weakness in his life, she had concluded, retreating.

Since then she had heard vague sounds coming from beyond that door but, listening attentively, had decided it was only Benbow preparing his master's bath. Calverstock himself had not yet come up.

She could have retreated to her boudoir and waited there but the adjoining room held no attraction for her, being altogether too pinkly fussy, frilly and garish for her taste. The decorations and furnishings there were at odds with those in her bedroom and Hero wondered who had been responsible. The embellishment of her bedroom looked recent and might reflect Calverstock's taste, albeit so different from that to be found in his own room, while that of the boudoir appeared to have been executed on relatively old-fashioned lines.

Arms crossed beneath her breasts, clutching her old cambric peignoir about her, Hero continued to pace. It seemed the only thing to do to ease the strain while waiting for her husband to keep his promise.

Drew sat as long as possible over his brandy. Benbow had his room ready, probably his bath, too, by now. Before long he would be down to warn him that the water was cooling. He sighed. If only things had turned out as he had planned. But those scathing words he'd overheard through Miss Langage's open bedroom window had killed his budding regard, withered forever the eager hopes he'd had of entering into a felicitous alliance. The woman he had chosen to wed evidently had no conception of the ease with which desperate people could find themselves condemned to the horrors of transportation and the possibility, almost certainty, of suffering extreme hardship and cruelty under the Draconian laws regulating their existence in a penal colony. Had he detected one scrap of softness in her voice, had she not gone on to scorn his mother's birth and his own worthiness to inherit the earldom, he would have considered explaining his actions to her. But she was as bad as her father. He should have expected nothing else. As a result of one moment of dazzled weakness he had leg-shackled himself to a selfish, unfeeling woman with whom he could expect to enjoy no true intimacy of communication or understanding.

How could he have been so misled? He had bumped into her and spilled his plums from her basket. They were his plums, he was assured of that, for he had been inspecting the orchard attached to the estate he had recently acquired only hours earlier and seen them hanging on the trees. He had not begrudged her fruit which would otherwise have gone to waste or allowed such a minor offence to dim the instant attraction he had felt for the young woman carrying them. When he'd heard her maid address her as 'Miss Hero', his heart had leapt, for he had realised that the delightful creature must be Lord Polhembury's daughter. The idea of demanding her hand in marriage had sprung into his mind as though by magic. It had seemed such an eminently suitable solution. Baron Polhembury would be left with his estate, though penniless, while he gained the desirable Miss Langage as his wife.

Desirable. Yes. Still desirable despite her contempt. His body craved her so badly that he feared it might betray him into revealing his need. Which explained his present reluctance to do what he most wanted to do—take the distracting creature into his arms and make her his.

He would do it, of course, he had told her so. But first he had to gain complete control over his emotions, for he must take her as coolly as he was certain she would respond to his advances. He must not give the impression that he was making love to her. Not that he felt so inclined, given what he now knew about her.

But in the throes of passion his guard might drop. He might imagine her the creature he had thought her to be, the young woman who had gazed at him with wide, dazed eyes while plums spilled unheeded about her small feet. That girl would have responded...

But there could be no profit in indulging in dreams. He had to face reality. He had made his offer on the most slender of evidence and must live with the consequences of his folly.

He drank down the last of the brandy in his glass and stood up, just as Benbow arrived to inform his lordship that his bath was ready.

Hero heard the voices, the splash of water. Her stomach clenched in a tight knot. Not long now. She should get into bed. Be ready for whatever might ensue.

Of one thing she was quite certain. She would give her father's unfeeling persecutor nothing, would not allow him the satisfaction of resisting his demands. Would lie still and endure. She was, of course, almost entirely ignorant of what went on between a man and woman in the marriage bed. Matty, the only woman she could have asked, was a spinster. Mrs Blackler, too, despite her honorary title. Mrs Cudlip must know, but Hero doubted whether she could have broached the subject to the vicar's romantic but genteel wife even had there been time. She took a last glance in the mirror, placed her frilly cotton nightcap over her cascading hair and tied the strings firmly under her chin. Huge, frightened eyes in a white face stared back at her. She tightened her lips impatiently. Why should she be afraid? She was no green girl! After all, every woman who wed endured the attentions of her husband. If they could do it, so could she.

With this determination held firmly in mind, Hero extinguished all but one candle, the one on a table by what she had decided should be his side of the bed, and threw off her peignoir, revealing the cotton nightgown beneath. Her best, with the smocking and embroidery at the shoulders, insisted upon by Matty. Finding nothing further to delay her, Hero at last slid in beneath the covers, pulled them up to her chin and lay rigid, awaiting the advent of her lord and master.

It seemed a long wait while her thudding heart beat out the seconds against her ribs but at last she heard the door handle turn. Her fists clenched and she shut her eyes, not knowing what to expect, afraid of what she would see, reluctant to look at the man who might have embodied all her dreams of a husband had she not discovered his true nature.

His feet brushed across the carpet and stopped by the side of the bed. She heard the rustle of silk, a quick puff of his breath followed by the acrid smell of a smoking wick. The bed sank under his weight, threatening to roll her across to his half. She resisted the movement, clutching the wooden edge of the bed to keep herself in position.

'Well, my dear,' his voice drawled, 'I trust you are not asleep?'

Hero's eyes snapped open. She turned her head to look at the shadowy figure leaning up on one elbow studying her face. He must have known by her breathing that she was not.

'Far from it, my lord,' she answered tartly. 'I have been awaiting your lordship's pleasure this age.'

His hand came out and touched her cheek. 'Did it seem so long?'

Suppressing an involuntary shiver at his touch, Hero jerked her head away. 'Long enough, my lord, after such a journey.'

'Then,' he said softly, 'I must apologise and waste no more time. Come, wife. Since I trust you are virgin I will endeavour to be careful. Believe me, any pain you suffer will be unavoidable.'

'Pain?' choked Hero.

'When I break your maidenhead, my dear.'

Hot shame rushed to Hero's cheeks. How dared he mention such a delicate subject, even to his wife? Even to explain something of which she was ignorant.

'I did not realise your activities would be painful on top of everything else,' she muttered resentfully.

'What else?' he enquired, his voice soft and silky.

Ignoring the warning implicit in his tone, Hero clenched her teeth and spoke through them. 'The indignity,' she informed him fiercely.

'Ah!' The exclamation sounded like a jeer. 'You find it an indignity to be touched by an ex-convict, my lady?' His hand deliberately sought her breast and squeezed it through the fine cotton while his thumb teased her nipple, which immediately hardened, thrusting itself against the pressure with mortifying abandon.

The shock sped down to her vitals. Hero's breath caught in her throat but she made no sound, no movement. She hadn't actually meant the indignity of being touched by a convict but of being in such a situation at all, of being at the mercy of any man apart from one who loved her as she loved him. That must surely make all the difference, she thought wildly as his hands, warm despite the insulating layer of cotton, went to work on her body, stroking, teasing, arousing sensations she distrusted because they were so enjoyable.

Still she lay immobile, tense under his experienced exploration. Even when he lifted her nightgown and found the most secret, unmentionable part of her she made no protest.

'It will hurt the more unless you relax.'

His voice came in her ear as he moved above her. She could feel hot, throbbing flesh against her thigh. Instead of relaxing, she tensed the more.

He did not kiss her. Had not done so once, except for that brief touching of her lips with his after the ceremony. She thought he should, should do something other than thrust himself into her unwilling body so that, despite all her resolution, she did cry out in pain.

He did not apologise, merely grunted. After allowing a moment for her to recover he began to move, swift, sharp, abrasive thrusts which gave her more pain, though now she was able to suppress her cries and endure as she had promised herself.

It was over quite quickly. An extra-hard drive, a few gasping breaths and he rolled aside and from the bed. While Hero watched through eyes glazed with unshed tears he picked up his gown and draped it over one arm instead of putting it on to hide his nakedness. Distraught as she was, dim as was the light, she could still appreciate the splendid proportions of his physique. A fine, upstanding-looking gentleman, Matty had described him. He looked it even unclothed.

'I will see you at breafast, ma'am. I trust you will sleep well. Goodnight.'

Hero had no answer to give him. She turned over on her side and curled herself into a miserable ball.

The tears trickled from her eyes to seep into the pillow. If that was marriage, she wanted no more to do with it. And Matty had been wrong, Calverstock was no gentleman to have treated her in so cavalier a fashion. She never wanted him to touch her again.

The next morning Hero, aching and sore in places she could not mention, decided that she would not present herself downstairs for breakfast but have a tray brought up to her bedroom. She ate scrambled eggs, hot rolls and butter and felt the better for having a full stomach. The previous night's events seemed less gothic in broad daylight, as did the boudoir she had scorned the previous evening.

Even if it did reflect the tastes of a bygone age, it breathed luxury and femininity. Perhaps Drew's grandmother had had it done in accordance with her taste. The pink was not quite so overpowering when seen in the sunlight and much of it was sadly faded. The curtains needed renewing and she could choose delicate stripes to blend in with the brocade of the gilt-wood cabriole chairs and the matching sofa. The mahogany sofa table, banded with satinwood, was exquisite and the upholstered window seats with high, curving ends looked promising, as did a comfortable chaise-longue. Hero wondered why she had taken such a dislike to the room the previous evening. She must have been feeling particularly jaundiced. It could be made her own, a room where she could retire to be private. Calverstock need never enter it, certainly not without her invitation.

Absorbed in plans for the future, all of which excluded the presence of her husband, Hero was interrupted by Matty with a message relayed by a footman.

'His lordship desires your presence in the library, Miss Hero.' She grimaced. 'Footman says immediately.'

'Does he?' muttered Hero, the quick colour staining her cheeks. Defying him would only delay a confrontation which must come sooner or later. 'Very well, I am as ready as I shall ever be, I suppose.'

She had donned the only other dress she had brought with her, an elderly blue muslin much faded from washing. But Matty had done her hair in a stylish chignon and covered it with a pretty cap, one of the late Lady Polhembury's things she had kept tucked away rather than lose all trace of the old mistress she had loved.

'You must wear a cap now you are a matron,' she had told a reluctant Hero, but once the cap was on her head Hero had admitted that it suited her and added dignity to her appearance. A dignity of which, that morning, she felt in need. 'His lordship will expect it,' Matty had added, almost aborting her victory, for the last thing Hero wanted to do was what his lordship expected. However, she had kept it on for her own reasons and now followed the footman down to the library, situated at the rear of the house on the ground floor, secure in the knowledge that the servants, at least, would have no cause to criticise her for appearing without one. They would probably look askance at her gown, though, she thought ruefully. But what couldn't be helped must be endured. Henceforward, that must be her motto.

When she entered Calverstock was sitting behind a huge desk in a room lined with an impressive array of books, except where long windows, partly opened to encourage a cooling draught and framed by tobacco-brown velvet curtains, gave on to the fine prospect she had seen from above. A door opened on to the terrace.

Her husband's polished boots, thrust through the kneehole by his long legs, withdrew from view as he looked up from some document he was studying, sprang to his feet, and moved round to meet her.

'My lady.' He took her hand and bent over it in a graceful manner but his lips failed to touch her skin. Despite this, the touch of his fingers, the warmth of his breath was enough to send a tremor of awareness streaking through Hero. She had hated last night but this morning, waking alone in the bed, reliving the moments when she had shared it with her husband, her mind had skittered between revulsion and a sneaking feeling that had matters between them been different the experience might have been extremely pleasurable.

She dipped a slight curtsy. 'You wished to see me, my lord.'

He stepped back and leant against the edge of his desk, crossing his arms over his chest. That morning he had chosen to wear a brown superfine coat, of much the same shade as the curtains, with buff pantaloons. The lapels of his shot cinnamon-coloured waistcoat framed a snowy neckcloth tied about the high collar of his equally pristine shirt with admirable dexterity.

Benbow knew his job, even if his haunted eyes and large hands did not immediately suggest him to be entirely suited to the position he graced with such an outward show of inscrutable dignity.

But now was not the moment to speculate over the earl's man. Her husband was scanning her person with blatant interest, his expression hovering somewhere between knowing enjoyment as he studied her figure and disparaging amusement as his eyes took in the nature of her apparel.

Hero felt her colour rise in an angry, embarrassed tide. How dared he mortify her so? She smoothed the cotton of her freshly ironed if unfashionable and faded skirt, and met his mocking gaze without flinching.

'My dress displeased you, my lord?' she enquired sweetly. 'I acknowledge that upon your countess it scarcely does your lordship's present noble status justice, but you must accept much of the blame.' One darkish eyebrow rose and she hastened to make her point, not attempting to keep the sarcasm from her voice. 'You should not have wed the daughter of a man you knew to be so far up River Tick.'

The eyebrow descended and he bestowed an amused smile, but not before she had noted the momentary tightening of his lips. He uncrossed his arms and ran a hand through his carefully arranged hair, of a lighter hue than her own mid-brown and laced with tawny streaks. Funny, she thought, eyeing the disarray he had created in his coiffure, that he should have darkish eyebrows and such seductively long, sweeping lashes to frame his grey eyes. The style achieved had suited him but he looked decidedly more human with his hair rumpled. Besides, the gesture revealed that he was not

quite so coolly in possession of himself as he would
wish her to believe.

But his next words disabused her of any idea that he
might be softening towards her.

'You are correct, madam, your present apparel does
your new status no justice at all. But it is not beyond
my means or capabilities to redress the situation to my
own, if not to your, satisfaction. One of London's
foremost modistes will wait upon you in your boudoir
at eleven. She will bring with her samples of fabrics
and a number of sketches from which you may select
a suitable wardrobe with which to enter London
society. At twelve, a milliner will join you and at
twelve-thirty a ladies' shoemaker will attend upon your
person. After some refreshment you will descend to
the music-room, where, at three of the clock, a master
will attempt to teach you the rudiments of dance.'

Hero stared at her husband in disbelief. He had
arranged all this without so much as mentioning it, let
alone seeking her agreement. She sighed and put the
back of a hand to her forehead, allowing her shoulders
to droop in artistic fatigue.

'I do not believe I have the energy for so full a
programme today,' she uttered in a weak voice. 'I fear
these worthy persons will be making a fruitless journey. Perhaps next week...'

She let her words trail off and glanced at Drew from
beneath fluttering lashes which were neither so long
nor so dark as his, curse him. The lines about his
mouth deepened ominously and his brows knitted
together.

'It is of no use your practising foolish female wiles
on me, madam. You appeared perfectly rested when

you walked into this room a few moments ago. You will oblige me by adhering to my timetable. By the end of September, a mere six weeks ahead, my wife must be fitted to move in London society. Meanwhile, since there are still a number of my acquaintances in residence here, you will exchange cards and morning calls. You will,' he insisted, his voice grim, 'take your place as my countess, accompany me to any function I wish to attend and entertain as necessary. Is that clear?'

Hero dropped her languid pose, straightened her shoulders and lifted a defiant chin. 'Perfectly, my lord. But I would remind you that, although I have sworn to obey you as my husband, I am neither slave nor convict labour and refuse to be treated as such. Do I make *myself* clear?'

'Indeed, madam.' His voice took on a harsher note. 'You will be neither flogged nor condemned to solitary confinement in a scorching tin shed.'

Hero's eyes widened with shock. 'Were you. . .?'

'No, ma'am. I managed to avoid such barbaric treatment. Benbow was not so fortunate.'

'Benbow?'

Drew inclined his head. 'Benbow was transported, too. He rebelled against the conditions a cruel master imposed and suffered the consequences.'

'Oh,' said Hero flatly. There were some things, she found, that she would rather not know. 'Very well, my lord. I will allow these tradespeople to attend me. And I will do my best to learn to dance, if that is your pleasure.' She did not think it necessary to tell his lordship that she could dance quite adequately despite the lack of society in Devon. The vicar's wife had been only too happy to teach her the steps she had been used to perform before her marriage. Nor did she choose to inform him that she could play the pianoforte and had an adequate voice. A small devil seemed to be driving her. 'Do you wish me to take music lessons?' she enquired. 'And mayhap a singing master would not come amiss.'

'Later, perhaps,' said Calverstock. 'You cannot be expected to learn everything at once. But dancing is an essential social skill.'

The devil in her made Hero give an awkward curtsy before leaving the room. His frown seemed to her like a reward. 'I must go and make myself ready,' she said, backing towards the door. 'I will bid you good-day for the present.'

'We will meet for dinner,' said Drew, returning her inept curtsy with an elegant bow. 'Mrs Deacon will have ordered it served at six of the clock.'

Hero frowned and stayed her departure. 'I am used to ordering my father's household at Polhembury,' she said.

'I am certain Mrs Deacon will take note of your wishes, my dear. I will instruct her to wait upon you tomorrow morning. But she is an excellent housekeeper; I could not wish for better. You will have much to occupy your time here. There is no need for you to concern yourself with the running of this establishment.'

Now it was Hero's lips which compressed into a tight line. She was not to be allowed to interfere in the daily running of his life. So be it. But she must make the housekeeper understand that her wishes, as well as Calverstock's, must be obeyed.

She inclined her head. 'She may wait upon me in the morning-room at eleven,' she said, turned about, and swept out.

Drew watched her straight back disappear and the door close. Only then did he move. Wearily. And sighed. What a disaster. And yet he still wanted her, had even thought for a moment last night that she might respond to him as he might wish. But, just as he had set himself to keep his emotions under control, so she had quite clearly determined to allow him his rights and nothing more. But she had been virgin, with no experience to draw upon and so had not understood the instinctive response he had elicited from her body, had tensed up and made the entire act difficult and painful.

He could not, in all honesty, blame her. Perhaps, when she had had time to adjust to her new life, to her status as his wife, things might change. Upon his return from Australia it had been devilishly difficult for him to come to terms with a civilised existence, let alone life as a member of the *ton*, but he had done it. So would she, he assured himself with sudden confidence. She had spirit and grace, despite that absurd curtsy she had given him. An unwilling smile tugged at the corners of his mouth. She had been determined to overcome any embarrassment she might have been feeling and to give as good as she got. He had to admire her for that. Perhaps, one day, he would be able to resurrect that lively, delightful young woman he had met in Polhembury village. She must be buried somewhere inside the new Countess of Calverstock. Just as the true Drew Challoner, gentleman, grandson of an earl, had lain buried inside Drew Challoner the convict for all those years, waiting his chance to emerge.

She had been shaken by his mention of the treatment Benbow had endured. Most people back home had no idea of the harsh conditions experienced by those transported to the other side of the world. Certainly, there were hardened criminals among them, men and women who deserved severe punishment, pickpockets and thieves who were a menace to honest folk and needed to be isolated from decent society. But most, he had soon found, were bewildered petty offenders unable to understand why they had been condemned to spend weeks in stinking hulks moored off Portsmouth, with iron weighing a stone riveted to an ankle, awaiting passage to Botany Bay or Sydney. Or why they should be chained together and daily made to shuffle through the town, a spectacle to all observers, to work in the dockyard. That, for him, had been hardest of all to bear. Like him, all most had done was try to feed their loved ones and to survive.

His mind shied away from the memory of the seemingly endless days at sea, chained four to a six-foot-square bunk in a fetid hold, most suffering agonies of seasickness, dosed with lemon or lime juice on doctor's orders but only allowed to see daylight, to breathe fresh air, to take exercise, for an hour here and there. It had taken them over three months to make the traumatic voyage. More than a few had not survived.

A tap on the door came as a welcome interruption to his unpleasant memories. A footman entered at his command to announce the arrival of Viscount Harrington.

'Archie!' he exclaimed. 'My dear fellow, I cannot tell you how glad I am to see you!'

CHAPTER FOUR

HARRINGTON entered the library, a smile of greeting on his pleasant but unremarkable face. Dressed, like Calverstock, in the height of fashion while managing not to appear dandified, he had nevertheless developed a languor of manner which amused Drew, who had no time for false airs and graces when applied to himself.

'Mornin', Drew. Saw the knocker back on your door. Everythin' go according to plan?'

Drew waved his visitor into one of the deep armchairs by the screened Adam fireplace and sank down in the other. He and Harrington had met by chance while riding in Hyde Park and found themselves in immediate rapport despite the difference in their circumstances. Archie Dalmead, a couple of years younger than Drew at almost eight-and-twenty, was still dependent upon an allowance from his father, Earl Dalmead, and would be until such time as he inherited the title. He had done much to help Drew to acquire the town bronze necessary for him to move easily in society.

Benbow and Harrington were his only confidants in the enterprise he had set himself. He looked across at his friend's expectant face and shrugged. 'More or less.'

With a well-kept nail, Archie flicked a speck of dust from his maroon sleeve. 'Do I collect that somethin' went wrong?'

'Yes and no.'

Archie's black brows rose over deceptively sleepy blue eyes. 'Bein' uncommon reticent, ain't 'ee, m'dear fellow?'

Drew laughed, though without humour. 'I suppose I am. I found my newly acquired estate of Wanleat in precisely the neglected state I imagined it would be, given the empty state of its late owner's pockets and the fact that he hadn't honoured the place with his presence for years. My stay there was primitive to say the least and it took Cuthbert all his time to keep the horses comfortable in almost derelict stables. Polhembury was in slightly better case thanks to the daughter, who had done her best to keep the place going.' For a moment he allowed his mind to dwell on the poverty Hero had been unable to hide. The faded elegance, the old, gleaming wood. The pride with which she had faced him in her outmoded gown. 'I married her,' he added abruptly.

A look of complete incredulity spread over Archie's face. 'You what?' he uttered faintly.

With a grim smile, Calverstock repeated his words. 'I married her.'

'You're leg-shackled?' demanded Archie, displaying such an anguished aversion to the very idea that Calverstock had to laugh, this time in genuine amusement.

'It did not seem such a bad notion—she is attractive, well enough born and I need a wife.'

'But her papa ain't a feather to fly with and it is common tattle she ain't in possession of a dowry,' frowned Archie. 'When you left here you had no such notion in mind.' He waved an expressive hand. 'We were agreed that even if she weren't a complete antidote, Miss Langage's chances of makin' any kind of a decent match were slender. We even wondered what the poor creature would do when you took possession of Polhembury!' He eyed his silent, pensive friend and comprehension dawned. 'I vow you're too devilish soft-hearted, Drew! You wed her because you felt sorry for her! You could have married any chit you liked, secured a sizeable settlement——'

'But I don't need more money,' pointed out Drew, shrugging. 'Polhembury will come to her upon her father's death. I shall secure the estate, but somewhat later than I had envisaged. And I'm not addle-brained enough to wed someone unsuitable out of mere pity, you should know me better than that. I now have a wife to grace my table—and my bed,' he added, with perhaps a little more grimness in his tone than he had intended.

Archie was quick to spot it and darted Drew a look which belied his indolent manner. 'Everythin' not quite right in that department, eh?' His only answer being an incomprehensible grunt, he went on, 'Well, there's always the beauteous Alicia. What d'you intend to do about her? Does she know?'

'No. And I haven't made up my mind,' admitted Drew sombrely. But courtesy demanded he warn her before the announcement appeared in the papers tomorrow. He'd have to call on her later in the day. When he had conceived the idea of marrying Hero Langage, part of the attraction had been the prospect of nullifying the need to continue the liaison with Alicia. Now, with his wife so obdurate, so unwilling to accommodate him, he was having second thoughts, for he would not plead and last night's experience had been more torture than pleasure. Alicia, Lady Willoughby, although approaching forty years and therefore ten years his senior, satisfied his needs with generosity. Sir Arthur, her elderly husband, was complaisant, since she had already provided him with two sons to secure the succession to his baronetcy and a daughter to charm his old age.

'Did Miss Langage turn out to be a beauty?' probed Archie. 'If you didn't marry the creature out of pity there must have been somethin' else, though you ain't much given to swoonin' over a pretty face...'

Drew stirred uneasily, remembering the instant attraction he had felt, the grinding disappointment on discovering her true nature, the desire the mere sight of her aroused in him, a desire he had barely been able to control last night. If he didn't keep away from her he'd be caught in her web, behave like a callow youth, a supplicant for her favours. And that he could never allow.

'No,' he denied abruptly. 'Not a beauty. She has more than beauty. Character.' Even if he had discovered it to be one he could not altogether admire. 'Grace. Spirit.'

Archie grinned. 'I wish I might see this paragon. Must pay me respects to your wife, y'know.'

'All in good time,' promised Calverstock abruptly. 'She is engaged with the dressmaker, milliner and shoemaker this morning. She will be available to receive callers in a day or two. She had no clothes fit to be worn.'

Archie pulled a face. 'That short of blunt, eh? Poor girl.'

'Yes,' agreed Calverstock. But she had not refined over her fate and sunk into a gloom. Neither the laughing girl he had met in Polhembury nor the scornful creature he had married had appeared as an object of pity.

'Comin' to St James's?' asked Archie idly, his interest in Calverstock's new wife satisfied for the moment.

Drew looked at the papers strewn over his desk, then shrugged. 'I might as well. Brook's or White's?'

Arguing amiably as to which club to visit, the two men left the house to step up into Archie's curricle and tool along Knightsbridge to Piccadilly and St James's Street. Fleetingly, Drew wondered how his wife was faring. He could safely leave her in Madame Ernestine's hands. A foremost modiste, she dressed Alicia. She was, of course, discretion itself. She would never mention the fact that he had paid for several of Lady Willoughby's gowns over the two years she had been his mistress.

Madame Ernestine, small, dark, voluble, dressed entirely in black, took one look at Hero, tut-tutted in dismay and ordered her client to remove her gown. After twenty years in London, having fled the revolution in her own country, unless she became agitated her French accent was slight.

'That is better!' she exclaimed, eyeing Hero's neat figure, scarcely hidden at all beneath her cotton chemise. 'Now I can decide what will suit you, madame.' She eyed her client critically, her bird-like head on one side, her dark eyes bright with enthusiasm. 'You will pay for being dressed well, my lady. I shall make you

the sucess of the little season, you will see! His lordship
is a generous gentleman. He will not begrudge the
cost.'

Hero stood still, Matty hovering near by, rather
amused by the antics of the little modiste. It did cross
her mind to wonder how Madame Ernestine knew her
husband to be generous but decided it would be unwise
to dwell upon the subject. Most gentlemen, particuarly
unmarried gentlemen, bought gowns for their mistresses. Her father not only gambled to excess but
spent lavishly on women, money he did not possess.
Calverstock would be no different to any other in his
position and—a blush threatened to betray her and
she fought it down—he was certainly experienced. He
could keep as many mistresses as he liked as long as
he did not trouble her again, she told herself fiercely.
The mental picture she conjured up of his making love
to some unknown woman sent a most peculiar feeling
through her. Since it could not possibly be jealousy, it
must be disgust.

Madame Ernestine ran a tape over her figure, dictat-
ing measurements to her pallid assistant. 'Such lovely
proportions!' she enthused. 'Neither too tall nor too
short. Good hips—thirty-seven inches——' she muttered in an aside '—an excellent bust—thirty-six—well-
covered bones but scarcely any surplus flesh to be
hidden, certainly about your waist—twenty-five—and
with the new lower waistline that is a great advantage.'

Under such critical yet enthusiastic scrutiny, Hero
began to gain confidence. She determined to show
Calverstock that she was more than able to carry the
role he had assigned to her. She would not sink under
the weight of his scorn.

Madame Ernestine had brought swatches, even bolts of material with her, which she spread about over the furniture. It seemed that pale muslins were beginning to go out of fashion except on very young girls, particularly for grand occasions. Certainly, such gowns would be suitable for wearing in the house in summer but, for the evening, gauze over silk or satin was much in fashion, with wider skirts and ribbon trimmings. For mornings her ladyship should consider gowns of various patterned materials in deeper shades which would suit her admirably. . .

So it went on. And Hero, entranced by the billowing swaths of sumptuous materials despite her annoyance at her husband's uncompromising attitude to her appearance, decided to stop concerning herself over choice or cost, to accept madame's advice and spend lavishly on new day dresses with matching pelisses, several exquisite evening gowns, shawls, cloaks, and a splendid ballgown of glowing amber satin with an overskirt of old-gold gauze.

And a new riding habit. The material, though green, was of a different shade to that of her old one and the style would be modish. Her husband kept a stable of horses. If no suitable lady's mount was numbered among them then he must purchase one. She would most definitely ride as soon as possible.

Hero donned her old gown again with some reluctance, not realising that, despite its age and madame's exclamations of horror, it had a simple charm her new gowns would never equal. Before the modiste had left the milliner arrived. Together the two women decided on a saucy top hat for riding, a number of bonnets and hats which would go with the day dresses, all lavishly trimmed with ribbons, feathers and flowers, and several headdresses for the evening.

'No caps,' decreed the milliner. 'Your hair is too beautiful and you are too young, my lady. I will create becoming confections from ribbons, flowers and beads.'

Gloves, muffs, reticules and fans were discussed. Hero felt her presence to be somewhat unnecessary, except to nod her approval of a purchase. By that time she would have agreed to almost anything they suggested. They were the best in their fields and who was she to argue if they felt that seed-pearls must decorate the bodice of her ballgown, long curling ostrich feathers were essential on a particular hat, or finest carved ivory the only possible material for a fan?

Hero felt rather like a doll being dressed up for the benefit of its owner. Calverstock! she thought grimly. Well, he would soon discover that clothing his wife in the style Madame Ernestine thought suitable cost dearly. She dared not think what the bill would come to. But he had set no limit, given no indication that he cared how much she spent. What use was it to be married to one of the wealthiest men in England if she could not disregard expense? It was a new and rather seductive experience to be able to forget money problems, to purchase anything she fancied. And it would serve Calverstock right if she spent more than he intended.

The others had scarcely left when the shoemaker presented himself, a rotund man who bowed obsequiously, eyed her with approval, and experienced some difficulty in getting down to measure her feet, huffing and puffing as he did so and having to be helped up again by his assistant. She chose shoes in finest kid or morocco, slippers in various shades of satin to match the swatches madame had left with her, riding boots in strong, supple hide.

By the time a small procession of footmen arrived at her boudoir door to serve a light nuncheon, Hero was exhausted. She ate the game soup, cold ham, rolls and butter with good appetite. The dinner hour here was set much later than that to which she was used at Polhembury and if she did not eat now by six she would be starved.

After her meal she stretched out on the pink *chaise-longue* and discovered it to be surprisingly comfortable. The gold was peeling off the woodwork in places and she wondered idly about having it restored before tiredness took over and she dozed.

Matty woke her an hour later.

'There's a Mr Reynolds waiting for you in the music-room,' she told Hero. 'Footman says he's here to give you dancing lessons.'

The outrage in Matty's voice made Hero smile, despite her reluctance to be disturbed. She sat up with sudden energy.

'I was expecting him, Matty, I forgot to say. His lordship informed me that he was coming. He may be able to teach me a few new steps, don't you think? You'd better tidy my hair.'

Matty's expression softened as she fetched a comb and began to tease some loose strands back into position beneath Hero's lacy cap. 'It'll be good to see you dancing and enjoying yourself at last, my chick. With the gowns you've ordered this morning you'll not lack for partners, I'll vow.'

'I can't imagine what Mr Reynolds will think of this gown and my old slippers. But still, they are the best I have for the moment. Maybe I'll be able to surprise him the next time he comes. Madame Ernestine promised that some of the dresses will be delivered within a couple of days.'

Mr Reynolds, a man in his late thirties, badly in need of a new suit of clothes and looking as though a good meal would not come amiss, greeted her with the greatest courtesy. He had brought a young girl of about sixteen with him, his daughter, Hero suspected, to play the pianoforte. She inspected Hero with large, anxious eyes, noted the elderly gown she wore and the quick smile with which Hero greeted them, and visibly relaxed.

'My eldest daughter, Lizzie,' Mr Reynolds introduced her, confirming Hero's suspicions. 'She is a good pianist and keeps excellent time.'

'Capital,' said Hero with another smile especially for the girl. 'Please make yourself at home, Lizzie. Perhaps you would like to try the instrument while your father tells me what he intends.'

'I have been engaged to instruct you in the dance, my lady,' murmured Mr Reynolds as Lizzie dropped a curtsy and made for the music stool. He spoke in cultured tones which indicated a good education and had good address. Perhaps a younger son down on his luck and without the prospect of even a mortgaged estate to inherit, guessed Hero. 'Do you have no experience at all?'

'Some,' she admitted, speaking over the sound of Lizzie's experimental scales, 'although because I have been living in secluded circumstances in a Devon village, my husband assumed that I had not. He failed to enquire before engaging you.'

Disappointment clouded Mr Reynolds's face. Clearly he had been relying on the money to be earned over a lengthy period of tuition. 'I see,' he said.

'I doubt it,' she rejoined, enjoying the prospect of conning Calverstock. 'I am certain I still have much to learn,' she went on encouragingly. 'I have had very little practice. Virtually none in the quadrille or the waltz.'

Relieved, Mr Reynolds beamed. 'Then we will concentrate on those dances, my lady. But first, allow me to join you in some steps from one of the older, more familiar dances.'

An hour later, flushed, happier than she had been for a long time, for she enjoyed dancing, Hero beamed at both Mr Reynolds and his daughter.

'I enjoyed that so much!' she exclaimed. 'Lizzie, you are a most accomplished pianist! I wish I could perform half as well!'

'Should you wish tuition I could recommend...' began Mr Reynolds, but Hero shook her head.

'No, not at the moment at least. I believe I can do well enough.'

She wanted to surprise Calverstock when the occasion presented itself. He had such a poor opinion of her that it would do him good to be proved wrong.

By the time it was needed, the yellow sprigged muslin had been washed, dried and ironed. Changing into it, Hero could not prevent a keen sense of anticipation. In only two days' time she would be able to dine wearing a real evening dress, provided Madame Ernestine kept her promise. Hero could imagine the team of cutters and sempstresses already engaged in producing her gowns, perhaps working late, sewing by the dim light of candles to finish the rush order in time. Older needlewomen often suffered from bad eyesight; it was a hazard of the job. Of course, plenty of other people had difficulty in seeing clearly, even members of the *ton*. But they did not have to rely on their eyes to earn a living and in any case could afford to buy a pair of spectacles should they wish to work or read. Or so Mrs Cudlip, who had connections with the minor nobility, had reliably informed her.

The five-minute gong reverberated throughout the house. Hero drew a deep breath and prepared to walk down to the floor below to meet her husband once again.

The kitchens occupied the semi-basement of the service wing, with store-rooms below. The vast entrance hall and staircase area took up much of the ground floor, though the library was located there, as she had discovered that morning, together with the morning-room and breakfast-parlour, reception-rooms, anterooms and a garden-room where impedimenta and boots were left. The first floor held all the formal rooms, the ballroom, the salon, the withdrawing-rooms, dining-rooms and the music-room.

The top floor housed the master suite at the front of the building and enjoyed an extensive view over Hyde Park and the Serpentine river. Other bedrooms were located at the back of the house and on the far side of the staircase. An empty nursery suite at the far end of the building included a schoolroom and rooms for nurse and governess. Benbow's and Matty's rooms were located near the staircase to be close at hand. All the other servants were quartered above the kitchens in the service wing, where the upper servants had their own sitting-rooms.

Hero had not yet inspected her new home in detail. Her information had come through Matty. Tomorrow, she determined, Mrs Deacon would show her around the domain she ruled, whether she wanted to or not. She, Hero, was the mistress and should be aware of everything the house contained. But things looked in such good order and seemed to run on such smooth wheels that she anticipated, as Calvestock had hinted, that there would be little need for her to exert herself in the ordering of the household. Which might be a pleasant change after the struggle she had had to keep Polhembury in even half-decent trim.

Hero descended to the elegant salon adjoining the dining-room, annoyed with herself because her legs felt weak with nerves. Calverstock stood by the window gazing out over the park, a glass in his hand. He turned at her entrance, his gaze appraising and wintry, his lips barely moving in a smile of greeting.

'Madam.' He inclined his head. 'May I pour you a sherry?'

'I would prefer a glass of ratafia if there is any, thank you,' returned Hero. For that evening she wished to keep a clear head, and did not feel the need for false courage.

He made no remark but his lips tightened as he turned to the side-table holding an array of decanters and jugs, and poured a small glass of the almond-flavoured cordial. Perhaps he thought she had asked for it to test the catering efficiency of the housekeeper, though she had not.

He walked back and handed it to her. 'Your ratafia, ma'am. We must not be long. The dinner is ready to serve.'

Hero drank quickly, set her glass down and stood up. 'I am perfectly ready, my lord.'

Drew tossed his own drink down, brandy by its aroma, disposed of his glass, and offered his arm. 'Then let us go in.'

Touching him had such a disastrous effect upon her nerves that Hero wished she could ignore the invitation. But, without showing herself to be completely without conduct, she could not. She therefore allowed her fingers to graze the sleeve of his informal evening coat, scarcely touching him but still aware of the flexed muscles beneath the dark blue cloth.

He was garbed impeccably but not extravagantly, wearing trousers rather than knee breeches for dining at home. He had, in fact, chosen to dress down and a tendril of gratitude threaded its way towards her heart. A more elaborate choice could have made her feel dowdy, have emphasised the poverty of her own attire.

Though they were to dine alone, the table glittered with crystal and silver. They took their places at either end of a table reduced to its minimum length but which still set them some ten feet apart, making conversation, even had they wished to indulge, difficult. Footmen carrying the dishes appeared from a small adjoining servery.

Hero frowned. She judged the kitchen to be below and to one side. She had not observed the food being brought up. It would be stone-cold if it had been waiting in the servery all that time.

The covers were lifted. Hero was offered a choice

between baked trout, roast fowl, and a steaming steak and kidney pudding, together with dishes of fried celery and oyster loaves. She realised she was unexpectedly hungry. The aroma rising from the pudding was irresistible. Having started with a small portion of the trout, she took a large slice of pudding packed with meat and running with thick gravy, and added some celery to her plate.

Drew chose a portion of pudding, too. As Hero sampled it she exclaimed over its delicious taste and its warmth. 'Yet it must have left the kitchen long ago.'

Drew laughed. She liked the sound. It held no hint of scorn, but simply genuine, proud amusement. 'Not so, my lady. After the meal you must take a look in the servery. The food is hoisted up from the kitchen by lift.'

How stupid of her to show her ignorance, thought Hero. Of course, she should have remembered Mrs Cudlip talking of the wonders to be found in the residences of the rich. Calverstock House would be equipped with every amenity, of that she could be certain. Although chamber pots concealed in night tables still abounded in the bedrooms, Hero had been introduced to a water closet which took the waste straight down to a cesspool in the garden. A closet had been put in on each floor, tiered one above the other. Although convenient, they tended to smell and Hero preferred to use her close-stool, which was emptied at frequent intervals.

'I shall be most interested,' she acknowledged, relaxing somewhat and offering a tentative smile. 'I expect to become better acquainted with the amenities

Calverstock House has to offer when Mrs Deacon takes me on a tour of the establishment tomorrow.'

'I trust you will approve. Would you like me to accompany you?'

The offer seemed genuine yet Hero could not imagine he really wanted to traipse about the house on her heels. Besides, she wanted to become acquainted with the housekeeper.

'It is kind of you to offer, but Mrs Deacon might prefer to show me heself,' she pointed out. 'I shall manage perfectly well.'

'I am certain you will.'

His flat tone told her she had, in some way, disappointed him. But that was absurd. She concentrated on her meal, following the pudding with an oyster loaf. The roll had been buttered and crisped in the oven, the oyster fried and tucked inside. It was delicious.

The second course was delivered. Chicken in a cream sauce this time, jugged pigeons and a variety of syllabubs, tarts and pancakes. Drew took some chicken and a spoon of potato pudding but Hero moved straight on to something sweet, choosing a pancake rolled round strawberry jam, which she followed with a raspberry syllabub. Drew finished with anchovy toast.

Wine had been served with each course. Although she had refused the sherry, Hero did accept a glass of wine, which she found both pleasant and stimulating. Perhaps it was that which loosened her tongue.

For when he asked her, politely but casually, how her consultation with Madame Ernestine had gone, she found herself giving a witty account of the little Frenchwoman's antics and a more enthusiastic description of the fabrics and styles than she intended. She had thought to be restrained, off-hand about the luxury being lavished upon her, for his reasons for generosity were not worthy of true appreciation. But something in the atmosphere, some strange contentment at sharing a pleasant tête-à-tête meal with her husband, made her forget her resolution to treat him with the contempt he deserved for ruining her father and claiming her hand as part-payment of the debt.

Drew looked along the length of the polished table, bare now that the cloth had been removed. Above the bowls of fruit and decanter he saw a charming girl in a faded blue gown, saw in her eager, animated face, her suddenly softened manner, the delightful female he had deluded himself into thinking her. If he did not watch himself she would succeed in seducing his senses again. It was the money being lavished upon her she appreciated, not him. He gripped the stem of his glass and sent her an icy stare.

'I trust the account for all this extravagance will not exceed your dress allowance,' he remarked coldly.

Hero's ease slipped abruptly back into tension. 'Allowance?' she enquired. 'What allowance?'

'Did it not occur to you, my lady, that you would receive an allowance? You cannot expect to have your every whim satisfied from my pocket.'

'I will cancel the order, ' said Hero through gritted teeth.

'No.' The denial was final. 'I will not have Madame Ernestine, the milliner or the shoemaker inconvenienced.' He had no intention of preventing her from making a show in society. He intended to be the envy of every blade in London. And scuttle the fond hopes of all the mamas at one go. As well as discourage other bored women, like Alicia, who pursued him with unflagging energy. For the first time the thought of Alicia brought with it a feeling of slight distaste. The interview this afternoon had not been pleasant. Alicia had flown into a jealous fury; then she had begged. He had given her no definite promise for the future and had left without taking her to bed.

Damn the creature he had made his wife! Was she to spoil even that pleasure for him? His voice when he continued sounded harsher than he intended.

'I will meet these first bills in full. But hereafter you will receive a quarterly allowance, which will be available from my bank. You will be issued with a chequebook. I think you will find the sum adequate but I would advise you to keep within it and to spend it wisely.'

'I have learned to do that the hard way,' gritted Hero. All her pleasure in the new gowns, the intimate meal, had disappeared. For a while she had forgotten Calverstock's ruthless nature. It would be a long time before she forgot it again. 'If you will excuse me, I will retire to my room. I have spent a tiring day.'

Calverstock rose as she did, bowed over her hand and wished her goodnight. He did not mention coming to her later.

Hero prayed he would not. Yet she lay for hours wondering whether he would and when she at last heard him come up prepared herself for his invasion of her privacy and her body.

But he did not trouble her. And she was not at all sure whether the tears she shed before falling into a restless sleep were because she was glad or sorry that he had not.

CHAPTER FIVE

THE announcement that a marriage had taken place between the Earl of Calverstock and Miss Hero Langage took the beau monde by storm. Teacups clattered as tongues wagged. No one had seen the new countess and curiosity was high. Before the day was through cards had begun to appear on the tray in the hall of Calverstock House.

Hero remained unaware until late in the afternoon when, her tour of the establishment completed and a satisfactory relationship with Mrs Deacon established, her nuncheon consumed and boredom set in, she descended to the library in search of something to read.

She gave a cursory knock before entering, not expecting to find Calverstock there at that hour, but he was, busy with the papers he had neglected the previous day.

He glanced up and then swiftly rose to his feet as she hesitated in the doorway.

'You wished to see me, ma'am?'

'No—I came to find a book to read, but it is of no consequence.' She half turned as though to go.

He made a sweeping gesture. 'You are at liberty to choose any book you wish. What kind of reading interests you?'

'History, geography—anything. I wish to improve my knowedge,' Hero explained somewhat breathlessly.

Calverstock's unexpected presence had confused her. 'The library at Polhembury was limited for choice. This one looks more promising.'

He nodded. 'It is reasonably extensive. But if you find nothing to your taste here I suggest you join a subscription library or visit Lackington's bookshop in Finsbury Square.' He appeared to hesitate for a moment before indicating copies of various news-papers, which lay on a table near the door, folded open at the announcement he had paid to have inserted. 'Have you read the papers today?'

'No. I did not know they were here.'

'You did not breakfast in the parlour,' he observed, a faint note of censure invading his tone. He had been irritated by her non-appearance. Not that he particu-larly wished to see her, of course, but her avoidance of him rankled. 'They are first available there. The announcement of our marriage is in them.'

After a startled glance at him Hero looked down to see the paragraph, boldly marked in pencil. She read the short, bald statement of fact and looked up again, her cheeks slightly flushed.

'So the world now knows.'

He acknowledged her statement with a slight bow. 'And in consequence many of those still in town have already left or will shortly be leaving their cards. Once Madame Ernestine has delivered suitable apparel for you we will begin to return the courtesy and make our calls. Everyone is eager to meet my wife.'

'You will accompany me?' asked Hero faintly, not sure whether she wanted him to. She had been nervous of making the necessary morning calls on her own, but his presence at her side could surely do little to diminish her apprehension.

'I think it would be wise.'

'Very well, my lord.'

He waved an expansive hand around the book-lined room. 'Please feel free to make your choice.'

As she moved forward he seated himself again and began to write. Hero remembered that she wished to ask him about the possibility of riding while in London. She cleared her throat.

'Excuse me, my lord, but there is something I wish to ask you.'

He looked up, a slight frown marring his forehead. 'Yes?'

Don't be so idiotish, Hero scolded herself silently as agitation threatened to overcome her. You are only making an enquiry! He cannot eat you! Besides, it was too lowering to acknowledge herself unnerved by the prospect of her husband's displeasure.

'I wished to ask if there is a horse in your stable suitable for me. I have ordered a new habit in the expectation of being able to ride. Exercising on horse-back was something I enjoyed at Polhembury until Papa had to sell most of his cattle.'

Calverstock's expression relaxed. He actually smiled and Hero felt her own tension dissolve.

'There is bound to be. I keep a horse trained to a lady's saddle for the use of a possible guest. You may use that until I can find a suitable mount to purchase for you.'

Hero's face glowed. 'Thank you! And. . .may I order a carriage should I wish to go somewhere—Finsbury

Square, for example?' she added quickly, remembering his earlier suggestion about the purchase of books.

He nodded. 'Naturally, my lady. You are my wife. The servants are at your command, the amenities at your disposal. I shall not always be available to accompany you on your social calls.'

'You are most kind,' murmured Hero, and meant it. He seemed in a most accommodating mood. 'I will not disturb you much longer,' she promised. 'It should only take a moment to choose a book.'

'You do not disturb me,' he returned coolly, returning to his letter.

But he did disturb her, thought Hero as she quickly scanned the shelves for a likely title. She was far too aware of his virile frame, of the way his capable hand moved down the sheet, filling it with his bold, decisive script. In the end she chose almost at random, took the book from its shelf and made her retreat.

That evening at dinner conversation flowed more easily. He enquired about her tour of his establishment and she was able to enthuse over the general size, layout, furnishings and convenience of Calverstock House. He looked gratified. 'How did you find Mrs Deacon?' he enquired.

'Efficient but a trifle stiff,' acknowledged Hero. 'I think she imagined I might wish to usurp her authority. I managed to calm her fears. We have agreed that she will present herself for a consultation each morning, immediately after breakfast. She will receive my instructions regarding any entertaining we may do and seems willing to include in the menu any dish I may suggest. Provided, of course, Monsieur Vodin agrees to cook it!'

This she said with a wry grimace which brought a brief smile to Calverstock's lips. 'Inform me should you encounter any difficulty,' he said.

Hero silently decided to ignore that suggestion. She would manage the cook without his help. She went on to inform him of the book she had chosen, an amusing account of a gentleman's travels around England. He asked her when Madame Ernestine hoped to deliver her first gowns.

'Tomorrow,' said Hero. 'She promised both a morning and an evening gown delivered by noon.'

'Then you may tell Mrs Deacon that we shall be entertaining tomorrow evening—a single gentleman,' he added quickly, seeing the consternation on Hero's expressive face. 'My particular friend, Viscount Harrington. He wishes to meet you.'

Hero relaxed again and nodded. 'I will inform her.'

'And now, my lady,' he said as he finished his port. 'Shall we retire to the small drawing-room? I will not linger at the table this evening. I am engaged to attend my club in an hour's time but we may drink tea together before I leave.'

He was, thought Hero, offering a small olive branch. She would not reject it. They might never achieve closeness, even friendship, but if they were to share the same house they could not exist in constant enmity.

Hero descended to dinner the following day endowed with a new confidence. Madame Ernestine had delivered the two simple gowns promised, had brought them herself and insisted upon a fitting before she would allow Hero to appear in them. She had brought tacked-up editions of several of the more elaborate garments, too, and her visit had developed into a full-scale session. Her assistant had made minor alterations to the two finished dresses—a tuck here, an adjustment to a seam there—while the modiste gave more detailed attention to the fit of the other, more complicated designs.

The evening gown Hero wore as she entered the salon to greet her first guest as Calverstock's countess, though simple, suited her to admiration and displayed her figure to advantage. The soft rose-pink silk clung lovingly to her generous bosom before falling in elegant folds to the floor, the colour lending its glow to her creamy shoulders and face. Sprigs of artificial flowers decorated the neckline and hem. Matty had taken care over her hair, which was piled on top of her head, displaying the slender length of her neck. In lieu of a headdress not yet delivered by the milliner, Matty had substituted a bow of dark pink velvet ribbon, the ends of which trailed fetchingly down the back of Hero's head.

The man lounging in a chair talking to Calverstock sprang to his feet as she entered, as did her husband. Their guest was a little shorter than Drew, slim, dark and handsome in an aristocratic way. He looked nice, thought Hero as she braved the scrutiny of his lazy blue eyes and answered the slow smile which spread itself over his face as she approached.

'My dear,' said Calverstock formally, 'allow me to introduce Archie Dalmead, Lord Harrington. Archie, my wife.'

Archie made a most elaborate bow to which Hero responded with a deep curtsy. A graceful one, Drew noted wryly. Seeing her dressed in the manner to

which she was entitled, albeit simply, had taken his
breath. If he had thought her verging on beauty before,
how much more must he admire her looks now. He
longed to be able to take her hand without embarrassment, to go to her bed without guilt. Guilt for desperately desiring a woman who despised him.

The emotion had kept him from her since that first
night. How could he so debase himself? Yet. . .

Through a haze he heard Archie congratulating him,
and responded automatically. The butler offered him
another glass of brandy, which he took. He seldom
drank deeply, having too much respect for his dignity
and a deep desire to keep in possession of keen
faculties which had stood him in good stead on many
an occasion. Others in the penal colony had chosen to
drown their sorrows in any rot-gut they could lay their
hands on and here men at the gaming tables indulged
freely as they risked their fortunes upon the turn of a
card, the fall of the dice. But he had always resisted
the urge and had no intention of changing his habits
now and certainly not over a woman.

Hero, despite a certain nervousness, enjoyed the
evening more than those she had so far spent in
London solely in her husband's company. Archie
Dalmead, despite his indolent manner, supported an
interesting conversation, recounting anecdotes of
members of the *ton*, setting the scene for Hero's entry
into society. Before the meal was over she felt she
already knew many of the people she would be meeting in the next few weeks.

'You'd better keep an eye on this clever, fetchin'
countess of yours,' drawled Archie with a mischievous
glance at Hero. 'Just the sort to take the beau monde

by storm, I'll warrant. Have all the gentlemen about town eatin' out of her hand, I wouldn't be surprised.'

Hero blushed and glanced uncomfortably towards Drew, who eyed her, she thought, disparagingly—no change—before saying in his most top-lofty manner, 'So they may. I anticipate that many men will admire Lady Calverstock once she is introduced into society. But, should my wife be tempted to betray me, when it comes to pistols at dawn I fear no man.'

Hero went cold. She had a dreadful feeling that he meant it.

'I say, old man, doin' it a bit brown, ain't 'ee?' enquired Archie with a lazy grin. 'Wasn't what I meant at all. Just tryin' to pay your delightful wife a compliment, that's all.'

Watching her husband's expression relax, Hero felt a sense of relief. Until that moment she had been truly enjoying herself for the first time since leaving Polhembury. She liked Archie and in his company Drew had behaved more easily towards herself. Not that he had ever shown her other than the outward courtesy good manners demanded, but beneath the surface she had sensed disdain, even anger in his attitude. Perhaps because of his friend's presence he had relaxed that evening and the underlying censure had been muted, as had her resentment towards him. The two men were comfortable in each other's company and she had discovered a side of her husband's character which had previously been hidden from her. With Archie acting as a buffer, a kind of rapport had been established between them. Until that unfortunate turn in the conversation.

But the incident was soon forgotten and the evening

proceeded in a most pleasant manner. The men lingered at the table for a short period while Hero retired to the small drawing-room to await them and the arrival of the tea tray.

Drew's reaction to the merest hint of the possibility of her infidelity had not only chilled, but also amazed her. He did not love her, did not even want her were the last few nights any indication of the depth of his desire, yet he had shown himself ready to demand her fidelity and challenge any man rather than play the cuckold. Yet she was certain he would think nothing of keeping a mistress himself. A gentleman could behave in the most blatantly indiscreet manner and his wife could remonstrate in vain. But let that wife step only slightly out of line and she would be condemned by both husband and society, become an outcast unfit to be received. It did not seem fair.

Not that she had the slightest desire to flirt or dally. Her husband's absence from her bed was welcome. Although...his indifference to her charms was inclined to make her feel rejected, and that was not a comfortable state in which to live. In truth, she scarcely knew what she wanted.

But she would give the matter no more thought. Drew had married her for some mysterious reason of his own—he could have ruined her father without insisting on making her his bride. She owed him nothing more than duty demanded. She would otherwise live as she pleased, enjoy the chance to explore London and to attend the routs and balls, the theatre and the opera, perhaps obtain a voucher for Almack's, that pinnacle of acceptance, of which she had heard so much. She would, in fact, make the most of the chance to sample the delights of living in town. After being buried in Polhembury for all her twenty-three years she would enjoy spreading her social wings for once.

Over the next weeks Drew gradually introduced his wife into the society which had, at first, regarded him as an interloper. His manner, but above all his fortune, had soon secured his acceptance. As it would that of his countess.

Most of society had returned to their country estates well before the first of September for the partridge shooting. Many would remain there until after Christmas, even until the start of the next season. But others preferred to return to town in October and arrange routs, dinners and balls before departing again for Christmas. Calverstock escorted Hero to make morning calls on all those currently residing in town and who mattered, and arranged to attend her when the calls were returned. At the fashionable hour he sometimes drove her in the park in his curricle, where she was introduced to yet more of the beau monde. It rather amused Hero to think that she had become part of the procession of smart carriages she had watched from her window.

A couple of weeks after her arrival in town, with her new habit delivered, Hero ordered a mount and groom to meet her next morning for a ride before breakfast. To her surprise and pleasure she was greeted by a beaming Ned Tribble. She had forgotten he was to travel to London to take up the duties of head groom and coachman there. Despite still holding him in some displeasure for leaving her father's employment, she nevertheless felt warmth spread through her at sight of a familiar face.

'How are you, Ned?' she enquired as he gave her a lift to mount.

'I'm fine, miss. . .my lady,' he returned.

He looked fit and healthy, happier than she had seen him for some time.

'The new position suits you, I collect.'

'Indeed it does, my lady. And, no disrespect, but my wages are paid regular.'

Arrested, Hero gazed down into his weatherbeaten, open face. 'They were not paid regularly at Polhembury?'

He flushed beneath his tan. 'No, my lady. I was owed a full year's pay. I couldn't have carried on much longer.'

'You should have applied to me,' said Hero grimly.

Since their steward had been dismissed because the estate could no longer support his salary, at about the same time as her horse had been sold, she had undertaken his duties. She had collected the rents, accepting them from the farmers on quarter days, and from the cottage tenants, visiting them in their homes once a month. She had kept the books of the estate, retaining just enough of the rents she collected to pay the household bills, including the wages, and then handed the remainder to her father. Ned and the boy's remuneration had been included in her careful calculations but she had given the cash to her father and trusted him to pass it on, since the horses were his and the running of the stables the only thing of interest to him. It had been a mistake. She had not believed her father capable of such blatant dishonesty.

And Ben Foster. Had he been driven to steal garden produce because he had not received his wages? If so, why hadn't he told the magistrate?

'I didn't like to complain, my lady,' said Ned awkwardly as he mounted his hack and they began to walk the horses towards Hyde Park Corner.

Probably Ben Foster hadn't liked to tell, either, for fear of retribution should he be acquitted. He would certainly have lost his job and most probably been driven to commit far worse crimes in his efforts to help his family. She wondered where he was and how he was faring in that far-off land. Poor Ben.

'You were too loyal,' she told Tribble, the last of her resentment towards the groom disappearing. Her father had brought Ned's defection upon himself, like so many of the troubles which had resulted in her own unhappy marriage. And now the staff at Polhembury had no one to look after their interests. Were they being paid? A new worry occupied her mind.

She had already written to the vicar's wife, as promised. Now she determined to write again to ask her friend Mrs Cudlip to investigate her father's and the servants' welfare.

She had to wait two weeks for an answer and when it came she did not know whether to be glad or infuriated. Now that she was no longer there to do it, her father had taken to collecting the rents and so far had paid the servants their wages, but as far as Mrs Cudlip could discover he did nothing else. The tenants informed him of their complaints and worries, but the baron did little about them, and he kept Mrs Blackler desperately short of housekeeping money. He paid the wages rather than be deserted, thought Hero bleakly.

Perhaps losing the services of Ned Tribble had taught him a lesson. And she could guess at how her father spent the rest of the money he collected: on brandy, gaming and women, in that order.

The report was not reassuring. She made up her mind to send Mrs Cudlip a draft every quarter to cash at the bank and give to Mrs Blackler to augment the housekeeping and make up any shortfall in the wages should her father fall behind. She felt her solution far from satisfactory but it was all she could do. The worry did not go away.

She rode out most fine mornings, as did Drew, but they never arranged to ride together. On a couple of occasions they met in the park and he turned and accompanied her. On those rare occasions they engaged in an exhilarating canter, to their mutual enjoyment. So far there had been no sign of the new mount he had promised to purchase for her but since the one she rode suited her well this did not trouble her and she did not mention the matter again.

October proved a busy month socially, so Hero should have had little time to feel sorry for herself, yet she did. She was lonely and bored, mainly for lack of anything useful to do, she thought. She had been kept busy at Polhembury, had found no time to repine over her lack of friends, her limited social life. But she had no wish to interfere with Mrs Deacon's smooth running of Calverstock House and possibly cause an upset. So she had nothing to do all day but socialise with people she scarcely knew and did not particularly like and, now that many of the *ton* had returned to London, attend hot, stuffy receptions and routs, listen to indifferent performances on the pianoforte and endure the trilling of those with no pretension to a voice. And feign an interest in all the latest, scandalous *on dit* flying about town.

She now had a score of acquaintances but not a single friend. And she had met no one she wished to cultivate. The ladies appeared so superficial, interested only in gossip and fashion, except for some of the government ministers' wives, like Lady Castlereagh, married to the foreign secretary. But she could scarcely expect to make a friend of her, despite the cordial relations existing between their husbands.

The new wardrobe had been delivered in good time. Drew had called her to the library and spoken harshly, shaking the resultant sheaf of bills under her nose.

'Your extravagance is far worse than I had anticipated. Did you not question the need for all these gowns?' he demanded coldly. 'No less than five evening and ballgowns, several morning gowns and house dresses, two riding habits, numerous walking gowns and pelisses, hats, gloves and headdresses by the dozen, not to mention unlimited underwear and enough shoes and slippers to equip an army——'

Hero cut in acidly, 'I offered to cancel the orders, but you would not hear of it. You instructed me to be guided by Madame Ernestine and the others you had called upon to attend me. They considered the gowns and accessories no more than an adequate wardrobe for someone of my rank.'

'And you did not question the opinions of tradespeople?'

'No, my lord,' said Hero, wide-eyed and innocent. 'Not since you had placed me in their hands. I accepted their advice as being yours and did not question the cost. After all, you are reputedly an exceedingly rich man.'

Drew's normally shapely lips compressed into a thin, straight line of annoyance. The chit had hoist him with his own petard. 'I will, of course, meet these accounts,' he stated haughtily. 'But many a gentleman has been ruined by his wife's extravagance. You will, in future, keep your expenditure within the allowance I promised you.' He turned back to his desk to throw down the bills and retrieve some other documents, which he handed to her. 'Here are the details. You may draw cheques as you please, but the bankers have instructions not to allow you to exceed the sum deposited each quarter.'

Hero glanced down and almost staggered as she read the size of her personal allowance. Just in time she regained her poise. He must know it was far more than she had had at her disposal with all the expenses of Polhembury to meet. But she would not give him the satisfaction of seeing her surprise. Since he was grumbling about her initial expenditure, it must have been immense. A trickle of guilt entered her mind but she forced it out. He had deserved nothing less.

She inclined her head. 'Maintaining my position in society will no doubt be expensive, but now I need merely to augment my wardrobe from time to time and occasionally replace damaged or worn items. This,' she tapped a careless finger on the written sum, 'should prove adequate, I believe.'

The merest twitch softened the severe line of his mouth. She had accepted his generosity with complete poise and calm. Only the faintest tinge of pink in her cheeks had given her surprise away. She was, he thought with admiration, a worthy opponent. A woman he could so easily admire and love.

'I am confident it will,' he said, repressing the urge to take her in his arms but unable to resist a compliment. 'The gowns you chose become you. I have been proud to present you as my wife.'

Hero glanced at him, almost overset by his sudden change of attitude. The gleam of appreciation in his eyes suggested that his initial severity had stemmed from a desire to punish her. In fact she had long suspected that he held some grudge against her, something more than simply the fact that she was her father's daughter. A grudge that had not been there during that first encounter in Polhembury village, although then he had not appreciated who she was. Just as her grudge against him had been absent then, for how could she have known him to be an ex-convict and a man who bought up debts and used his power to ruin his victims?

For her father was not the only peer he had brought to ruination. Despite the favour he had found in many quarters she had discovered one or two ladies who held him in deep disgust for what he had done to someone of their acquaintance. They had not spoken openly, but, knowing what she did of his dealings with her father, she had realised immediately the cause of their disparaging remarks. Yes, she knew why she nursed an underlying resentment against him, although when he behaved as he was behaving now it became hard to sustain. He was such a difficult man to understand. But the cause of his antagonism to her remained obscure. Could it be due to something her father had said or implied?

She wished she knew. Wished they could return to ignorance of each other, return to being the two people who had met as strangers in Polhembury and instantly felt an affinity.

But dreams were for green girls. She swept him a graceful curtsy. 'I am glad you are not altogether displeased with our bargain, my lord. I shall do my utmost to perform my part of it.'

'Capital. We shall deal well enough together, I collect. Perhaps you would like to take a drive in the park?'

'I would account it a pleasure, my lord.'

'Then we will leave in half an hour, if that will suit?'

Hero smiled. 'I shall be ready, sir.'

Only one incident since then had broken the cool truce existing between them.

Shortly afterwards, as she presented herself dressed for an evening's entertainment, Drew had given her coiffure a critical stare. 'You must employ a skilled lady's maid,' he had decreed abruptly. 'Matty is not competent to turn you out in a manner due your station.'

Hero stared at him, dismayed. Did he wish to break her last close link with her past life? And, after so many years of faithful service, what would happen to Matty?'

'Matty knows me and I know her,' she protested. 'I have no desire to change her for a stranger. And there would be nothing for her back at Polhembury without me there.'

Drew threw her an exasperated glance. 'I did not itend to deprive you of Matty's company. But the little season is about to begin and you need to acquire more town polish, my dear. Matty may remain as your companion, if you so desire, but I insist that you employ a woman skilled in the art of dressing someone of your rank. I will advertise tomorrow.'

'In that case, thank you. Matty has been like a mother to me. I could not bear to lose her.'

'I know.'

Relief that Matty was to remain made Hero more complaisant over the appointment of a new maid. She smiled her acknowledgement of his consideration. 'And I may make the final choice?'

'Naturally. All those sent along will be competent. You have only to decide who will be most congenial to you. I shall not interfere.'

They had departed for the evening's entertainment in amity once more.

The dancing classes had proceeded smoothly but it was not until November that she attended her first ball. They had been invited to attend the banquet given at the Guildhall to mark the inauguration of the new lord mayor of the City of London and a ball was to follow. How Drew had come to be invited remained a mystery but he did know Mr Vansittart, the chancellor of the exchequer, and they had attended the Countess Bathurst's drum the previous week. The earl, her husband, was the minister responsible for the colonies and both would be present at the Guildhall. Plenty of official guests had been invited but, for the first time, Hero would be mixing with those men who had made their money rather than inherited it. Perhaps Drew's banker had invited him. The bank must be keen to keep such a wealthy client, whatever his history.

That evening Hero knew she looked her best, resplendent in cream satin trimmed with seed-pearls and with fine gold lace about the neck and sleeves. The elaborately decorated hem, which trailed the floor behind, was designed to be lifted to facilitate the dancing afterwards. Jackson, her new maid, was indeed proficient at her job. Hero's hair, arranged in smooth pleats behind with ringlets about her face, gleamed with health. Jackson, however, refused to place in position the headdress the milliner had created to match the gown.

'I have received instructions from his lordship to leave your head bare, my lady,' she excused herself when Hero commented. 'He wishes you to wear a jewel, I believe.'

'His lordship must, of course, be obeyed,' said Hero, hiding a certain bitterness, for she had thought the confection of gold ribbon and lace became her. She almost decided to challenge the whim of her husband which decreed she must adorn her head according to his dictates, but decided that it really did not matter. It was his overbearing manner which rankled, not what she wore on her head, and her complaint against him could be dealt with at leisure.

At first Matty had watched with jealous eyes as Jackson wrought her transformation, but she had long since accepted her own limitations and found a greater pleasure in her role as Hero's companion. Her duties were lighter, which suited her age and rheumatism, and she, too, had acquired a wardrobe more suited to her new status.

'Enjoy yourself, my chick,' Matty admonished as Hero prepared to descend to join her husband.

As Hero entered the room where he waited, he looked up from his contemplation of his shoe and stood to receive her. She approached swiftly and as she did something stirred in the depths of his eyes. Could it be admiration? Hero hoped so. For the limbo in which they were living irked her. He was meticulous in his attentions when necessary, but for the remainder of the time he disappeared. He dined at home when they entertained, but that was seldom. Otherwise, unless they were invited out, he went to his club, leaving her to share a tray with Matty in her boudoir, for neither of them fancied eating in the stilted atmosphere of the dining-room. Once or twice he had absented himself for two or three days—called away by urgent business out of town, he said, but Hero wondered.

'Congratulations,' he murmured after making his customary bow. 'You look very well. Come here.'

His tone was neither curt nor cold, the instruction an invitation rather than a command. Perhaps, after all, he did not intend to be provoking. Maybe he had a good reason for the order he had given Jackson. If so, then his manner of transmitting it to her left much to be desired.

So Hero complied, though the constriction in her throat brought on by the sight of her husband arrayed in full evening dress threatened to deprive her of breath. His black cutaway coat revealed a narrow margin of white satin waistcoat, a high-collared frilled shirt and cravat tied with Benbow's usual expertise. White satin breeches clung lovingly to his muscular thighs, descending to meet white silk hose held up by ribbon ties fastened by diamond clips which matched the buckles on his black pumps. She had never seen him looking so fine.

He reached behind him to pick up a piece from a jewel box lying open on the table.

'Turn round.'

Hero tore her eyes away from the sparkling stones spilling from his palm and tried to ignore the *frisson* of awareness that ran through her at the touch of his fingers on her nape as he fastened the necklace about her throat. His hands on her shoulders turned her back to face him and she saw that he held another piece of jewellery. He inspected her hair, and smiled. 'This will suit you to admiration,' he decided, placing the gold hoop with its swirls of colour on her head and tucking the ends securely in the folds of her hair. 'These are but two pieces I picked out from among the family heirlooms. The most valuable are set entirely with diamonds but I thought, since your gown was decorated with pearls, this mixture of stones and pearls would suit it best.'

Hero moved to stand before the mirror placed over the mantel. The colours, set in gold in both necklace and tiara, were exquisite, a mixture of aquamarine, amethyst and beryl set off by an interweaving of pearls set in finely wrought gold scrolls. The necklace rested about her throat, the drop at its base nestling into the hollow between her breasts; the tiara framed her face and set off her hair. Both could have been designed for her.

'They are beautiful,' she said, touching the fine workmanship of the heirloom necklace with loving fingers.

Drew's face appeared behind her in the mirror, his

features softened, his eyes smiling and holding a gleam she was unwilling to interpret.

'*You* are beautiful,' he murmured.

'Fustian!' cried Hero turning, blushing with pleasure. 'You are bamming me, sir! I fear I shall never be a beauty.'

'Ah,' he responded quietly, 'but beauty is surely in the eye of the beholder.' He grinned. 'I dare you to call me a liar.'

Embarrassed, not knowing how to deal with this new, flirtatious man she called her husband, Hero giggled. 'You will turn my head, my lord. I think we should depart!'

He immediately offered his arm. 'The carriage awaits you, your ladyship. Let us hope the streets will not be too crowded, or we shall be late.'

CHAPTER SIX

IN THIS amicable mood they descended to the carriage and began the journey into the City of London.

On first passing through the streets of the capital, Hero had been stunned by the number of buildings, the quantity of traffic. Carriages and carts, horses, drays, donkeys and pedestrians jostled for room. Many of the vehicles melted away to make room at the approach of so splendid an equipage as the earl's town chariot, crested and gleaming, drawn by a pair of matched greys, with Tribble and a groom wearing beaver hats on the box and two bewigged and uniformed footmen up behind. For Drew insisted that when she travelled without him she was as well attended as when he accompanied her.

Even with the carriage windows shut, new and unwelcome odours had assailed her nostrils. The rattle of iron wheels on cobbled streets, despite being muffled by the malodorous layer of dung and slime, had threatened to add a headache to a turned stomach the first time she went calling in Mayfair. Although she was by now accustomed to it, she always returned to Kensington Gore thankful that the Calverstock residence had been built in several acres of grounds on the outermost limits of London and overlooking a vast open space where the air was fresh and the noise of traffic too distant to be heard.

The heart of the City was new territory for her. She

therefore peered out of the windows of the carriage regretting November's early advent of darkness, for she could see little. The gas lamps, already lit, supplied only fuzzy pools of muted brilliance because of the mist, which almost completely obscured her view. Buildings lined the streets and the carriage appeared to be moving through a murky canyon filled with ghostly crowds, people who, having earlier watched the lord mayor's procession proceed along the Thames, disembark and drive through the City streets, now hoped to catch a glimpse of the dignitaries arriving for the banquet. Unused to the conditions, afraid of losing his way, Tribble drove carefully.

Despite its being a City rather than a society occasion, plenty of the *ton* attended the function, if the number of crested carriages caught in the crush of vehicles attempting to set their passengers down at the steps of the Guildhall was any indication. Hero found the arrival at functions a tedious business, but nothing had prepared her for the frustrating wait while Tribble edged their coach and pair into the waiting line and inched forward as one after another of the carriages discharged its load.

Arrived at length, they were greeted by the new lord Mayor, Mr Alderman Atkins, and his lady, before being ushered through to the council chamber, where the guests, including members of the government, foreign ambassadors and other dignitaries, many in the livery of famous London guilds, were gathering prior to processing through to dinner.

'Allow me to introduce you to our prime minister, Lord Liverpool,' said Drew, and Hero found herself curtsying to the head of His Majesty's government.

Faces and names flashed past her after that, Lord Bathurst, Lord Sidmouth and Mr Vansittart, all members of the cabinet, among them. She was by now quite used to being introduced to some of the cream of London society and made the appropriate responses without nervousness. Drew entered into a deep conversation with Earl Bathurst, presumably discussing the state of the colonies, leaving Hero to be entertained by Mr Vansittart, the chancellor of the exchequer.

She was not sorry when that gentleman was called away, for, charming as he was, they had no point of contact and making small talk had been difficult for both. Before leaving her he introduced her to the man on whose arm she was to enter for dinner. Mr Rudge, although not currently an Alderman, was an important man in the City and proved to be a round, cheerful draper of middle age, who dealt in woollen materials and was reputed to be vastly rich.

To him she could talk easily about cloth and fashion and he urged her to visit his main emporium, where she could command his personal attention. While they spoke he escorted her on a tour of the paintings hung in the chamber, some of historical interest, others of more contemporary importance. For a rich cit Mr Rudge showed considerable address and an agreeable degree of knowledge of the topics on which he chose to expound.

'Our prosperity depends upon the Navy's mastery of the sea,' he explained when Hero wondered why so many admirals featured among the portraits. 'Without men like Nelson, Howe and Rodney to command and ensure that our shipping lanes are kept open through war and peace, trade would suffer. The City owes them much.'

The pageantry outdoors had been, by all accounts, lavish; indoors high ceremony was maintained. The dining hall itself, Gothic in its architecture, almost defied description. As she went in to take her place, just one of some nine hundred invited guests, Hero marvelled at the brilliant lighting provided by myriad candles and lamps, at the glittering decorations, the livery banners, the lavish table ornamentation, the silver and glass, all displaying the wealth and importance of the City.

They stood while a band slowly led in a procession which included all the ancient symbols of the City's history and power.

Aldermen, sheriffs and judges in full regalia were followed in by the lord mayor in his, which included several heavy chains of office. The mayoress wore court dress, a hooped gown of the last century. Once they had all taken their seats grace was said and the banquet began.

'The men wearing the armour have to be small,' explained Mr Rudge as they took their seats, 'for, although that is King Henry the Fifth's armour, it would fit no one larger. And the City presented the helmet the other knight is wearing to Henry the Seventh. Can you believe, it weighs fourteen pounds?'

Hero tried to imagine such a weight of iron enclosing her head and resting on her shoulders and failed.

'I should not like to have to don it,' she acknowledged with a smile. 'But, if those are full-sized suits of armour, men must have been smaller in those days.'

'Undoubtedly,' put in Drew, sitting opposite with

Mrs Rudge. He smiled encouragingly, obviously pleased with her perception. Hero silently fumed at his condescension.

Mrs Rudge was, she thought when she had recovered from her pique, rather overwhelmed by finding herself partnered by an earl. The pairing had elevated the Rudges from their normal order of precedence. Mr Rudge, secure in his ability, his wealth and his influence, suffered from no such susceptibility.

The dinner was much like others she had attended, although so much larger and more lavish. Each course, the food of superlative quality, was carried in and removed by an army of footmen. Fortunately she was not required to speak much, for the noise level in the hall rose as the meal progressed and to make herself heard she would have been forced to shout. Her partner seemed content to enjoy his food and wine, pausing only to serve her and speak an occasional word of approbation of a dish. Drew gave his attention to Mrs Rudge, who, like her husband, had a well-padded figure, and her colour soon became high. This did not prevent Calverstock from exerting his charm to put her at ease, Hero noted, and he soon had the woman hanging on his every word. Hero did not know whether to admire his manners or feel jealous of the attention being lavished on such a creature. Sharply she caught up her thoughts, reminding herself that how Calverstock behaved to other women was of no consequence to her, none at all.

She was not sorry when toasts were given, for the noise level fell. Once they were over and the speeches made—they seemd never-ending—everyone rose from

the tables to make their way through to the splendid
ballroom.

Drew immediately claimed the first set of dances.
He smiled slightly as he said, 'I must check on the skill
of Mr Reynolds in teaching his art.'

'I have enjoyed the lessons,' said Hero truthfully
and, unwilling to allow overt discord to obtrude that
evening, said no more. He would surely discover for
himself that the instruction had been unnecessary. She
had known the steps since leaving the schoolroom and
made no attempt to appear clumsy or awkward, allowing her natural grace to carry her through the movements with accomplished ease.

If Drew was surprised he made no comment. As the
music stopped he made his bow and escorted her back
to the chair she had found. He bowed again as he
prepared to leave her sitting with Mrs Rudge for
company.

'I shall claim you for the first waltz,' he informed
her, his eyes intently quizzical. 'I am certain you will
not lack for partners, my lady, but I must look to my
duty elsewhere.'

'Of course,' assented Hero, strangely forlorn at the
idea of his leaving her side.

Drew stood up next with Mrs Rudge, and Mr Rudge
claimed Hero's hand. Like so many stout people, the
merchant proved light on his feet and perfectly at
home with the steps. As, thought Hero, watching her
husband and his partner whenever the pattern of the
dance allowed, did Mrs Rudge, who, despite her ple-
beian accent, appeared to be as good-hearted and well-
mannered as her husband. Drew, she saw with amusement rather than scorn, was still bathing his partner in

soothing, courteous charm. As he would every female he danced with. Even her.

Between dances, Hero chatted with Mrs Rudge and was introduced to some of that lady's friends. Isolated as she had always been from the company of matrons whose husbands were in trade, Hero had never realised how unjustified most of the *ton*'s criticisms of their manners and behaviour was. They did not possess quite the polish of the pampered ladies of the nobility and quite possibly many vulgar, ill-mannered men and women were to be found engaged in trade and commerce, but vulgarity and lack of conduct were to be found in the loftiest circles. Who had not come up against a duchess with appalling table manners, an outspoken countess who put the company to the blush, a duke too high in the instep to notice his inferiors, an earl given to drunken debauchery?

Watching closely, she noted that those members of the government and the *ton* present seemed disposed to mix freely, even intimately, with their hosts. But then, of course, so many of the landed aristocracy had invested in roads and canals and other commerical ventures their forefathers would have disdained. And government depended heavily on the taxes paid by the merchants and financiers. Of course, there would always be those who considered that anyone making money in any way other than through the land was beneath their notice, but times and opportunities were changing and perhaps, eventually, it would be they who were considered strange.

Social revelations were not the only ones to be offered to Hero that evening. Drew came to claim his waltz and she found herself in his arms for the first time since he had consummated their marriage.

She had danced often with Mr Reynolds, perfecting her expertise in the waltz, and being in his arms had not affected her in the least. But the moment Drew laid a hand in the small of her back and took one of hers in his warm clasp, a tide of such self-consciousness overtook her that Hero found herself stumbling over his feet.

'I am sorry,' she mumbled, her face scarlet.

'Do not concern yourself,' murmured Drew. 'You lack practice, that is all.'

No, she didn't, thought Hero desperately. She knew she would be able to dance the waltz faultlessly with any other man. It was being close to Drew that was causing her to perform badly. But he seemed entirely undisturbed.

In truth Drew was regretting the impulse that had made him request the pleasure of a waltz with his wife. For weeks now he had kept his distance, her presence in his house, in a bedroom so close to his own, a constant irritant, a source of unending temptation. He carefully kept the prescribed foot of space between their bodies as they danced but that did little to prevent his desire from rising to an almost disastrous level. He had been a fool to think that he could partner her calmly and assess her ability.

But as his agitation, well-disguised, grew, hers appeared to subside. He found himself guiding an accomplished, feather-light creature among the throng of other dancers. Reynolds must be a miracle-worker unless, as he began to suspect, she had hidden her talent in the face of his admittedly autocratic assumption that she was without any of the finer accomplishments required to move easily in society. He remembered again that purposely awkward curtsy and knew he was correct. Against his will a smile twitched the corner of his mouth. He wanted her, he admired her. She was his wife. Why should he not take her?

The music speeded up, signalling the end of the dance. He drew her close, whirling her into a finishing spin, felt her soft body mould to his. Her nearness intoxicated him and he resolved that tonight he would deny himself no longer but taste again of her sweetness. . .

As the music died away he smiled down into her flushed face to murmur, 'You confound me, ma'am. I must congratulate you. I have not enjoyed a dance so much this age.'

She was quite out of breath and for an instant he saw an answering lilt tip her lips before she seemed to recollect herself. She stiffened and quickly evaded his encircling arm. Her face lost its animation, became an inscrutable mask.

'Your approval overwhelms me, my lord,' she returned sarcastically. 'We are not entirely without accomplishment or conduct in the country. 'Tis I who should congratulate you. I believe my situation afforded me a superior opportunity to acquire the necessary graces than did yours. Or were you able to find the chance while you were. . .abroad?'

His face closed up and he answered her with cold civility. 'There is always someone able to play a fiddle while others dance. We made what pleasures we could.'

Hero immediately felt a vast wave of shame engulf

her. She had not meant to taunt him so but his presence was compelling, his nearness so overwhelming that she had been in danger of succumbing to his charm as easily as Mrs Rudge, of allowing him to see that she did not hold him in such abhorrence as she once had. That she would welcome his presence in her bed... So she had reacted badly, had struck out blindly and delivered an unintentionally telling blow.

But she could not apologise as she should or she would give herself away. 'I am certain you did,' she answered stiffly. 'As did we in local Devon society.' Before she had been forced to withdraw from it.

Back at her seat, he bowed. 'I shall be in the card-room should you want me,' he informed her. 'I ordered the carriage for two of the clock. I will return for you then.'

Hero inclined her head. She could not have spoken to save her life. Mrs Rudge saved her from having to do so by chiding Drew on being like all the gentlemen, more inclined to favour the gaming tables than the ballroom.

Drew made some smiling reply and walked away. Hero watched his tall figure for as long as it was in view.

'He is such a charming, fine-looking gentleman,' observed Mrs Rudge chattily. 'On his way to ruin another luckless gamester, I collect. As I said to Mr Rudge, it is difficult to imagine a member of the nobility being transported. I'm sure he did not deserve it. It must have been a mistake.'

She was, of course, probing. Hero had no intention of discussing her husband's past with a self-made merchant's wife, however agreeable. She swallowed and forced herself to speak calmly.

'I know nothing of it, ma'am. I look to the future, not the past.'

'And quite right too, my dear. But Mr Rudge says it don't do to cross a man like him. His experiences have made him a hard man. No mercy on those as owes him money, so he's heard.'

'I really would not know,' said Hero faintly.

'It's the talk of the City,' said Mrs Rudge confidentially. 'He's been the ruination of at least two important men. One of 'em, old Grimshaw, was a justice of the peace, too. Not that many had much room for either of the poor creatures, as they wasn't liked, but still, you can't help feeling some pity for 'em, can you?'

'I didn't know,' murmured Hero, attempting to hide her shame at being wed to a man who showed such lack of compassion. But had she really imagined her father to be the only victim of Calverstock's machinations? She simply hadn't thought about it until gossip forced her to.

'Well, I suppose I shouldn't be gabbling on embarrassing you,' admitted Mrs Rudge with belated finer feeling, 'but there you are, don't take no notice of me. *I* don't hold him any the worse for it. In my opinion a man shouldn't get into debt, not if he can't pay up. Mr Rudge is forever having to sue customers who don't pay their accounts. Think he's made of money, they do, and I'm not denying he has plenty,' she added somewhat smugly, 'but he wouldn't have if he let them get away without paying. Business is business. He don't deal direct with the *ton* if he can help it,' she confided loudly, 'they depend upon their tradesmen for all their fine things yet they take it as an insult if you ask 'em to pay.'

'Yes,' said Hero, bereft of other words.

At that moment an elderly alderman claimed her for a dance. Hero performed the steps automatically, kept a smile fixed on her face and said yes and no in what she hoped were the correct places.

Mrs Rudge's utterances revolved around her distracted mind. Was Calverstock really the dreadful creature he sounded? Was he really ruining one man after another? She had seen and heard him deal with her father. She had no doubt he could be equally ruthless with others. Yet, normally, he appeared to be an essentially honest, amiable man, a charming gentleman still languished over by the younger ladies despite his changed marital status, frowned upon by previously ingratiating mamas but otherwise popular with most in the circles in which he moved. Harrington would surely not consort with him if he thought him in any way dishonest or overly ruthless in his dealings, for Archibald Dalmead was the most chivalrous of creatures. He often hovered near by to rescue her from the attentions of dubious gentlemen and the questions of formidable peeresses when Drew was otherwise engaged. And Mrs Rudge had not sounded censorious. Just curious.

Yet she knew to her cost that her husband could be harsh and unforgiving. He was a puzzle she would dearly like to solve.

She longed to leave the ball before the time Drew had set but refused to be so weak as to seek him out and ask him to take her home. She spent as much time as she reasonably could in the room set aside for the ladies to replenish their toilet. After what seemed a lifetime Drew came to escort her to their carriage.

The dancing was still in full swing as they took their leave of Mr and Mrs Rudge. Hero looked in vain for any hint of censure in their manner towards her husband but could detect none.

'We are sorry you have to leave so early but quite understand, since you have a long journey home,' said Mr Rudge after Drew had expressed their appreciation of the hospitality of the City. The many others to whom they made their parting devoirs appeared quite affable towards him.

If government ministers, members of the *ton* and city gentlemen all accepted his behaviour, why should she feel at odds with him? Because, she realised, his conduct had turned her life upside-down, had unsettled her and made her face realities about her father she would rather not have admitted. And because she did not wish to grow fond of a wolf in sheep's clothing.

In the darkness of the chariot she pressed close into her corner. She did not think she could bear for any part of Drew's body to touch hers. It had been difficult enough to depart the ball on his arm, her fingers all too aware of the living flesh beneath the fine, silky cloth. But Drew, too, had withdrawn, sat close to his side of the carriage. A chilly space separated them. The moment the step was lowered Hero descended quickly and, without waiting for Drew, fled into the house. She wanted no cosy tête-à-tête with her husband and anyway it was far too late.

'I am tired,' she threw behind her as he entered the hall. 'I will retire immediately.'

'As you wish, my dear. I shall not expect to see you
at breakfast.'

Since both so often rode early they met in the
breakfast parlour afterwards. They spoke little, yet a
quiet companionship had developed as both perused
the morning papers. Drew could not know how much
she had come to cherish those moments of shared
interest. Occasionally one or the other would remark
on some item of news and a short discussion would
ensue. Hero was learning about government and poli-
tics, things she had never dreamt of studying in the
isolation of Devon. News had come second-hand, for
her father was no reader and newspapers were not
delivered to the house. Although Drew had not as yet
taken his seat in the House of Lords, he evinced a
remarkable knowledge of what was transpiring in the
country and the world. Small wonder that government
ministers were happy to discuss matters with him.

'No,' agreed Hero. 'I shall instruct Jackson not to
disturb me until noon. Goodnight, my lord.'

'Sleep well.'

The words floated up the stairs after her. Did she
detect a hint of mockery in his tone? He knew very
well that the events of the evening had disturbed her.
That she was fleeing his presence. That she would
probably lie awake most of the remaining hours of the
night thinking about him.

What she did not know was that five minutes later
Drew left the house again to walk off his frustration
by beating the bounds of his extensive grounds.

She slept eventually but not until the late winter
dawn had brought faint grey light to filter round the
edges of the window drapes. She woke again, heavy

eyed and listless, just before nuncheon. She instructed
Jackson to bring out a simple house dress of dove-grey
muslin, over which she wore a fine cashmere shawl to
ward off the chill and the draughts. She almost always
partook of the light meal in her boudoir, for Drew was
seldom at home during the day. Any more than he was
in the evenings. With the nuncheon came the news
that his lordship had taken his horse to Kent shortly
after breakfast, with Benbow in attendance. Jackson
had received the news from the butler and been
enjoined to convey his lordship's regrets, but he did
not know how long his business would keep him away.

Hero's spirits dropped even lower at the news. She
should have been glad to know that she did not have
to face him again so soon yet instead she felt nothing
but disappointment and a sense of being abandoned.
Her appetite quite deserted her.

But she really must pull herself together. The low
sun cast an alluring brightness over the park and the
promise of fresh air drew her. She pushed her food to
one side and ordered the barouche brought round.
Changed into a warm blue carriage dress and pelisse,
wearing a deep-brimmed velvet bonnet over which she
tied a silken scarf to protect her ears so that she could
drive with the hood down, she descended to join the
last of the throng who paraded in Hyde Park at the
fashionable hour. Meeting a few acquaintances and
exchanging greetings might remove some of the lone-
liness from her heart.

She drove alone in the carriage, for she could not
subject Matty to the rigours of a chilly promenade.
Tribble knew her favourite route by now and pro-

ceeded at a sedate pace, drawing up beside another carriage the instant she indicated her wish to stop.

'Why, Lady Calverstock!' The greeting came from one of the many matrons with whom she had acquaintance and although this one was a duchess Hero wished her at Jericho, for Duchess Fanny was one of the most determined of the gabble-grinders among the *ton*.

There was nothing she could do to avoid the encounter. Tribble had already reined in the horses in response to the duchess's gesticulations.

'Your grace.' She greeted the woman with a polite inclination of her head. 'I fear we must not linger, or the horses will take a chill in this weather.'

'I will not keep you, my dear Lady Calverstock, but I simply had to ask! Is your husband ill?'

'Ill?' Hero looked as bewildered as she felt. 'Why do you ask?'

'I was in Harley Street this morning, visiting, you know, and I saw the earl coming from a doctor's consulting-rooms there. Or perhaps it is one of your servants who is suffering from some malady? He did have a young woman with him. They appeared well-acquainted.'

'Not that I know of, ma'am.' Hero kept her countenance and control of her voice by sheer will-power. 'I will enquire the moment I return home. But he has said nothing to me.'

'Don't want to worry you, very likely,' said the duchess. 'But I see he ain't driving with you today. I do hope he does not ail. Wish him well for me.'

'I will, ma'am. Thank you for your concern, but I am sure there is a simple explanation. Some lady who fainted in the street, perhaps, whom he felt bound to help.'

'Of course, that is most probably the case,' agreed the duchess, her manner conveying the impression that she did not believe a word of Hero's explanation. 'His man was holding two horses. I should not have worried you, perhaps, for I could have been mistaken—it might not have been Calverstock at all.' That, it was plain, she believed even less.

Hero did not believe it either.

The carriages continued on their ways and Hero ordered Ned to drive straight home. He and the footmen had heard the exchange but all their faces remained expressionless.

As she dismounted from the barouche she addressed Tribble. 'His lordship must have found it necessary to visit Harley Street before he set out for Kent.'

'Yes, ma'am,' said Ned.

The footmen's faces remained impassive.

Of course, she would be the last to know, poor Miss Hero, thought Ned as he drove the carriage back towards the stables. But you couldn't keep secrets from servants. He'd been regaled with all the gossip. His lordship had a number of women he visited on a regular basis. Benbow always accompanied him and clamped his lips together when questioned, only opening them to insist that there was nothing wrong in what his lordship did. But he would volunteer no explanation, so what was everyone to think? And that house in Kent he had most likely gone to visit now. Young Jem had been sent there once with an urgent message. He'd been told not to linger but he'd seen enough. A woman and kids, he reported. This had fuelled gossip for weeks. Perhaps the earl was secretly married! But then he'd arrived home with Miss Hero as his bride. So, unless he was a bigamist, that couldn't be the answer. For all the speculation no one really believed he was up to no good. Just a bit of a libertine, they'd decided with sly smiles. And why not, after the terrible time he'd had in the penal colony? They enjoyed the scandal and didn't blame the master for keeping a number of mistresses. He was generous and they all liked him far too much to want to lose their places. So they were careful with whom they gossiped. Servants who did so outside their own households were likely to end up without a job. Ned and Matty, concerned as they were for Miss Hero, kept their own counsel. Matty, he knew, was far from convinced that what they all suspected was true. His lordship had gained a stout defender in her.

For Hero the next week dragged past. She heard no word from Drew. She continued to ride when the weather allowed, to attend functions to which she was invited and to receive callers, but there was no pleasure in any of it.

Drew had a mistress. There could be no other explanation for what Duchess Fanny had observed. And discreet enquiries had revealed that the doctor he had visited specialised in women's complaints, particularly pregnancy. He had a mistress and she was increasing. That seemed to be the only logical explanation of his presence there. She had heard whispers about his former mistress, Lady Willoughby, of how spiteful she had become now he had dropped her. So it was only to be expected that he would seek satisfaction elsewhere. And this time he had chosen someone from the lower orders, for the duchess had taken the woman for a servant and she would not have been mistaken.

Misery ate at Hero's heart. Why had he not turned to her to satisfy his needs? Because, common sense told her, she had as good as rejected him.

And she'd reject him again! He'd forced her into a marriage doomed to failure, for quite apart from anything else she disliked the life she was expected to lead in London. Oh, it was exciting for a while and her presentation to the Regent at Carlton House in October had been an event she would not have missed. But to live the life for long would soon push her into a fit of the dismals.

She was already in a fit of the dismals. She could not deny it. And Drew's defection was the chief cause.

And then, on the seventeenth of the month, the Queen died and on the Saturday Drew returned to London.

CHAPTER SEVEN

HERO's joy at seeing Drew was quickly swallowed up in resentment at the aggravation he had caused her. She longed to confront him with what the duchess had seen but prudence won. He was back, even seemed a little glad to see her again, judging by the manner in which he greeted her. And the news of Queen Charlotte's death swamped every other consideration.

'Did you ever meet her?' asked Hero of her husband.

He nodded. 'I was presented at a drawing-room soon after my return to this country. Under her guidance the court remained both grand and decorous. She was a most gracious lady and devoted to King George. I doubt he will live long now she is gone,' he added sadly.

'So we shall have a new king. We already have him in all but name.' She sighed. 'I cannot like the Regent and I doubt very much whether he will maintain his mother's high standards.'

'He lives sumptuously and spends lavishly—his debts are huge—but his schemes provide work for many of his subjects, you know. He is an inveterate builder and a great connoisseur of the arts. Think of the men employed on building his palace at Brighton and on the works going on now to build the road to join Carlton House to Portland Place and Marylebone Park.'

'I suppose so. If rumour is correct the park will soon be renamed Regent's Park.'

'The road will be named after him too, no doubt. I know he is unpopular with the people because of the manner in which he treats the Princess of Wales, but he was forced by his position to enter into the dynastic marriage when he had already been through a form of service with the woman he has always loved, Mrs Fitzherbert. She is his true wife and by all accounts the Princess is an impossible woman. I have no great liking for him myself, but he has great charm and will be no better and no worse than many of the men who have sat on the throne of England.'

Hero grimaced. 'Despite their high birth, our kings and queens are all but men and women trying to perform a difficult task. Shall you attend the funeral?'

'That is my intention. Do you wish to accompany me?'

'I had thought I might. The procession will proceed from Kew Palace to Windsor, but not until the second of December. We have time enough to procure mourning. I have already bespoken a suitable gown, since court mourning is ordered. It will be delivered on Monday.'

Drew nodded approval. 'I visited Weston on my way here. Everyone will be wearing black, not just the court, and all entertainments will cease until after the funeral. We shall have a quiet ten days. I shall not be sorry.'

'Nor I.'

'You have been well-entertained during my absence, I trust?'

'Excellently, I thank you. I have been out almost every evening. Matty accompanied me.'

Drew's brows rose. 'As a married woman you scarcely need the services of a chaperone!'

'No, but a congenial companion is of great value. And her presence staved off the worst of the improper advances made to me during your absence.'

Let him make what he liked of that, both a prick of his conscience at deserting her and a reminder that while he chose to absent himself others vied to attract her attention.

For Archie's prediction had been vindicated. She was a success; to her surprise, men did gather round her eager to dance and flirt. And more than one had hinted at their desire for a liaison. Archie stood in for Drew as protection when he could but he was not always available. So she had taken Matty with her and Matty had thoroughly enjoyed herself watching her mistress attract so much attention.

'I cannot understand his lordship,' she had said on one occasion, 'going away and leaving you alone! He should be here with you.'

'He would be,' Hero had rejoined bitterly, 'except that he prefers to be elsewhere. He did not marry me for love, Matty, and there is no use your trying to pretend otherwise. Ours is a marriage of convenience, nothing more. I do not expect him to pay me much attention.'

'Then he's more of a fool than I thought him to be,' Matty had muttered darkly, but had said no more.

But now he was back and frowning at her words. His aristocratic nose lifted and he regarded her down its length. 'Am I to understand that you have suffered annoyance, ma'am? Tell me who has presumed on my absence to trouble you and he will answer to me!'

'Oh, no, my lord,' said Hero hastily. She had momentarily forgotten her husband's possessive streak, though why he should react the way he did when he did not want her himself was beyond her imagination. 'There has been nothing I cannot deal with myself. But Matty's presence was an insurance.'

Drew looked doubtful but pursued the matter no further. 'I see. I will dine here,' he said. 'It looks as though there may be a fog later.'

They spent a reasonably amicable evening together, though his response to Hero's enquiry as to whether his business had been completed satisfactorily brought merely a vague response. He had, it appeared, ridden back from Gloucestershire, not Kent.

'Well enough. I will not regale you with the details. They could be of no possible interest to you.'

His reticence did not surprise her but it did infuriate her. As though she had no claim to any knowledge of his affairs! Again she almost confronted him with the duchess's report but again did not. What did it matter? A wife had to expect such peccadilloes. He was with her now and she had the legal claim to him. The idea came to her to try to cut out his woman—or women. Other men appeared to find her attractive, so it should be possible... But that would be a fool's game. For if he rejected her advances she would never be able to respect herself again.

Drew had been right about the fog. The next day a remarkably thick yellow pall blanketed London. Even in Kensington one could scarcely see one's hand before one's face. Neither Drew nor Hero ventured out in the murk even to attend church, and afterwards were glad, for London had never known so many accidents. People were knocked over at crossings, carriages clashed with each other despite the torches used to guide them and the pickpockets were out in force.

The fog cleared by dawn but there were no routs, suppers, balls or performances for them to attend together during the week of clear weather that followed. Hero saw little of her husband. He dined at his club with Archie while she ate in her boudoir with Matty. He might just as well have remained in Gloucestershire.

On the Wednesday of the funeral they started out early. Carriages had already begun to pass through Kensington on their way to Kew and soon they were caught up in a mass of carriages, horseback riders and pedestrians, all intent on watching the procession start out for Windsor. The Calverstock carriage, with many others, would follow the cortège all the way.

Progress was slow. It took all day to reach the castle and as darkness fell the way was lit by torches held by soldiers lining the route. The flames made their helmets gleam with fire, illuminated the hearse, flickered on every part of the long, solemn procession of coaches and horses bearing all the trappings of death. Both the Calverstocks wore weepers, Hero a black veil over her face, Drew a band with streamers tied round his hat. The coachmen and liveried footmen all wore mourning. For the entire length of the route door knockers were wreathed in black crêpe. And the people lining it, half hidden behind the line of soldiers, had all assumed the same sombre garb. Everyone mourned and many were in tears as they bade farewell to a much respected Queen. It was a state occasion Hero would not forget in a hurry.

At long last they arrived at Windsor and the coffin was carried into the Royal Chapel of St George. The internment took place in the dim light of the vaulted crypt. The Regent and close family and friends followed the coffin down to observe the final committal, as did the prime minister and other statesmen. Hero and Drew remained in the chapel with the bulk of the mourners.

Afterwards refreshments were offered to all the guests. Hero was both thirsty and hungry, since she had eaten nothing since dawn. Drew remained by her side, plying her with food and replenishing her glass with lemonade the moment it became empty. He himself ate well but drank sparingly of the wine.

Then began the long journey back, faster than the funereal pace out but still slow because of the press of traffic. By the time the carriage arrived at Calverstock House in the early hours of Thursday Hero was fast asleep in her corner.

Even the bustle accompanying their arrival failed to wake her. Not until she felt herself being lifted in strong arms did Hero stir, to realise drowsily that it was Calverstock who held her, Calverstock who was carrying her easily up the steps and into the house.

She should, of course, have forced herself awake, demanded to be put down and walked up the stairs to her room. But she was far too comfortable. She could feel the steady beating of Drew's heart against her side and with a sigh of content her arms reached up to wind about his neck as she settled more securely into his embrace.

His heartbeat quickened and began to race as Hero's
fingers teased the hair at his nape. She seemed to have
no will to stop her seductive caress and why should
she, when he had picked her up and his hold was
having such a devastating effect upon her? Why, she
wondered drowsily, did she always tremble when he
touched her? Why did she feel that if she did demand
to be put down and attempt to walk to her room her
legs would refuse to carry her? Why did she feel so
relaxed, so comfortable, so *at home* in her husband's
arms? Why, when in fact she despised him for a
heartless, manipulating creature incapable of any of
the softer feelings, let alone love?

They reached her room before she had even begun
to answer her own questions. Both Matty and Jackson
were waiting for her though both had obviously been
sleeping in chairs and had woken reluctantly.
Calverstock took no notice of either but strode straight
over to the bed and laid his burden down. He raised
Hero's veil and untied the bonnet-ribbons beneath her
chin. She saw his fingers shaking, the result of his
racing heart. He was not the cool, controlled man of
the image he liked to project. He wanted her, wanted
her badly, there could be no doubt of that. So she did
have the power to rouse him. The surge of jubilation
at the realisation of her feminine power brought her
fully back to her senses and for a delirious moment
she toyed with the idea of seducing him.

But she could not. Could not bring herself to invite
his attentions. The memory of that first night, when he
had all but forced her to his will, flashed blindingly
across her mind. No, she could not. But were he to
ask, to woo, to suggest. . .

Then she would become a compliant wife, taste, perhaps, the pleasure other women found in the marriage act. For undoubtedly they did, if not with their husbands then with their lovers. That much she had most assuredly discovered since coming to London.

The scale of the infidelity practised by both men and women in what had become her circle both astonished and disgusted her. To Hero, marriage vows, however reluctantly made, were inviolable. So because she had been forced into this marriage if she did not find pleasure in Drew's arms she would never know the joyous depths of passion that others hinted could be experienced between a man and a woman. This dismal fact was already clear to her. Yet she could never easily allow herself to surrender to him as her body seemed to demand.

The decision was taken from her. Drew sucked in a harsh breath, straightened up and spoke, his expression cold, his voice curt.

'You are tired, my lady. Jackson, undress your mistress immediately. She has had a long and exhausting day. I shall not expect to see you at breakfast, my dear. Goodnight.'

Hero watched him leave with eyes heavy not so much with sleep as some other emotion which, she realised with some dismay, must be longing. If only he had sent the others away and remained with her. But he had not. He could not want her as much as she had imagined. Or as much as she wanted him.

But as Jackson came forward to tend her and Matty bombarded her with questions Hero's main emotion was one of deep disappointment. Quickly followed by equally deep resentment against the man who had caused it.

London burst back into life the next day. People continued to wear mourning but attended the reopened theatres and other entertainments, taking up the social round again with undiminished enthusiasm.

It was during the interval at the threatre the following evening that Hero overheard a conversation from the next box. Drew and Archie, who had accompanied them, had gone to fetch refreshment, leaving her blessedly alone for a few moments. They had closed the door of the box behind them and Hero sat back in the shadows, unwilling to invite intrusion from anyone. The group chattering behind the thin partition must not have realised her presence.

'So Blacklock is ruined,' came an accusing female voice.

'So I hear, my dear. He has been trying to raise money to pay off his debts but of course no one is willing to risk their fortunes to come to such a blackguard's aid.'

'He will lose his estates, I collect.'

'All but the house in Gloucestershire and a few acres, which are entailed to his son,' answered a gentleman Hero assumed to be the lady's husband.

'I feel sorry for Gatby. He does not deserve to lose his inheritance.'

'Sons often suffer for the excesses of their fathers,' responded the male voice grimly.

'Gatby is an effeminate fool. To think he will become a marquis one day! And you surely must not hold Calverstock responsible,' chimed in a much younger female voice. 'Blacklock is an odious man who has squandered the family wealth and in order to restore it is trying to wed his useless son to a fortune, as you must know since he tried to negotiate for my hand. I would never marry a man like Gatby, for I do not believe he likes women. It is my guess he does not wish to take a wife.'

'You would have wed the man had I chosen to order you, miss!' rapped the gentleman.

'But you did not, dearest Papa, and for that I thank you. Blacklock deserved to be brought to ruination. I can feel no sympathy with him at all and very little for Gatby. I admire Calverstock for bringing him down.'

'But who will be next?' demanded the father rhetorically. 'We know nothing of Calverstock except that he has found an unusual way of adding to his own property, which must be extensive by now.'

'I think him a positive benefactor,' declared the young voice firmly. 'I would have had no objection to wedding him had he not chosen that Polhembury girl. Why he did I cannot imagine. It cannot have been a love match, for they are merely polite to each other.'

'You foolish chit!' came the girl's mother's sharp voice. 'To cherish a *tendre* for such a man, and a married man at that! The sooner you are wed yourself the better. You could do worse than young Harrington.'

A silvery laugh rang out. 'Do not worry, Mama, I do not refine over Calverstock! I like Harrington enormously, but it will take a better woman than I to bring him to a declaration! He positively shudders whenever the question of marriage is mentioned!'

'Then he has something in common with Gatby,' observed her father drily.

'Oh, no, Papa.' The young voice sprang quickly to Archie's defence. 'It is not the same at all. Harrington adores women. He is known to keep a mistress. It is simply the thought of being leg-shackled that horrifies him.'

A wistful note had crept into the girl's voice and Hero longed to know who she was. Archie was much sought-after by all the mamas and had long ago learned to evade their scheming and the daughters' lures. But he needed a wife, and the girl sounded as though she had a sensible mind of her own as well as a good dowry.

At that moment the door of the other box opened and a hearty, booming voice rang out.

'What a squeeze! But I have your lemonade, my dear Lady Felicity. I have only spilt a little.'

'Thank you, sir,' came the girl's voice, all animation wiped from it. 'I apologise for sending you on such an onerous errand but I was exceedingly thirsty.'

'Not at all, not at all. Pleasure to serve you, my dear.'

'I believe the curtain is about to go up again. You should return to your seat, Harcourt.'

'Indeed, my lord, so I should. I will return to pay my respects again in the next interval.'

Receiving no response to this, Hero presumed, unwelcome promise, Harcourt departed just as Drew and Archie returned with refreshment, the lamps were dimmed and the curtain went up on the second act.

Hero accepted her lemonade and tried to concentrate on the play but found her thoughts wandering irresistibly back to the conversation she had overheard.

So Calverstock had not deserted his mistress to travel to Gloucestershire to administer his estate, but to ruin another man. Lady Felicity had seemed to admire him for it, but Hero could not convince herself to do the same. She knew, at first hand, how much misery his actions caused. Few people deserved to be pursued in the way Calverstock was hounding his victims. Her father had not been blameless in his dealings but had surely not deserved the harsh punishment Calverstock had administered.

But even as she fulminated over her husband's misdeeds her mind wandered back to the girl in the neighbouring box. Did Archie realise she cherished a *tendre* for him? He must know her. Hero determined to make the girl's acquaintance as soon as possible and the next interval seemed as good a time as any.

As the illumination in the auditorium increased she shot a sideways look at the people occupying the neighbouring box and glimpsed a young woman with fair hair cut to a fashionably short length. Like everyone else, she wore mourning and the black enhanced the fragility of her appearance.

'Are you acquainted with a Lady Felicity, my lord?' Hero enquired as soon as the applause for the second act had died away.

'Lady Felicity Charteris? Of course,' responded Archie airily. 'Daughter of the Earl of Beltinge. Kent, y'know. In the next box, as a matter of fact.'

'So I believe. I heard her mention your name.'

Archie shifted uncomfortably. 'Did she, now?'

'You must have seen her,' put in Drew, glancing

towards the next box and giving her a quizzical look. 'Tall chit, quite a beauty, sizeable dowry. Must have received plenty of offers.'

'But not from you or Harrington, I collect,' said Hero drily.

'Lord, no!' exlaimed Archie with a shudder. But his colour remained high.

Poor Lady Felicity, thought Hero. But Archie, she deduced from his manner, was not entirely indifferent to the lady's charms. With a little assistance from h r...

'I should appreciate being presented to the Beltinges,' she informed Drew. 'I liked the sound of Lady Felicity's voice.'

Drew shrugged. 'Now? Why not? You would meet her before long in any case. The family returned to town for the funeral, no doubt.'

'Coming, Lord Harrington?' asked Hero sweetly as she prepared to leave the box on her husband's arm.

'Don't think I will,' muttered Archie. He had risen when Hero had and left the box with them but hurried off in the opposite direction on some unspecified errand.

'He is shy of her,' murmured Hero.

'Shy of any woman who shows an interest in matrimony,' chuckled Drew. 'Archie has a horror of being snared.'

'He has never fallen in love, then.'

Drew did not reply to this remark for he had rapped on the door of the Beltinges' box and a call came for them to enter.

By this time Hero was quite used to the interest she created upon being introduced by Calverstock as his wife. Having overheard so much of the earlier conversation, she was a little embarrassed, watching for any sign of censure in Lord, but particularly Lady, Beltinge's attitude towards her husband. She did detect a certain coldness in the latter, which seemed to disturb Calverstock not one whit. He maintained his most charming manner throughout. Lady Felicity greeted him in a calm, open fashion which greatly appealed to Hero and the smile the girl turned upon her was both appraising and friendly.

'I have been longing to make your acquaintance, my lady,' she told Hero confidentially as the others spoke together. 'The female who could persuade Calverstock to enter into matrimony earns my greatest admiration!'

'My hand was part of a bargain he struck with my father to save him from ruination,' Hero told her honestly, since everyone must suspect as much. 'I gather that both he and his friend, Lord Harrington, had been given up by most mamas long since.'

'Perhaps, now Lord Calverstock is wed, Lord Harrington may come up to scratch,' murmured Felicity.

'He shows little sign at the moment, but I do not despair of him.' returned Hero with a smile. 'Lady Felicity, would you do me the honour of taking tea with me one day? I feel we could become friends. I knew no one in London when I arrived and so far have made only acquaintances.'

'I should be delighted, Lady Calverstock,' cried Felicity, so warmly that Hero could not doubt her sincerity.

'Then let it be soon,' she said, smiling. 'Are you engaged tomorrow?'

'I do not believe so. I must consult Mama.'

It was agreed that Felicity should visit Calverstock House the following afternoon. As the third act was called Drew escorted Hero back to their own box and soon afterwards Archie rejoined them.

Hero scarcely heard a word of the last act. She was too busy planning—what she would say to Calverstock regarding his dealings with people who had fallen into debt, and how she could advance the cause of Lady Felicity Charteris with Lord Harrington.

They arrived home late. Hero went straight to her room, removed her black dress and wrapped herself in a dressing-gown.

'I will see myself to bed, Jackson. I wish to sit up for a while. You may go.'

'Very well my lady.'

Jackson curtsied and left. Matty had already departed for bed, having seen her chick safely home. Hero went through to her boudoir intending to recline on her day bed for a while but after a few moments sprang to her feet and began to pace the floor.

It would be prudent to wait until the morning before tackling Calverstock over the matter of his dubious activities in using his money and position to ruin people but she knew that she would never sleep if she did. She had to get it over with. She had been bottling up her resentment for too long, putting off the moment because she hated the thought of the unpleasantness which must follow. But her discoveries that evening had brought her feelings to the boil and not even the prospect of Felicity's visit the next day could calm them. She must speak with Calverstock now.

He had not come upstairs yet. He was most likely in the library, his favourite haunt while in the house. She would go down and tackle him this instant!

The thought was no sooner formed than she was out of her door and descending the stairs. The servants were all abed apart from Benbow, she supposed, and a boy on duty, dozing by the front door. He did not see her as she flitted across the staircase hall and entered the library without knocking.

Calverstock was there. He had removed his jacket and lay back in a comfortable chair, his newly fashionable closely trousered legs ending in pumps which rested on a brocaded footstool before the leaping flames of a revived fire. Their light gave the snowy sleeves of his shirt a pink tinge while nearby candles illuminated the rumpled waves of his brown hair, turning it almost golden. Hero's heart fluttered in appreciation of the sight of him.

Perhaps he was dozing. It took him an instant to realise that someone had entered the room. When he saw who it was he sat up and rose languidly to his feet. As she advanced towards him Hero saw his eyes lose their sleepy look to focus upon her dishabille. Too late, she realised that she should not have appeared before him so scantily clad. The nerves in her stomach quivered.

But she had not come to admire or dally. She steeled her resolve. 'My lord.' She addressed him coldly, hoping to kill off any sign of ardour before it had time to develop. 'I desire a word with you.'

He bowed slightly. 'Indeed, ma'am, I am at your service. To what purpose do you wish to speak?'

Hero moistened suddenly dry lips. But she had remained silent too long.

'I was forced to wed you for my father's sake, to save him from ruin, and now I must listen to tales of your contemptible behaviour towards others. I wish to make it plain that I find your activities despicable. I had thought my father your only victim but I discover this is not so. That there have been several other persons, even magistrates, brought to the end of their ropes, and that while you were in Gloucestershire last week you bankrupted Lord Blacklock, forcing him to make over all but his entailed lands to you.'

Calverstock's spine stiffened and his expression hardened. 'You judge harshly, ma'am. You know nothing of the circumstances——'

'No circumstances could exonerate you from shame at the way you set out to buy up a man's—or a woman's, for I believe at least one of your victims has been a woman—debts and then demand their property, their very livelihood, in recompense. Shame on you, sir! This is not the behaviour of a gentleman!'

'But then,' retored Calverstock in his most top-lofty manner, 'I have little to recommend me as a gentleman. I make no pretence. You know what I am,' he went on, bitterness suddenly edging his voice and stripping it of hauteur, 'an ex-convict. From the age of fifteen I was reared in a strange, harsh environment where every man and woman had to fend for himself or herself. What else, ma'am, should you expect of me?'

Hero swallowed, suddenly regretting her attack. The bitterness in Drew's tone spoke louder than his words. And he had proved himself considerate on occasion, could be most agreeable when he liked. The harshness was surely a veneer adopted to cover his true, softer nature.

'A little pity,' she whispered.

'Pity? Who has ever shown me pity? You may expect none from this quarter, madam. I see now that I have been too lenient with you thus far. It is time you realised I am no society fop to be twisted around a woman's finger!'

Hero gasped as he took two long strides to reach her. His fingers dug painfully into her shoulders as he shook her. Her head nodded violently so that her frilly nightcap, tied loosely beneath her chin, became dislodged and fell back and pins scattered, releasing a tumble of lustrous brown hair.

Drew's breath caught. Next instant his hard mouth came down on hers. Taken by surprise in the middle of a wild, involuntary nod, her lips parted in protest, Hero felt the impact shudder through her. His hands left her shoulders as his arms clamped her body to his while long, powerful fingers tangled almost painfully in the mass of waves hanging down her back. She had no time to think, no time to protest—the assault was too sudden.

His proximity, his touch, always a threat to her nerves, devastated her. To be held so closely, kissed so fiercely, his tongue filling her mouth with his essence, threatened imminent disintegration. Hero felt her resolution to resist diminish with the same speed as the strength in her limbs. She sagged against him.

Needing air, Drew released her mouth and looked down into her drowning face. With a soft curse he

swept her up into his arms, strode from the library and
began to ascend the stairs.

Hero lay completely limp in his arms, lacking the
ability to even hold on, let alone resist. Yet by the
time he reached the door of her bedroom and flung it
open she had regained enough of her normal equilib-
rium to utter a hoarse protest against what she instinctively knew was about to happen.

'No, Drew. Not like this!'

Breathing heavily from the exertion, 'Like what?' he
almost snarled. 'What other treatment can you expect
from someone as uncivilised as a convicted felon? My
God, woman, you have been driving me demented
with your untouchable presence in my house. I am
wearied of playing the gentleman. You are my wife.
And tonight you will once more fulfil your marital
obligations.'

While he was speaking he had flung her on the bed
and stripped off his waistcoat. His shoes and trousers
followed so fast that Hero had no time to collect
herself before, still breathing heavily, he was on the
bed with her, his fingers at the fastenings of her
dressing-gown. He threw it back and dealt expertly
with the buttons on her snowy cambric nightdress.
Hero did not resist. Apart from calling for help, which
was unthinkable, she knew there could be no escape.
And a part of her rejoiced.

He moved over her, his weight pressing her down
into the feather mattress. His head descended and his
mouth began a merciless attack on first one bared
breast and then the other while his hands roved at will
over her body. Possessively, roughly, but not bruisingly
as she had feared.

The first time he had made love to her Hero had not known what to expect. Now she did and a half-hearted attempt to suffocate at birth the response he was evoking failed. She was already too deeply under his spell, lost in the painful pleasure of her body's awakening. The excitement gripped her, would not be quelled. She had wanted him to come to her for weeks. Now she could no more resist the longing that had been building up in her than fly to the moon.

Her senses reeled, her brain ceased to function. She could only feel and respond with mindless abandon as tumultuous sensation took control.

She did not notice when Drew began to woo rather than demand, when what had been a passion born of anger and desperation became something quite different. No less intense, but sparked by new, softer emotions. Yet in the end uncontrollable desire swept them both up in its irresistible tide so that Hero welcomed the hard, deep, penetrating thrusts which eventually sent her whole being spiralling into uncharted regions of ecstasy.

As she descended once more to cold reality she discovered Drew lying on her as one dead. She could detect no trace of a breath. In a panic she began to push at him, to call his name in frightened tones.

To her infinite relief he gave a great shudder and came to life. In the light of the candles she had not extinguished she saw the bewildered look in his grey eyes give way to one of awed realisation. And then the shutters came down.

'The devil, wife, when you are roused you are a wanton piece!' he declared as he rolled from her to retrieve his discarded clothing.

His crumpled shirt and tousled hair bore silent witness to the truth of his words. Shame burned brightly on Hero's cheeks. He was disgusted with her behaviour. With a half-suppressed sob she turned over and buried her flaming face in the bedcovers.

CHAPTER EIGHT

A DISCONCERTING surge of shame almost swamped Drew as he allowed Benbow to prepare him for bed. His servant knew where he had been, of course, and would later go down to the library to make the fire safe and extinguish the candles left burning there. It was not his loyal servant's knowledge of his recent activities that caused his discomfort but the anguished look in his wife's eyes as she had turned away to hide her face from his derisive accusation.

He had censured her for wantonness for no better reason than to hide his own remorse. Guilt so overwhelmed him that he doubted he would recover in a hurry.

He had lost control. He, who had prided himself on his coolness under extreme pressure and provocation as a convict, had allowed himself to be propelled into such immoderate behaviour that he undoubtedly owed her an apology.

But did he? She had first roused his anger by repeating ill-informed gossip and accusing him of dishonourable intentions, and had been in no mood to listen had he attempted to explain. *His* feelings, *his* point of view were the last things she would ever consider, for she had thought him despicable from the first. Except on that one occasion when she had not known he was a convicted felon and had accepted him at face value. As he had accepted her and fancied she would make him an admirable wife. But on discovering his identity she had allowed his past to colour her opinion of him, had condemned him unseen.

And for her to appear before him so temptingly, so scantily clad! Unless she was a complete innocent she must know the effect such a sight would have on any man! Yet, he acknowledged, almost groaning aloud, in many respects she *was* an innocent, especially in the ways of men. Her feelings must have been strong enough to bring her to his presence on a surge of such righteous indignation that she had forgotten all else.

Once again he was moved to reluctant admiration for her spirit in pressing her opinions, misplaced as they were. If only he had not overheard those words of hers spoken before the wedding he might have found her perfect in every way. But he could not forget them, or forgive her for condemning him out of hand. He might have much of which to be ashamed, but she had more. He had no need to apologise. Besides, an apology would allow her the whip-hand.

On this comforting thought Drew closed his eyes and immediately fell into the slumber of a man released from physical frustration, not waking until Benbow came in to open the curtains.

The dull grey light which invaded the room did nothing to indicate the time of day. Yet instinct told him he had slept late.

'Ten o'clock, my lord,' Benbow informed him upon being asked.

'The deuce! Why did you not wake me, man?'

'You have no urgent appointments today, sir. You have not rested well for several nights now. Since you did not wake I left you to sleep your fill.'

Devil take him, Benbow was right. He had slept badly while away and even worse since returning to London. He had spoken nothing but the truth when he had accused Hero of driving him insane by her presence. And it was of no use his attempting to relieve his frustrations by turning to another woman. He had tried that and found himself impotent for the first time in his life. He remembered the occasion with deep mortification. Damn Hero Langage!

But he would, he *must* recover from his obsession. Quite apart from anything else, he would no longer deny himself the pleasures of the marriage bed. There could be no valid reason for him to refrain from intimacy simply because they despised each other. He despised whores but in the past he had used them effectively. His body stirred at the memory of his wife's unexpected capacity for passion, the feel of her, deliciously soft, feverishly responsive in his arms. Superior to any whore or mistress he had ever known.

And he had foolishly made her ashamed of her desire. But no matter, he reassured himself confidently, there would be plenty of opportunity in the future for him to teach her that a man seldom objected to active participation by his wife during the act of love, whatever young females might be taught to the contrary.

Meanwhile he must control his deuced libido or it could betray him at an inconvenient moment. The very thought of Hero threatened to render him a trembling wreck. Thank heaven he wore a nightshirt or he would be *afraid* to get out of bed, not simply reluctant! Deuce take the woman, what had he done to deserve entanglement in such a coil?

Knowing his master well, Benbow bore the brunt of his ill-temper stoically as Drew snapped, 'You take too much upon yourself, Benbow! You know I am out of sorts for the rest of the day if I do not gallop early in the park!'

'Indeed, my lord.' Benbow inclined his head in acknowledgement of the reprimand. 'I have your shaving water in the dressing-room. It will lose its heat if you do not use it soon.'

'Then you will have, perforce, to send for more! You have already informed me that I have little need to stir myself today.'

'Breakfast is on the table in the parlour. With respect, you should rise now, sir.'

'Do you think I brought you back here to bully me, man?' demanded Drew.

'No, my lord.' Benbow, imperturbable as ever, paused before adding, 'I believe her ladyship was up and about betimes.'

'Was she?' growled Drew. His reluctance to rise grew with the prospect of facing his wife. Perhaps she would choose to remain in her boudoir. 'Has she taken breakfast yet?'

'Not as far as I am aware, my lord.'

'I shall go to my club,' decided Drew abruptly, flinging back the covers to reveal a striped nightshirt. 'Damn thing,' he grumbled, turning his back to strip it off. 'Can't think why I allow you to persuade me into wearing it.'

'Because you know it is expected of you, sir,' rejoined Benbow, the faintest of grins touching the deep lines of his face. 'Supposing a maidservant were to enter and discover you naked?'

'I slept naked in the Colony,' Drew reminded him.

'Not the same thing at all, sir. We even worked half naked most of the time.'

'True. We would freeze to death clad like that here.'

Drew remembered the heat, the sweat which had poured from his back beneath the coarse cotton shirt he had sometimes, in sheer desperation, thrown off—but seldom in the full heat of the burning sun. One dose of sunstroke and agonising sunburn had been lesson enough. Eventually his skin had hardened, as had his muscles, until he could work stripped for long periods and toil all day without undue exhaustion.

With the prospect of a confrontation with his wife shelved, Drew's temper recovered. Having pulled on the underwear Benbow had laid out for him, he wandered through to his dressing-room and sat patiently while his valet shaved him. No sound came from the room beyond. Hero must either be in her boudoir or down in the breakfast parlour. By the time he met her again at dinner that evening, after which they were due to attend a rout, he would be fortified, his irrational sense of guilt pushed firmly where it belonged—out of his mind. When he finally took up the ribbons to drive his curricle to St James's he was whistling under his breath.

He returned in time to change for dinner and the evening engagement, to find the house in uproar.

Grindley, the butler, greeted him as he entered the door, his normally expressionless face lined with worry.

'My lord! Thank goodness you are returned home!'

'Why? What is amiss?'

'It concerns her ladyship, my lord. Lady Felicity

Charteris called earlier. She had engaged to take tea with the countess at three o'clock.'

'Yes, I heard her make the arrangement.'

'But her ladyship was nowhere to be found in either the house or grounds and on enquiry I discovered that she had not been seen at all today. Jackson says that when she went in to attend her ladyship she had already dressed and left her room but she thought nothing of it, as her ladyship often rises early without calling her. She is a considerate mistress.'

'But her ladyship did not return?'

'No, my lord. But even then Jackson was not concerned, having discovered that Miss Bright was also missing and must be with her.'

Drew swore under his breath. 'Foolish woman! Did she not think to inform me? Benbow knew I was at my club.'

'She did not believe it necessary to trouble you or anyone else, my lord. It was not until Lady Felicity arrived that she began to question her ladyship's absence.'

'The devil!' Drew's hands clenched into fists and the hard lines of his face settled into a look of such cold displeasure that Grindley flinched.

'Lady Felicity waited a full hour before leaving, so certain was she that her ladyship would return,' he hastened to add uncomfortably.

A scowl descended on Drew's brow, adding to the formidable expression already on his face. 'But she did not.'

It was a statment, not a question, but Grindley answered it just the same. 'No, my lord. She is still absent, as is Miss Bright.'

'Then where the devil are they?' barked Drew.

'I have ascertained that they departed before dawn, about six-thirty, my lord. A housemaid cleaning out the grates saw them leave the house. She thought they were embarking on a walk in the grounds.'

'At that hour? By God, but I am served by idiots!' Drew's voice rose to a shout. 'Benbow! Where the deuce are you?'

'He went out, my lord. To question hackney drivers, I believe.'

Drew's scowl deepened. What in Hades was Benbow up to? 'Send him to me the instant he returns. I shall be in her ladyship's rooms,' he snapped.

No one had mentioned a note but if she had intended to disappear—as Benbow must suspect—she would surely have left him some word—of reproach, most likely. For he had no doubt that his wife's defection could be attributed to his own behaviour the previous night. She had determined to teach him a lesson, he supposed. Well, he thought as he searched her boudoir and bedroom in vain for any missive, when she did reappear he would not offer an apology.

Her absence had revealed to him that the idea of living in the house without his wife's presence was even less agreeable than with it. She might frustrate and irritate him and drive him to dementia but she was there. Without her to share it his life would stretch ahead like the outback, which had claimed the lives of so many absconding convicts. It was an unwelcome revelation. He had not realised the extent to which he had come to rely upon her company, how much he enjoyed watching her take society by storm. How jealous he was of any man upon whom she smiled.

How much he admired the manner in which she conducted herself as hostess or guest. How proud he had become of his countess. But he would never admit as much to her.

And his concern was unnecessary. She would not dare to disappear for long. She would return in time to dress for dinner and the evening engagement, he assured himself. She must simply have forgotten her arrangement to take tea with Lady Felicity, or been delayed. Otherwise she would have left a note.

Jackson appeared and he wanted to berate the woman for not raising the alarm earlier, but refrained. Hero was a free agent; she could go out without telling her maid if she so wished. And, unlike him, what reason could Jackson have had to suspect that her mistress had run away?

'I expect her ladyship will return at any moment,' he said, affecting a casual air upon Jackson's bobbing him a curtsy and expressing her puzzlement over her mistress's disappearance. 'What was she wearing?'

'Her black gown and bonnet, my lord, and the cloak she wears in the rain. All her lovely things are here, except that I think she took a change of underwear and a few personal items, slippers and a comb and suchlike, in a small valise.'

Drew's lips firmed and a cold hand seemed to clutch at his vitals as Jackson delivered her blow. Benbow's search for a hackney driver who had taken up his wife began to make more sense, as did the general air of panic among the staff. For no doubt Jackson had disseminated her discovery to everyone.

Only he had not known. 'Why was no one sent to

inform me when you discovered this?' he enquired acidly.

'Mr Grindley sent a footman to your club, my lord. He returned to say that you were not there, had left an hour since.'

A grunt was Drew's only answer to that. He had driven round to call on his lawyer, having thought of some business he needed to discuss. Of course no one had known where to find him.

'I must change. I'll be in my room,' he told Jackson as he opened the communicating door and left her standing irresolute in his wife's empty bedroom.

Where had Hero gone? Back to Polhembury? She had dressed in her simplest clothes, taken little with her. He had checked her jewel case and the pieces he had given her were still there. But she had no need to sell her jewels—she probably carried with her enough cash drawn from her allowance. And she had access to what remained in her account at the bank. She would not starve and had enough funds to buy herself out of trouble or to pay her way to Devon if she wished.

He no longer believed she would be back in time to dress for dinner. She had gone.

A stab of fury pierced him. How dared she? She was his wife! And despite her possession of money and the presence of Matty she must have been aware of the dangers of travelling alone and unescorted by a man. The two women had walked from the house, apparently to take a stroll in the garden, or so the stupid housemaid had thought. How far had they wandered through the streets of London before finding a hackney to carry them? Not too far, for Matty could not have walked a great distance.

Drew discovered anxiety coupled with anger to be a heady, painful mixture. He wanted to shake her until her teeth rattled and yet, at the same time, he wanted to hold her safely in his arms, close to his heart. And then to make passionate love. . .

His imaginings were cut off at that moment by Benbow, who presented himself breathing heavily, as though he had been hurrying.

'Any news?' demanded Drew without preamble.

Benbow shook his head. 'No, sir. None of the hackneys I could find was on duty early this morning. We shall have to wait until tomorrow and try again.'

Drew punched a balled fist into his other palm. 'We cannot do that, man! She may be in danger!' Fearful pictures of the two women being set upon by footpads or lured into some den of iniquity filled Drew's mind and he sounded quite desperate as he growled, 'I must know where she went and how. Besides,' he added, 'I want her back here before anyone discovers her to be gone.' It would do neither his nor her reputation any good were her escapade to be discovered. He would have to make sure that Lady Felicity was given a believable explanation for Hero's absence earlier. He must scribble a note, but not now.

'It may not be possible to discover anything quickly——' began Benbow, only to be cut off by an impatient oath.

'I will send a reliable footman to enquire at all the nearest post houses. She may have hired a chaise.' Benbow nodded and moved to the bell-pull as Drew went on, 'And I'll order our horses saddled. We will make all haste to the Gloucester Coffee Tavern in Piccadilly. The mail coaches will not leave until eight.

We may find her still there if she waited to travel in more comfort and safety on the Quicksilver to Exeter rather than take a slower, crowded stage. Though I doubt it.' Common sense told him she would have departed on the first stage coach available, whatever he might hope. 'We will enquire about the passengers who have left on them, too.'

'You think she may have gone back to Devon?'

'Where else?' enquired Drew grimly. 'If we have no further news by tomorrow night I shall depart for Polhembury early the next morning. Help me to change. Move, man!'

'Yes, sir,' answered Benbow, a thoughtful look in his eye as he went to lay out his master's riding clothes. He had rarely seen his lordship so disturbed. 'The Exeter coaches pass the door,' he pointed out. 'She may have hoped to board one further out from London. Hounslow perhaps?'

'Then someone must enquire in that direction, too,' decided Drew.

The senior footman knocked and entered at that moment and instructions were given, together with admonitions of secrecy. 'If I hear a word of this outside the house I shall seek out the culprits and have them dismissed without a reference,' declared Drew sternly.

Seeing the look on his master's face, the footman knew the threat to be real. 'Mr Grindley and Mrs Deacon have already warned the staff against gossip, my lord,' he said as he made a dignified withdrawal and went to pass on the orders he had just received.

'Help me off with this,' said Drew as he began to struggle out of his blue superfine coat. 'We have little enough time to spare if we are to find her.'

'Should I inform Monsieur Vodin to hold dinner, my lord?'

Drew shook his head as Benbow, having removed his shoes, presented him with a pair of shining hessians. 'We will do that on our way out. Curse these things!'

The struggle with the boots over, Drew stood to draw on his riding coat. Cut more generously than the garment he had discarded, it required little assistance to don.

'The weather is foul,' remarked Benbow, handing his master a many-caped greatcoat. 'It was wise of her ladyship to wear her thick cloak.'

'Huh!' snorted Drew, glaring at his servant. 'I account it nothing but the height of foolishness for her to embark on such an irresponsible venture in whatever garb she chose.'

'She is a spirited young lady, sir,' murmured Benbow.

Drew glared. 'I have no need of you to tell me that, curse it!'

After a sleepless night Hero knew that she must leave Calverstock House and her husband as fast as she could. She had no clear idea of what she wanted to do and decided to seek refuge with her Aunt Augusta and so remain in London.

She could not fly straight back to Polhembury. There, she would have to face her father's wrath. For her leaving Calverstock might mean his debt being called in. Besides, she was not certain that she did want to leave him, not for good. But she must make some protest at the way he had treated her, the aspersions he had cast upon her character.

And she simply could not face him. She couldn't even face herself in a mirror. How could she have behaved with such abandon that Calverstock had thought her wanton? Her cheeks burned anew. Yet while it was happening it had seemed the most natural thing in the world to return his caresses, to cry out her need, to welcome the release his possession had brought. The first time, an inexperienced virgin, she had managed to remain calm and impassive under his skilful assault. But last night she had been unable to sustain a similar coolness because her body, having known it once, had longed for his touch, the fulfilment of his final possession, had responded automatically to his ardour.

She knew instinctively that he had enjoyed the encounter as much as she. But he had acted in a cloud of anger, had been punishing her for daring to accuse him of the pitiless accumulation to himself of others' wealth. She, while protesting her wish not to have him take her in such a mood, had made but a feeble protest; her resistance pitifully weak, she'd tumbled headlong into a trap set by her senses. Had responded to a passion born of anger and lust rather than love and respect, and been punished for it.

If she remained with her husband the same scene would be re-enacted again and again. He would take her, despising her, and she would respond, unable to help herself. So, unless his attitude changed, she could not remain. But could not, for long, continue to draw upon her allowance.

Unwelcome choices lay ahead. Unless she returned

to an impoverished Polhembury she would be forced
to find some remunerative position as governess or
companion in order to live. And if she returned there
and Polhembury was taken from her father, she would
be faced with a similar dilemma. And she must ask
Matty to uproot herself again. Dear, loyal Matty, who
scarcely argued when she invaded her tiny room long
before dawn and begged her to leave Calverstock
House immediately.

'Why, my chick?' she asked, rubbing the sleep from
her eyes. Then she sat up suddenly, her nightcap
askew, to demand. 'Has your husband ill-treated you?'

'Not really. But. . .he said things. . .Matty, I simply
cannot remain here any longer.'

Matty grunted as she threw back the covers and left
her warm bed. 'I don't know how I came to be so
deceived by him,' she muttered. 'I'd have sworn he
was an upright, honest gentleman, kind-hearted
despite his manner at the wedding. And I thought he
held a *tendre* for you, my chick, though he seemed
determined to hide it. But there,' she finished as, roles
reversed, Hero aided her to don her warmest clothes,
'he's not an easy man to read.'

'He holds me in disgust,' Hero said, her voice
quivering. 'So, you see, I must leave him.'

Matty said no more. She packed a few of her things
in a similar valise to the one Hero carried and together
they left the house, the bags concealed beneath their
cloaks. She knew her aunt's address in Dorset Square,
knew it was located north of Oxford Street, north even
of the new road linking Paddington with the City.

They walked to Hyde Park Corner and through the
toll gates before, for Matty's sake, she hired a hackney

to Portman Square. From there they walked aimlessly for a while before taking another hackney to Dorset Square.

They arrived at Aunt Augusta's front door as the family was taking refreshment with two other callers.

Hero regretted her lapse in not calling on her aunt before. Such a politeness would have saved a great deal of commotion now. Having been announced and ushered into a cheerful room overlooking the square, a much gratified Mrs Edward Dashper greeted her niece with astonished delight, introduced her daughters and friends, and extended an immediate invitation to her to sit down near the fire and partake of refreshment.

Hero indicated Matty, standing quietly at her shoulder. 'Miss Bright is my companion, Aunt,' she explained as she removed her cloak and handed it to a hovering maidservant. The valises had been left in the hall. 'She may join us?'

At this suggestion Aunt Augusta's face lost its look of effusive welcome. 'Matty Bright?' she murmured, recognition dawning. 'Was she not our nursemaid, your mother's and mine?'

'She was, Aunt, and mine, too. Now she is become my dearest friend.'

'I see,' murmured Augusta. 'Very well,' she agreed reluctantly, 'Matty may join us.'

'Thank you, Aunt Augusta,' smiled Hero, wishing with all her heart that her aunt had been alone, that she could have told her at once of the circumstances surrounding her visit.

'We saw the announcement of your marriage, my dear Hero,' Mrs Dashper declared as her new guests took their seats and accepted dishes of tea. 'Just fancy, I said to my dearest daughters, didn't I, girls? Just fancy, your cousin is become a countess!'

A murmur of approval came from Mrs Dashper's friends, both of them matrons, both clad splendidly but tastelessly in black of the latest fashion and appearing quite overset at meeting a real live countess. At least Aunt Augusta and her daughters, although in deepest mourning, were dressed with more taste, thought Hero, smiling at cousins Dorothea and Chloe. Aunt Augusta, the daughter of a baron, despite having made a poor marriage by society's standards, since her husband had no expectation of a title and little money, had retained much of the benefits of her upbringing.

Dorothea, the eldest of the sisters, who looked to be almost at her last prayers, smiled back shyly and quickly lowered her rather prominent pale blue eyes in confusion. A shy, lumpy girl, ill-suited by the black she wore, she would make little impression on the gentlemen, thought Hero with pity.

Chloe, younger by several years, fashionably fair and of a more lively disposition, exclaimed, 'Oh, yes, cousin. We were so excited. We did so hope that you——'

'Chloe!' cut in her mother severely. 'Guard your tongue!' She turned to Hero with an apology. 'Dear Chloe is so inclined to chatter. I tell her that forward, boisterous young ladies are not admired, that in company she should behave with the utmost decorum.'

'You must not count *me* as company, Aunt, I am family, though I am afraid that I have called in a most uncivil fashion——'

'Oh, but my modest establishment is honoured by

your visit, as are my friends! And one has no need to follow form when calling upon relations!'

Eventually the two matrons rose to depart, no doubt to spread their new, enlivening *on dit*. 'We will leave you to have a comfortable coze with your niece, my dear Mrs Dashper,' said one, while the other nodded assent, her head bobbing and wobbling her several chins.

Adieus were said and the ladies seen out. Aunt Augusta hurried across to the tall window and peered through the lace curtain to watch them descend to the road. She turned back to Hero with disappointment written all over a thin face which, in repose, could look discontented. Beside her stout friends Aunt Augusta had looked positively elegant.

'Did you not bring your own carriage?' she asked.

'No, we came by hackney,' explained Hero, realising that her aunt's disappointment stemmed from the fact that her friends would not see a crested coach drawn by splendid horses being walked outside her door. Its not being there would reflect badly upon the consequence of Mrs Edward Dashper.

'I suppose his lordship required its use,' speculated her aunt archly.

'No, Aunt, we have more than one carriage for our use should it be required. I owe you an explanation, but I would prefer to make it to you alone. Is there somewhere. . .?'

She allowed the question to trail off. Her aunt frowned in perplexity but immediately told her daughters to leave the room. They departed reluctantly.

Matty stood. 'I will wait in the hall, my lady,' she informed Hero. Hero nodded and Matty left the room.

'Now,' said Aunt Augusta, frowning austerely, seating herself opposite Hero. 'What is it you have to explain?'

'I came here hoping you would give me refuge, Aunt. I found it necessary to leave Lord Calverstock, no matter why.'

'And you wish to stay here?' demanded Augusta, unable to disguise her shock at this turn of events.

'If I may, Aunt. Matty, too. You are the only relation I have, apart from my father, and you live near by. I did not wish to return to Polhembury.'

'Well, I have no desire to pry,' declared Aunt Augusta in the manner of one denying her dearest wish, 'but I have never heard of anything so addle-witted! Left your husband indeed! My duty must be to send you straight back!'

Hero paled. She had not expected her aunt to welcome her with open arms, but had not foreseen opposition. 'Pray do not, dear Aunt. I may return in due course, but for the moment I need to escape Calverstock House while I decide what to do. The world is privy to my husband's past. The marriage was arranged by my father. You must realise that I had no say in the matter.'

Augusta exclaimed, 'Naturally not! No chit of a girl knows what is best for her! Your father's choice was impeccable. Since inheriting the title his lordship's reputation has been second to none. You should be the happiest of creatures!' She shrugged bony shoulders. 'But I can tell that you are in some distress. For your mother's sake I shall not turn you away.'

'You have my deepest gratitude, Aunt.'

'Honoured as I am to have a countess under my

roof, you must realise that this is not a large house. Matty will have to share the room with you. Have you any objection to that arrangement?'

'None at all.' Hero knew she would be glad of her old nurse's company.

Augusta's sharp eyes studied Hero's exhausted face thoughtfully. 'And the earl has no idea where you are?'

'None, Aunt. I was careful to leave no trail he could follow.'

Augusta pounced on this statement. 'So you believe he will wish to find you?'

Hero plucked at the folds of her skirt, her fingers trembling; not with fear, but some other emotion she could not name. Of course he would search for her. He considered her his property, part of a financial bargain. Perhaps the sentiment causing her such distress was resentment. Or disappointment that he would not seek her out for herself. 'I fear so.' Unconsciously, she sighed. 'He is not a man who likes to be crossed.'

Her aunt nodded. 'I dare say he is not. Well, my dear, you must stay here until your future is decided. Mr Dashper will be surprised to find you here when he returns. You have not seen him since you were a child.' She stood up. 'Dorothea will show you to your room. You will have time to get to know your cousins before dinner, which we take early.'

'Thank you, Aunt. I will try not to be a nuisance to you. I hope my stay will not be of long duration.'

'I doubt it will be,' replied Augusta somewhat ambiguously.

CHAPTER NINE

DREW paced the floor of the library, unable to relax.

'Do sit down, my dear fellow,' pleaded Lord Harrington, who, informed of Hero's disappearance, though not of the reason for it, had come to support his friend in his hour of need. 'Walkin' up and down like that will only wear a hole in an expensive carpet. I doubt she is at any hazard.'

'It's fine for you,' muttered Drew. 'She is not your wife.'

'And I ain't in love with her.'

At this blandly spoken observation Drew stopped his pacing to stand and stare coldly at the speaker. 'Meaning what, pray?'

'Nothin', nothin' at all,' drawled Archie with a bland smile. 'You ain't, of course. You can't be, you'd never be in such a takin' if you were.'

This irony was not lost on Drew. 'She is my wife,' he informed Archie with unnecessary violence. 'Her action, if it is discovered by the gabble-grinders, will reflect upon us both.'

'Never known you to care what the gossips said before.' With deliberate unconcern, Harrington took out his snuff box, flicked it open and offered it to Drew.

Drew waved it away. 'This is different. They will invent a lover where there is none.'

'You are certain of that?'

'Of course I am, damn you!' Drew controlled his reaction to Dalmead's deliberate provocation with difficulty. Archie knew as well as he that Hero was not the sort of woman to fly to another man's arms for solace. Archie simply wanted him to acknowledge the fact, a point borne out by the smug quirk on his friend's lips. 'She is new in society,' he went on more calmly. 'It will prejudice her position. The hostesses may not receive her. She will be ruined.'

'Stop tormenting yourself, Drew.' Archie sniffed up his pinch of snuff before adding comfortingly, 'All will be well, you'll see.'

Drew turned on his heel and walked over to stare out of the window, the fine vista an unfocused blur. 'At least we can now believe she is still somewhere in London. She was not seen boarding any West Country stage or mail in the capital.'

'And this mornin' you found a hackney driver who took her to Portman Square,' soothed Archie. 'Benbow and the others will soon be back from searching that area for further news.'

'Their enquiries can only increase the risk of her disappearance being discovered.'

'Perhaps we should visit our club and behave as normal? Put 'em off the scent, you know.'

Drew shook his head at this eminently sensible suggestion. 'I must remain here. But you could do me a service, if you would.'

'Anything within reason, my dear fellow.'

Drew sat at his desk and began to sharpen a pen. 'I have just remembered I must make my wife's excuses to Lady Felicity. She failed to keep their engagement yesterday afternoon.'

He scribbled quickly, read through what he had written, then sanded the sheet before folding it, reaching for wax and flame, and fastening it with his seal.

'Deliver this, if you will.'

Harrington looked down at the paper thrust into his hand as though it might bite him, the look on his face bringing a faint smile to Drew's lips. Even caught up in his own turbulent preoccupation, he could not miss Archie's reluctance to execute the commission.

'You do not need to hand it to her personally,' he drawled. 'Unless, of course you would welcome the excuse to call upon her?'

'Couldn't you send a footman or a groom?' asked Archie anxiously, his normally languid air quite deserting him.

'They are all otherwise engaged, as you know. Come, now, my dear fellow, you are surely not afraid to knock upon the door of the Beltinge residence?'

Archie rose stiffly to his feet. 'No such thing. But I do not wish to place myself in a position to be caught in parson's mousetrap.' He blushed. 'I have paid her quite enough attention recently. The gabble-grinders will begin their work.'

'If you like the girl wed her,' advised Drew. 'She cherishes a *tendre* for you, you know. You could do a lot worse.'

Archie shuddered. 'I have no desire to wed,' he declared in a pained voice.

'The wedded state is not the end of the world,' revealed Drew.

'Even when your wife leaves you?'

'Not even then. Do get along there, Archie, there's a good fellow. Just hand the letter to a footman if you must. By the way, I've said that Lady Calverstock was taken ill while out shopping and sends her apologies. That she will be in touch when she is fully recovered.' He grinned. 'In case you should see anyone to speak to.'

Archie grimaced. 'Devious devil! You simply want to see me as leg-shackled as you are yourself!'

'I want to see you happily wed,' said Drew sincerely. 'It can be the most felicitous of states.'

'But you ain't found it so!' Archie pounced on Drew's inconsistency to defend himself, moving towards the door. 'I'll see myself out. But,' he said, his hand on the knob, 'your lady is a diamond of the first water. Thought so from the first, and now we are better acquainted I'm sure of it. If you ain't happy, then neither is she. Pity.' He shrugged one shoulder languidly. 'She missed you while you were away, y'know. Should do something about it. I'll call back later to see if there's any further news.'

He closed the door behind him without giving Drew a chance to answer. Drew slumped into his chair and buried his face in his hands.

Could he make himself forget those searing words of hers? Could he change her opinion of him? Unless he could do both, happiness would elude them.

A short while later a locally recruited housemaid, doing duty for an absent footman, knocked and entered. By this time frustration with his enforced inactivity had Drew pacing again.

'Yes?' he barked.

'There's a lad 'ere, me lord. Come to the back door, 'e did. Says as 'ow 'e 'as a messidge for the earl, must give it into 'is own 'and, 'e says.'

'Then send him in!'

As the girl turned to obey Drew strode impatiently towards the door. The boy, who had been waiting just outside, appeared on the instant. A grubby urchin with a running nose. Drew stopped short.

'What is it you want, boy?'

'Got a messidge for the earl. You 'im?' demanded the boy with a noisy sniff and gulp.

'Course 'e is!' put in the housemaid, but turned and sped off as she met Drew's imperious glare.

'I am,' confirmed Drew, holding out his hand for the soiled paper clutched in the lad's fist. 'Is that it?'

'The lady said as 'ow you'd give us a tanner,' muttered the boy, parting with the note reluctantly.

'You'll get it.' Drew broke the seal and perused the letter's contents with rising exhilaration. His first real smile of the day lit his face as he placed the note on his desk and took out his purse. 'Here is a shilling for you,' he said, dropping the coin into the boy's filthy palm.

'Cor!' The boy bit it to be sure it was genuine before tucking it safely into a pocket. 'Ta, guvner!'

'Thank you for delivering the letter so promptly.' Drew tugged on the bell ribbon. 'Someone will come to see you out.'

Hero sat, sharing a sofa with Matty, in the room where she had first met her aunt and cousins the previous day. She had slept badly for the second night running. Bruised circles had already made their appearance beneath her eyes. She wondered when she would enjoy a good night's rest again.

Her aunt chattered on, asking innumerable ques-

tions Hero did not wish to answer. Mrs Dashper
occupied a position on the fringes of society, moving
in a lower circle than that of her niece. Despite a
certain restless jumpiness of manner, she was anxious
to hear all the latest gossip and scandal circulating in
first circles.

Hero did her best to respond but her mind was
elsewhere. What was Calverstock doing? Was he
angry? Worried? Indifferent? Or merely piqued that
she should dare to leave him? Where was he? He
could, she supposed, be on his way to Polhembury,
thinking she would return there. Her aunt's address
had been held in her head, she had left no written
record behind, so he would have no immediate way of
finding her here in Dorset Square.

Her head ached. She would be glad when the light
nuncheon Aunt Augusta had promised for two o'clock
was served, though she doubted whether she would
have the appetite to eat. But a dish of tea might ease
her malaise.

The morning seemed interminable. At every rattle
of carriage wheels outside her aunt jumped up to peer
from the window. Hero watched resignedly as she
leapt up yet again. She had never known anyone so
inquisitive about her neighbours' movements.

This time, however, Mrs Dashper gave a little cry.
'Girls, tidy yourselves! We have a visitor! No, do not
rush to the window, Chloe, it is unbecoming behaviour
in a young girl. Sit where you are. We will wait for
Lily to announce the visitor in form.'

She returned to her own seat, arranged her skirts
and sat, hands clasped in her lap, listening for the
knock on the door.

'Who is it, Mama?' asked Chloe.

'Patience, my dear. A gentleman, I believe.'

Her aunt's expression held a mixture of excitement, guilt and triumph. Foreboding made Hero glance anxiously at Matty, who shook her head, frowning and giving a slight shrug. Only one thing seemed certain: Mrs Dashper had been expecting a caller. She was up to something.

A few moments later a familiar voice in the hall confirmed Hero's worst fears. She turned angrily to her aunt.

'You betrayed me!' she accused in a low tone.

'For your own good, my dear,' replied her aunt self-righteously.

The door opened on a knock and Lily, the parlour maid, announced Lord Calverstock.

He strode into the room, his eyes immediately seeking Hero's stricken face, but she refused to meet his gaze. Remembering his manners, he made his bow and addressed himself to his hostess.

'I must thank you for your communication, ma'am, which I received but an hour since. We are not acquainted but no doubt my wife will be pleased to make the introductions. My dear?'

The buzzing in her ears, caused by anger and mortification, not to mention the frantic leap of her pulses at sight of her husband, made it almost impossible for Hero to respond. Had it not been for Matty's reassuring squeeze of her arm she would probably have failed to find her voice altogether. As it was she managed to make the introductions, though in accents she scarcely recognised as her own.

'Do please be seated, my lord,' gushed Aunt

Augusta. 'A tea tray and some light refreshment will be with us in but a moment. You and my dear niece are both most welcome in my humble abode. My daughters are enchanted to have renewed acquaintance with their cousin. Are you not, my dears?'

'Yes, Mama,' they responded in unison.

'Both Dorothea and Chloe are "out", of course, but our social circle here is restricted. Perhaps, with their cousin's influence. . .?'

Hero cringed for her relation. How could she be so obvious?

'They could extend their expectations.' Drew finished the sentence for his hostess. 'Quite so, ma'am. When we return to town for the next season we must consider introducing them into our circle, must we not, my dear?'

Drew's tone was dry. In due course both he and Hero would be expected to pay for the services rendered them by Mrs Dashper. His wife looked quite crushed by her aunt's presumption. But in the euphoria of finding Hero again he really did not care.

The refreshments arrived. Hero drank her tea thirstily and nibbled dutifully at a scone. Drew ate with relish. But then, it took a lot to put him off his food. She watched him surreptitiously, seeking some indication of his attitude towards her. She could detect no trace of softness in his manner, which had been courteously polite from the start, but no anger, either. And he had come after her. Perhaps he had been just a little worried.

He had given no indication of his intentions. He may simply want to confirm her whereabouts. Hero did not really believe that and waited for his next move, her nerves stretched almost to snapping point.

If he commanded her to return with him, as though she were his property, she would resist. Much depended on his approach. His feelings were well-hidden; she found it impossible to read his thoughts or divine his intentions.

With the refreshments consumed and the tray removed, Drew at last broached the reason for his visit.

'Ma'am.' He addressed Mrs Dashper with due formality. 'I would account it a great service if I could speak to my wife in private?'

Augusta jumped to her feet. 'But of course, Lord Calverstock! I personally will show you both into the drawing-room. You will be undisturbed there.'

Hero rose reluctantly. She had regained much of her composure but the prospect of facing Calverstock in private threatened a return of debilitating emotion. Yet she must stand up to him, must convince him that she was not a wanton, that his accusation had been false...except that, when she remembered her bewildering behaviour in bed, mortification swept back to render her helpless before his censure.

The door closed behind Augusta. Drew, denied the gentleman's normal tactic of warming his back in the heat of a blazing fire, stood before the empty grate with one foot on the ornate fender, a hand resting on the mantelshelf beside a ticking clock.

'Well, wife,' he began austerely, 'I trust you have an explanation for your peculiar behaviour?'

Hero, her hands clasped before her, drew a deep breath. Now was the moment. She must be brave. 'I could not remain to be insulted, husband.' If he could call her 'wife' she could address him so, midway between formality and intimacy. 'I wished for time to consider my future. Had my aunt not betrayed me. . .'

'She did her duty.' He paused only briefly before looking down at his boot and asking, 'Did you not consider the anxiety your disappearance would cause?'

'I had Matty with me. I did not think you would care.'

'Not care?' He moved swiftly to stand erect, towering over her. 'When my wife leaves me? What sort of a fool does that make of me, pray?'

'I would rather be called fool than wanton.'

Hero's voice, scarcely above a whisper, shook. In the face of her evident distress Drew's anger, largely induced by anxiety, crumbled. He had sworn he would not but. . .

He swung away from his position by the fireplace to stand with his back towards her. He spoke jerkily. 'I owe you an apology, Hero. If you will but return with me I will prove to you that my words were said in the heat of passion, that they were not meant.' He turned to meet her gaze full on. 'You must allow me to take you home.'

There was no humility in his voice. He had made a statement of fact. Yet he had used the word 'allow' and his tone held a touch of strain. Hero knew he was sincere.

The colour came and went in her cheeks as she struggled to control her wild emotions, to subdue a mortifying desire to cry. She wanted to return with him. Life had become so desolate since she had walked out with Matty. Would Matty think her foolish to give in so easily? Probably not, for she had always held Drew Challoner in high regard, despite his unfortunate past.

As she hesitated, Drew's voice came again. 'Madam, I will not plead but it is necessary that you return. Gossip may already be rife, although I have done my best to avoid it. I sent a note to apologise for your discourtesy in failing to keep your engagement with Lady Felicity——' At Hero's gasp he gave a grim smile. 'You had quite forgot?'

'Yes,' gasped Hero. 'Oh, how could I?'

'Easily enough, it seems. I made the excuse that you had been taken ill while out shopping. Whether she will believe this, since she waited a full hour for you to return and to the best of my knowledge no one mentioned where you had gone, for they did not know, I cannot say. However, if you wish to avoid scandal and its consequent effects upon your position in society, you should return at once and make your own apologies to Lady Felicity.'

'I care little for my own position,' murmured Hero, making a dismissive gesture with her hands, 'but I would not wish to offend Lady Felicity or to make a mock of you.'

Drew shrugged. 'As to that, I am accustomed to being the object of speculation, censure and, in some cases——' he made a grimace of distaste '—pity. I mislike it but am well able to ignore it. Other people's opinion does not concern me. I trained in a hard school.'

Beneath the bold assertion Hero, for the first time in their association, caught a hint of vulnerability. It stirred her deeply yet still she made no response. Drew

took a step towards her. 'If you return we will leave
for Ashworthy almost immediately. There, perhaps,
we can begin again, learn to know each other and
hope that affection will grow between us.' He drew a
breath. 'I need you, Hero. I must provide an heir and
as my wife it is your duty to bear me one. I believe
that if we both try we can deal well enough together.'

An heir. Yes, she was the only person who could
supply him with a legitimate son. And a baby might
compensate her for the love her husband could not
give her. She determined to fight for her marriage, not
simply give it up.

She nodded. 'Very well, Drew. I shall enjoy to see
Ashworthy. I like living in the country. I have missed
Polhembury.'

He took her cold hand and kissed her wrist. A shiver
ran up her arm to end as a quiver in her heart.

'We will inform your aunt.'

'I must ask Matty to pack. We did not bring much
with us.'

In a dry voice he responded, 'So I have been given
to understand.'

'Drew.' Hero hesitated, feeling guilty for imposing
the problem her new-found relatives could present in
the future. 'I am sorry you have been forced to
recognise Aunt Augusta and my cousins. Shall you
mind very much if I bring the girls out in society? I
feel sorry for them.'

Drew shook his head. 'Edward Dashper is well-
regarded in gentlemen's circles and both parents are
nobly born.'

'You made enquiries,' said Hero flatly.

'Naturally. I wished to know with whom I might be

forced to deal. I discovered that the family is merely poor. I shall not object to anything you may be able to do for them.'

Hero smiled, if rather ruefully. Her hands had stopped shaking. Her husband was nothing if not thorough, but she could return to him with renewed confidence in the future. 'I had better have a word with Matty.'

Upon their return to Calverstock House the servants were given much the same explanation for Hero's absence as Drew had sent to Lady Felicity. They knew she had left the house early and so the story was elaborated a little and the note delivered by the urchin was said to have originated with her. Drew rewarded the men who had been engaged in the search for her with a bonus and the tongues of the staff were stilled by Hero's own cheerful reappearance.

Apologies were sent to several hostesses whose invitations had been accepted for the next week. Hero called upon Lady Felicity and invited her to visit Ashworthy for the Christmas festivities. Lord and Lady Beltinge gave their permission and so it was arranged. Hero believed she would enjoy Felicity's company. Her presence, and that of several other guests already engaged to spend two or three weeks at Ashworthy, might ease the strain between her husband and herself. That Lord Harrington would be one of the guests Hero had not thought it necessary to mention. But if Felicity could not fix Archie's interest during that time then she was not the young woman Hero took her for.

From the moment of her return Drew had shown

greater consideration for her welfare. He spent much of the slow journey down to Gloucestershire in the coach with her and Matty, leaving the driving to Tribble, who led a procession of lesser carriages loaded with servants and luggage. The removal of the household to Ashworthy took a deal of organisation, which was accomplished by Drew and Mrs Deacon with enviable efficiency.

Mrs Deacon had been left behind to supervise the annual cleaning of Calverstock House by the small staff retained there. That done, she would see it maintained in a state of readiness to receive its owner at a moment's notice, although the household would probably not return to London until April.

The housekeeper at Ashworthy, Mrs Pilcher, greeted Lord Calverstock with an unmistakable affection which she seemed ready to extend to Hero.

'We are delighted to welcome you here, my lady,' she cried, her round, cheerful face beaming with genuine goodwill as she bobbed a respectful curtsy. 'I do hope you will find everything to your liking. The notice of your early arrival was short but we were already almost prepared to receive you. The entire staff hopes you will be happy here, ma'am, and offers you their best services.'

'I like it here already,' Hero returned with truth.

The chef, the butler, their personal servants and several footmen and maidservants had travelled down with them. Except for Matty and Jackson they were all familiar with the place, most having served the Calverstocks for many years, and, like their masters past and present, had spent more time at the country estate than in London. Hero was glad to see a few familiar faces as she settled into the vast, draughty stone pile Drew had inherited so unexpectedly upon his uncle's sudden and heirless death.

The driveway to the house wound through undulating parkland, the views obscured in many places by trees and undergrowth. They had rounded the base of a low rise and emerged from surrounding woodland to see the mansion spread before them. Hero had given a gasp of pleasure and surprise. Even on that overcast winter day the Cotswold stone had appeared warmly welcoming. The sprawling building, built over many generations, looked picturesque and intriguing with its stone mullioned windows and steeply sloping gabled roofs dotted with dormers, the whole topped by a veritable forest of tall chimneys. Unlike Polhembury, Ashworthy looked to be in a good state of repair. Not until she stepped inside and traversed the various corridors and galleries had Hero realised how deceptive the aura of warmth given off by the cream stone had been.

The rooms were kept warm by blazing fires but no female dared venture into a draughty corridor without first wrapping herself in a shawl. The maids wore theirs folded into a triangle with the ends crossed over in front and tied behind. After the first evening Hero carried a fine woollen or cashmere shawl with her wherever she went. But despite this discomfort she quickly came to love Ashworthy.

Drew loved it, too. 'It needed complete restoration when I inherited,' he told her as he escorted her on a tour of inspection. 'Perhaps I was prejudiced, since I had always found my grandfather and uncle to be uncharitable, odious creatures, but I felt the place

needed cleansing of their presence. I set about reno-
vating it from basement to attic.'

'You did an excellent job,' acknowledged Hero.

Drew accepted the compliment with a smile. 'I hired
the best help available. The servants were wonderful.'

'They did not object to the upheaval?'

'Scarcely any of them, and those who did were soon
replaced.' He shrugged self-deprecatingly. 'They
seemed inclined to prefer my rule to that of my
predecessors. Mrs Pilcher, in particular, has blossomed
since I took over.'

'She adores you,' grinned Hero without rancour.
There was scarcely need to be jealous of the adulation
of the stout, middle-aged woman and Drew seemed to
attract all females, whatever their position in society.
She could not forget the woman Duchess Fanny had
seen him with, the covert speculation over his dealings
with women of a lower class rife in London. No one
had been overt in their accusations but the hints had
been too numerous to ignore. She hoped that here, in
his ancestral seat, his women left behind, she would be
able to win his regard and satisfy his needs sufficiently
to render all competition redundant.

Since her return he had played the charming considerate husband both in public and private but he had
not come to her bed. They occupied the master bedroom as was expected of them but Drew had chosen
to sleep in the bed made up in the large adjoining
dressing-room. Hero did not understand this. He had
said he needed an heir. He must surely come to her
soon. And when he did, how was she to behave?

She feared she would be unable to maintain the
unresponsive modesty required of a woman of fashion

being favoured with her husband's attentions. Drew had promised to prove to her that he had not meant the words he had spoken. He would teach her how to respond. But what if, she having once demonstrated passion, he asked for more than it was possible or decent for her to give? Some gentlemen, she knew, visited houses of ill repute or kept a mistress to slake the baser instincts their wives could not, or would not satisfy. She did not like to think of Drew being driven to such lengths. No one had suggested that the women he visited were other than normally obliging. Surely he would not need to indulge in behaviour she could not condone?

He had suffered a rough upbringing during his growth from youth to manhood. Had mixed with the lowest classes of criminal society, could have sunk to depths she could only dimly imagine. He had emerged, apparently, as a perfect flower of the nobility, but she could not be certain of what lay beneath his smooth exterior.

He had proved himself capable of harsh, even vindictive behaviour. In London he visited Jackson's gymnasium and he enjoyed watching a good mill. According to Benbow, who was inordinately proud of his master's capabilities, the earl possessed a useful bunch of fives, could plant a facer and acquit himself well in a brawl if necessary. And, quite apart from his acknowledged mistress, Lady Willoughby, he reputedly kept a harem of other women.

He gave no sign of dissolution. He looked hard, tough, yet she now knew of his kindess, the consideration with which he treated his inferiors. And he had only to smile...

Hero sighed. She seemed no nearer to fathoming her husband's personality than when she'd married him. Doubts still plagued her but did not stop her from experiencing emotions which bordered on love.

Leaving him had been like tearing herself apart. If it had taught her nothing else it had made her realise how deep her feelings for her husband had gone. Despite all his faults, real and imagined, she had begun to hold him in deepest affection and to feel tenderness towards him. Add passion, and surely that amounted to love?

She wanted to tell him, show him, but how could she when he did not want her love or even his marital rights?

She could not take the initiative. He had branded her wanton once. She would not lay herself open to that charge again. Patience and quiet affection, her only weapons, seemed singularly frail.

She lay that night, their second at Ashworthy, in the large canopied bed in which generations of Calverstocks had been born—including Gerald, Drew's father, but not Drew—the glow from the dying fire the only light to alleviate the darkness. The candle by the bed had long since guttered out.

The already comfortable room had been improved by new silken hangings to cover the walls and the addition of thick rugs, heavy curtains and a draught roll at the bottom of the door. It was one of the cosiest rooms in the house—the library and her small sitting-room being others—and she wished Drew would come and share it with her instead of banishing himself to the far less agreeable dressing-room. But he could not know how much she so longed to be held in his arms, to hold him in hers. . .

She must have dropped off as her mind wandered in the realms of fantasy. But she was not so deeply asleep that the slight sound of a door opening failed to wake her. No one should intrude at this hour. Matty and Jackson were both long abed. In her confused state she did not at first realise that it was the opening of the door to the dressing-room that had woken her.

She lay still, feigning sleep, ready to scream for help if the intruder proved hostile. One of the servants, perhaps, intent on theft? Or a stranger who had broken in with the same objective? Every nerve tense, her mouth dry, her hearing strained for any sound, Hero lay waiting.

Footsteps brushed across a rug, approaching the bed. She made herself lie still, breathing steadily, until, suddenly, she realised who it was. The familiar scent of her husband, compounded of sandalwood and his own distinctive odour, filled her nostrils.

Her heart began to hammer. Almost, she said his name but something stopped her. Somehow she controlled her breathing. He had come to her like a thief in the night. Why?

She could hear his breathing as he leant over her. It seemed to catch. A touch came on her forehead, so feather-light that she thought she had imagined it. But then, as fleeting as the brush of a butterfly's wings, she felt his lips on hers. On a breath he whispered, 'Sleep well, my wife.'

Hero's eyes flew open. 'Drew!' she gasped and reached up for him.

He came down into her arms with a small grunt. 'I

thought you would be asleep. I did not wish to wake you, my dear.'

'Then why did you come?' she whispered.

'Because I could not sleep,' he admitted ruefully. 'I have tried to give you time but I lay in the next room wanting...' He broke off and took a deep breath. 'I came in to look, to touch, to go away again and hope to sleep.'

Such an admission! Hero's arms tightened about his shoulders. 'Did you not realise I would welcome you, my lord? I have waited, it seems, so long...'

'Then you have forgiven me? You will allow me to make amends for my previous mistakes?'

'If you will forgive mine,' whispered Hero.

'You made no mistake that night, never think it. A man whose wife exhibits the passion you honoured me with is fortunate. I knew it and was overwhelmed. My reproof was born of other causes. But now, my wife, allow me to teach you how to please me as much as I hope to please you. You agree?'

'If you wish,' murmured Hero.

CHAPTER TEN

DREW threw off his gown and nightshirt, slid under the covers and took her in his embrace. For long moments they lay quite still, absorbing each other's nearness.

Hero could feel his heart hammering, as was her own. It seemed to have swelled and risen inside her breast, blocking her windpipe so that she could scarcely breathe. When Drew at last moved it was to untie the strings of her nightcap and remove it, spread her hair upon the pillow and bury his face in its fragrance.

Fascinated by the hard contours of his muscular shoulders, Hero allowed her fingers to smooth over his silky skin and felt a shiver run through his body. She stilled at once.

He groaned. 'Don't stop!'

'You shivered. I thought I had offended you.'

'You must learn to recognise the difference between revulsion and delight.' His finger traced a line down her spine and despite the presence of intervening cotton she could not repress a shudder. 'You see?'

She nodded, although he would not see in the darkness, but he must have felt the movement. 'You really don't need this nightgown, you know,' he whispered, his fingers beginning to undo the buttons it had taken Jackson so long to fasten. 'It separates us. I want to feel you. . .'

'But——'

He interrupted her protest with gentle firmness. 'Do not fear for your modesty, my dear. Between husband and wife there should be no shame. One day I shall stand you before me in all your naked beauty. There can be no sin in that.'

A blush suffused her whole body. Memory flooded back. She had glimpsed him naked and, despite her misery at the time, still saw him so in her dreams, glorying in the remembrance of his strong, manly body. She remembered, too, the anguish of knowing he had taken her merely from duty. And the only other time he had taken her it had been in anger, though desire had been there, too, in full measure. But now he seemed willing to give tenderness and passion, even if he could not give her love. To allow him to remove her nightgown did not seem too depraved. She made no further demur as he continued with his task, turning the operation into an erotic adventure.

They lay close again, skin to skin, and Hero luxuriated in the feel of him, the rough texture of his body hair against her tender flesh, the awareness of bunched muscles and spinal indentations under her fingers as she explored the length of his back until she reached his taut buttocks and experienced an explosion of pleasure.

He had probed the secrets of her body before, but not in the careful, almost adoring fashion he did now. His mouth closed on hers in the way she had longed for, demanding yet tender, in a kiss which drew from her the willing response he sought.

He followed the kiss by tracing a searing trail of salutes down her throat to the hollow between her breasts. As he ran his hot, moist mouth over the swelling mound then bit gently at a peak, his hand found hers and led it to the part of himself she had not dared to touch. Hero's hips reared involuntarily as spears of sensation from his suckling pierced through to her core just as her hand discovered his throbbing flesh.

Her senses spun. 'Yes!' she gasped. 'Please, Drew! Please!'

Drew lifted his head just enough to murmur, 'Patience, my wife,' his voice thick, his breathing fast and hard. On a kind of desperate laugh he added, 'I shall not be capable of pleasuring you for long.' She wondered what he meant as his head dipped again and his mouth claimed her other breast.

Hero could not stop herself. She shifted and moaned, clutched at him urgently as he pursued his passionate assault with mouth and hands. When at last he turned her under him and entered her clamouring body she let out a cry of exultation. His groan of satisfaction chorused with it as her warmth closed about him.

To hold him became impossible. Her limbs had no strength, she lay under him like a rag doll, the enervation like nothing she had known before. She wanted Drew to remain exactly where he was for ever and ever. . .

His weight bore down on her, a welcome burden, until he stirred to prop himself up on his elbows.

'I'll last as long as I can,' he promised softly, 'but I have waited so long for this that I may not be able. . .'

He trailed off and began to move. As the new, exquisite sensations began to ripple through Hero the strength returned to her muscles. She moved under and with him, wound her legs to twine with his, clutched him with urgent hands, pulled him closer, strained to take him deeper to fill the void inside her.

How long they coupled she did not know but it was over too soon. Sudden frantic movement, a huge groan and Drew jerked and collapsed on top of her. Great shudders shook his body. Hero realised that he had lost control and understood what he had meant. He had not been able to carry on. And she had driven him to this abandon!

The emptiness inside disappeared as tenderness for her husband filled her. She held his inert body tightly in her arms and, without any conscious thought, pressed a flurry of hot kisses on his neck and shoulder.

The shudders subsided and he stirred at length to kiss her gently on the forehead, then on her nose and, lastly, on her soft, vulnerable mouth.

'I behaved like a starving youth, grabbing all the food on the table for myself,' he apologised ruefully, 'but next time, I promise you, it will be different, my dear. Next time, we will share in the feast.'

'What feast?' queried Hero, and added shyly, 'Husband, I have never known such pleasure.'

'Nor I.' He sounded surprised at the admission. 'It was so great, the need so urgent, that I failed to carry you all the way with me. You had less of a climax this time than last.'

Hero flushed at his reminding her again of the humiliation she had suffered. But she knew he was not throwing it in her face. Man-like, having apologised, he had already wiped his offence from his mind.

'Was that a climax?' she asked in surprise. 'I did not

know. And tonight I experienced so much more
delight in every way.'

He stroked the hair from her face as he slid to lie
beside her. She felt his withdrawal as a loss. But he
gathered her close again, pulling her to nestle against
him. 'I am happy you should feel so. But you will
reach greater heights of enjoyment, that I can promise
you.'

'I felt shockingly wanton,' she confided in a small
voice, daring to use the word with which he had once
condemned her.

He laughed, no trace of censure apparent, and Hero
sighed her content as her confidence returned.

'And so you should, my wife,' he murmured deeply.
'I shall not. . .object. . .as long as you confine. . .your
wantonness. . .to your dealings. . .with me.'

This statement he punctuated with several kisses to
her face. Instead of melting under this tender barrage
Hero stiffened and tried to withdraw. 'You may have
no fears on that score, my lord. I am fully aware of the
duties imposed upon me as your wife.'

His arms tightened possessively. 'Oh, Hero! Don't
ruin the mood between us by climbing up on your high
ropes! Can you not recognise a tease when you hear
it?'

Hero relaxed only slightly. 'Not from you, husband.
You have already shown a tendency to indulge in quite
irrational jealousy.'

'Irrational?' Indignation gave way to a rueful laugh.
'A natural emotion, wife, when your beauty drew the
attention of every man in a room and I was uncertain
of your response to me. But I know you better now,

my wife. You will soon, I pray, become the mother of my heirs. I shall not doubt you again.'

So her abandoned response had not offended him but negated his fears. He did not know she loved him and could therefore never betray him. His jealousy had been, and would be, rooted in possessiveness, not love. That was the crux of her lingering sorrow but something she would have to learn to live with. She sighed and curled into him again.

'You have no need.'

To her shock she felt his body rear against hers, waking immediate response. She gave a small moan and when he murmured into her hair, 'Again?' she breathed,

'Yes.'

The household was astir before they slept. A little housemaid crept in to clean the grate and light a new fire. Screened by bed-curtains, they lay still and silent while she went about her task. As the door closed behind her Drew rose to turn the key in the lock. Her eyes being accustomed to the dark, Hero watched unashamedly, revelling in the pale gleam of the male body that had brought her such pleasure. He had kept his promise and taken her with him to that place where thought ceased and the world became a cocoon of sensuous ecstasy, making her forget that he did not love her.

He went briefly through to the dressing-room before rejoining Hero in the bed.

'I've left a note for Benbow. We shall not be disturbed until we ring,' he informed her, running a hand over the swell of her breast, down into the valley of her waist, over the rise of her hips to rest on one slender thigh. But for the moment passion was spent. He turned her so that her back was against him, clasped her about the waist and murmured into her nape, 'Sleep well, my wife.'

Hero made a sound of assent, pressed his hands against her with her own and, secure in the knowledge that he did at least, quite unmistakably, desire her, complied.

They stirred at noon. Hero left the bed and drew back the curtains to find the countryside enjoying a bright, frosty December day. Drew rang for Benbow and Jackson and ordered breakfast to be served in the bedroom.

'Put on your riding habit,' he ordered as he disappeared into the dressing-room. 'After we have eaten we will ride round the estate.'

He looked relaxed, happy, energetic. Hero wished she did not feel as though she had been through a mill. He had been gentle but even so she ached in places she had never ached before. Still, she would enjoy the fresh air and the exercise might help.

With her usual efficiency Jackson, well-trained to be inscrutable whatever the master and mistress got up to, soon had her dressed. Matty had no doubt drawn her own conclusions and was keeping out of the way until called for. Not having been happy about their flight in the first place, she had been delighted at the reconciliation and Hero knew she held out strong hopes that here in the country everything would come right between the earl and her chick. After the night they had just spent together Hero began to hold out some hopes herself.

Drew led her to the stables, situated a few hundred yards from the house and covering an extensive area. The yard was busy. Hero saw Ned Tribble and immediately recognised Cuthbert, who crossed the yard to greet his master.

'You have the horses saddled?'

'Aye, my lord. I hope your lady approves of the gelding.'

Drew smiled. 'So do I!'

Several horses had been sent ahead from London, Drew's beautiful bay stallion, Samson, among them. A groom led him forward. Following behind came another, smaller but, to Hero's admiring eye, even more beautiful animal, a bright bay with white socks and a star on his forehead, carrying a new lady's saddle.

She gave a little cry and went straight up to the strange horse. He seemed to share her delight at the meeting, blowing into her palm and arching his graceful neck under her stroking hand.

'You like him?' asked Drew from close behind her.

Hero turned to him, her eyes shining. 'How could I fail? He is for me to ride?'

'He is yours, since you approve of him. I promised you a horse and both Tribble and I thought a gelding would suit you best. Cuthbert agreed and this one's temperament made him ideal. He is still young, but not too skittish. Many of my neighbours breed and I found him when I was last here.'

'Oh, Drew!' Even when he had left her alone in London he had not entirely forgotten her. Just in time Hero remembered the audience of grooms and stable-hands and stopped herself from flinging her arms round her smiling husband's neck and kissing him. But her eyes said it all as she murmured demurely, 'Thank you for the most wonderful gift I have ever received. What is his name?'

Drew's hand touched hers as he, too, fondled the bay's muzzle. 'His stable name is Samson's Boy—he was sired before I purchased Samson a couple of years ago—but you may call him what you like.'

'Boy will do. Hello, Boy!' She kissed the white mark between his eyes and Boy whickered his pleasure.

'Allow me to help you mount. Samson,' Drew pointed out with a grin, 'is becoming restive. He is jealous at all the attention being given his son and wants to be off.'

'Does he know. . .?'

Drew gave a delighted laugh as Hero put her foot into his laced hands and he tossed her into her saddle. 'I think not! Only human fathers recognise their progeny and even they would fail were they parted before the child had grown. Boy is just another horse to Samson and not even a threat where the mares are concerned. So they should give no trouble when we ride together.'

He left her then to mount himself and soon had Samson alongside. The two animals, no doubt used to riding out together on stable exercise, took little notice of each other as their riders proceeded from the yard and took a path leading through lawns and gardens and across the park towards the farmland and open countryside beyond.

Boy's muscles rippled beneath Hero as they came to a field and kicked the horses into a canter, making for the crest of a rise. Never had she felt such immediate affinity with a horse, not even her beloved mount of old. She leant over his withers and crooned softly into his ear as he carried her effortlessly up the hill.

At the top Drew called a halt. As the horses blew to regain their wind and jangled their harnesses to show their exuberance he swept an arm to indicate the fertile land stretching away before them, dotted with buildings and small wooded copses and criss-crossed with hedges.

'The Ashworthy estate stretches as far as you can see in every direction,' he informed her, quiet pride in his voice.

Hero looked about her in wonder. Some of the myriad fields contained herds of cows, others flocks of sheep. Many lay bare of any apparent crop yet were clearly under cultivation. A man plodded his way along a furrow behind a plough drawn by two huge horses. A narrow ribbon of water, shrouded in places by lingering mist, wound across the landscape to disappear behind a belt of trees.

She turned to Drew, sitting his mount with erect dignity, hard and proud, exhibiting as always that lack of soft effeteness which set him apart from his peers. He stood out in London society because of it. But the last vestiges of town affectations had dropped from him and, by the way he was eyeing them, these acres held first place in his heart. He employed stewards to help, but she had already discovered that he largely administered his estates himself.

'Have you always loved this place?' she asked.

He glanced at her quickly, then away again. 'I did not know it in my childhood.'

'Oh?'

'You have not heard?'

His tone had taken on a grim tone. Hero shivered without knowing why. She was almost afraid to ask, but she did. 'Heard what?'

'My father was banished from Ashworthy, cut off without a penny for choosing to follow his heart and wed for love, a penniless girl, a mere gentleman's daughter.'

The bitterness in his voice brought quick sympathy from Hero and a flood of sudden understanding. No wonder he had sounded grim. There was little she could say to assuage his hurt, but she tried.

'I feel the greatest admiration for your father, Drew. And it must be a comfort to know you were conceived in love.' Unlike me, she wanted to add, but instead observed, 'Your grandfather must have been a hard man.'

'You cannot imagine.' He gathered his reins. 'Come, let us go down to the river.'

He had changed the subject. Hero hid her disappointment and almost forgot it in the joy of exercise. They reached the river and Drew led the way along a track which followed its bank. Before long they entered the belt of trees she had seen from above so that, although not far from the house or the driveway, they were invisible from both. The track widened into a grassy bank and Drew again brought them to a standstill.

He dismounted and slung his reins over a nearby branch. Turning, he held out his arms to help her down. Hero did not demur, although she could have managed perfectly easily without help. She let him catch her, knowing the pleasure it would give them both as she slid down his body to reach the ground.

'It is lovely here,' she remarked rather breathlessly as he let her go and she turned to look about.

'I shall look upon it with more favour in the future. Until today it has been a place to bring me nothing but unhappy memories.'

He had led the horses to the river and stood waiting for them to drink. Hero followed after him and asked, 'Why? What happened here?'

He gazed broodingly into the water. 'This is where my grandfather's gamekeeper caught me and so where my journey to the penal colony began.'

His voice held no bitterness now. Hero waited, almost holding her breath, for him to continue. But the horses had finished drinking and he led them back to the path and tied their reins to low branches. As they began to crop the lush grass he indicated a fallen log. Hero sat down and he came to prop his boot on the bark beside her. Elbow resting on his braced thigh, he clasped his hands together as he spoke again.

'I had better tell you my story. I had hoped not to have to but it will not be long before you hear it from others and I had rather you had it from me. My version will be accurate.'

'Only if you want to tell me, Drew.'

He sighed. 'It is time I did.' He paused a moment and she knew he was still reluctant to confide in her. But he did go on. 'My father, Gerald Challoner, was the Earl of Calverstock's younger son. As so often happens with younger sons, he was bought a commission in the army, the 28th Foot. My mother's parents were clinging to their small estate by the skins of their teeth so his chosen one had no dowry to bring him except her love. But still, he defied the old man and married her.'

'He must have loved her very much.'

'He did; they loved each other. Living on a captain's pay was not easy. However, they managed it. Mother rented rooms near his barracks so that they could be together as much as possible. She took in needlework to pay for my education, the best available wherever my father happened to be stationed, as long as it was in England. But when he set sail for Egypt she had to remain behind and eke out a living for us both by her needle. We returned to this part of the world, where they had both been born.'

He paused and Hero asked, 'Could you not have lived with your other grandparents?'

The definite shake of his head made it clear that that had been impossible. 'No. They were both dead and her brother had squandered what remained of the family fortunes. He sold the estate, spent the proceeds and took himself off to the West Indies to make a new fortune but died of a fever. There was nothing left.'

'And she had no other relatives?'

'None with room or money to spare for us.'

'And your uncle, your father's brother? Surely he——?'

Drew broke in, 'He was worse than his father. Papa had betrayed his class, they would have nothing further to do with him. And then,' he went on sombrely, 'word came that Captain Gerald Challoner was dead. No wonder we had heard nothing from him. He died of wounds in March 1801 after the battle under

Abercromby near Alexandria. Mother was prostrate for weeks.'

Hero swallowed. 'How old were you, Drew?'

'Thirteen. Mother had worked herself almost blind to send me to a minor public school. She had to work even longer hours then and she lacked the stamina. Less than two years later she went into a feverish decline. I had not realised... I left school at once, of course, and took a casual job in the local forge to bring in a shilling or two each week. We had nothing saved, I had to look after Mama, the parish paid out a pittance, but quite simply we were starving. The rent had to be paid or we'd be thrown out and that would have killed her. I collected firewood from round about but there was never enough money to feed an invalid properly or to pay a doctor. So I came here to beg help from my grandfather.'

A picture of Drew as a half-starved youth desperate with worry for his mother brought quick tears to Hero's eyes. 'Did he give it?'

'He laughed in my face.' The bitterness was back in Drew's voice now. 'How I hated him! I'd walked ten miles or more on an almost empty stomach to see him and all he did was laugh!'

'Oh, Drew!'

Hero put her hand up to touch his clasped hands. She wanted to put her arms about him to give him comfort but she could feel the resistance in his taut body. Indeed, the instant he saw the tears in her eyes he took his foot from the log and turned away.

Head flung back, he declared, 'I demanded no pity then and I wish for none now. I decided to take matters into my own hands. Instead of leaving the property immediately I scouted round and found what I had been looking for. Rabbit traps. Rabbit broth would do my mother a power of good and if I was to provide for her I needed something solid and warm inside me. I found a couple of prize specimens struggling to free themselves and released the poor creatures, put them out of their misery by wringing their necks, hid them under my coat and began to make for home.' He glanced towards the undergrowth beyond the path. 'The traps have gone now.'

'Did you have them removed?'

He shot her a sardonic smile. 'How did you guess? I could not bear to see them every time I passed this way. I was unfortunate, you see. Midgley, the gamekeeper, happened along and caught me with my prizes. Stealing game is, of course, a heinous offence. And I made matters worse by trying to fell the fellow and escape. I did not know he had assistants within call.'

'But surely the estate belonged to your family——?'

'But not to me. I told Midgley who I was and he took me before my grandfather. He refused to acknowledge me. Told Midgley to hand me over to the law. The rest you know.'

She did not, not really. How could she possibly imagine what it must have been like for a boy like Drew to be thrown into gaol, convicted, transported to the other side of the earth to work for slave wages in a harsh penal colony? And what had happened to his mother?

Hero sensed that he wished to say no more, so she suppressed most of the questions burning the tip of her tongue. All she said was, 'Your mother?'

He paced to the river's edge and spoke with his back

turned. 'They allowed me to send her a message. At least she knew what had happend to me. I wrote from time to time and her letters came like a breath of fresh English air.' He drew some deeply into his lungs before swinging round and grinning wryly. 'It seems I was well-liked in the area and my misfortune awakened the charitable conscience of the doctor and others. Thanks to them she survived and continued to make a living with her needle. I worked as much overtime as I could and sent the money home. She is still alive.'

Hero frowned. 'I did not notice anyone who could be your mother on the list of Christmas guests. Is she not coming to Ashworthy?'

'No. She prefers to remain quietly at her home.'

'What a pity. I'd like to meet her.'

He turned. 'You will, one day. But not yet.'

Hero wanted to ask why not, but didn't. He was releasing Boy and held him ready for her to mount, making it clear that confidences were over for now.

'Tomorrow we will ride to the village. You must meet some of the tenants who live there. The farmers will all come up to the house to pay their rents after church on Christmas morning, since it is quarter day. You will meet them all then.'

'Mrs Pilcher mentioned the Christmas feast you give for them. They bring their families, I believe. I shall look forward to it.'

He untied Samson and sprang into the saddle. 'We help to serve them,' he informed her with a sideways, interrogatory glance. 'You will not mind?'

'No! I wish I had thought of doing the same at Polhembury!' A slight sadness crossed her features. 'I wonder how they will all fare there this year.'

'Your Mrs Blackler will dish up something special for the household, I'm certain. They will manage. There will be sufficient income from the estate if your father manages it well.'

'And if he does not?'

His shrug said it all. 'That is his concern, not yours.'

Drew disliked Baron Polhembury for some reason and she did not wish to make matters worse, so she could not mention the drafts she had sent to Mrs Cudlip or the report she had received of her father's neglect. Perhaps, one day, when the shadow lying between them had quite gone, she would summon up the courage. Ask his help. But not yet.

'I came to know them well,' she explained her concern. 'I would not like to think of them suffering because of my absence.'

'You are quite unlike your father,' Drew surprised her by saying as they emerged from the wood and turned along the drive, heading towards the house. 'You did have a care for your people.'

'I always did my best for them,' she assured him quietly.

'I believe you did. Our servants already adore you. The tenants will soon learn to do the same.'

She looked at him quickly, searching for mockery, but found none. He meant it. The unexpectedness of his praise set her nerves tingling and her heart singing. Could it be that he no longer despised her?

CHAPTER ELEVEN

In just over a week the guests would begin to arrive at Ashworthy for the festivities. Hero spent much time in conference with Mrs Pilcher discussing the merits of venison—deer roamed the park—chicken, mutton, rabbit and partridge and whether to serve trout from their pond, fish from the sea—would it be fresh enough?—smoked salmon from Scotland, salt cod or pilchards, or something of everything, baked, boiled or stewed. The varieties of soup for the remove, of pies, puddings and custards had to be decided upon. Ice stored in the ice house made iced puddings a possibility, fruit and vegetables grew in abundance in walled garden and hothouse, and the estate could provide flowers and plants to decorate the table and rooms.

Despite all her training and years of experience, Hero found the decisions difficult, for they had seldom entertained at Polhembury and she scarcely knew some of the people Drew had invited. The party would not be large, just a dozen guests including Earl Bathurst and his countess, a young viscount, Lord Edding, and his mother Lady Edding, Archie and Felicity and, most alarming to Hero, Lord and Lady Castlereagh. Most would stay until the New Year. But, she consoled herself, if the choice on the table was wide enough, surely there would be something to please everyone!

The guest rooms had already been prepared and

allocated according to precedence. It remained only
for her to arrange flowers in them on the day of
arrival. Drew was showing an efficient aptitude for
organising the entertainment. Card tables, billiard-
room, smoking-room and library were all inspected
and dispositions planned. A small ensemble of piano,
violin and flute had been engaged to entertain the
company with music on Christmas Day and to provide
the music on St Stephen's Day, a Saturday, when they
planned to introduce a little dancing. The older guests
would surely stand up in such circumstances. And on
New Year's Eve they were to throw a ball to which
many of the local gentry had been invited.

In addition to the invited guests and the servants
they brought with them, the musicians also had to be
accommodated, but Ashworthy was large enough to
house twice the number.

In her new role as Hero's companion, Matty helped
in any way she could. She dined with them now, for
Hero considered it her due, but Matty refused to join
them when they entertained.

'I've not been bred to it, my chick,' she protested
when Hero suggested that she should do so during the
coming festivities. 'I'd be that nervous—I'm fine with
just you and his lordship, since you've been so kind as
to ask me, but I shouldn't feel right sitting at table
with Lord Castlereagh! No, I'll have a tray in my
room, or eat with Mrs Pilcher. I'll be much happpier,
never you fear.'

'But you'll join us at other times, won't you?' Hero
pressed. 'I'm relying on you to help me to entertain
the guests. And to act as chaperone to the young

ladies! We must allow no misconduct under this roof or I shall be ostracised from society!'

Matty grinned, showing her gappy teeth. 'I'll do that right enough, my chick,' she promised.

Hero retired each night tired but, on the whole, happy with the arrangements being made. Drew joined her in the master bedroom, where they shared hours of warm intimacy and passion.

She learnt to know his body as he knew hers. One night she had stood naked, proud and unashamed, while he circled her, a branch of candles held high, feasting his eyes on the firm roundness of her hips, the fullness of her breasts, the neatness of her waist. Afterwards he had shown particular passion during his lovemaking.

Yet she knew that although Drew wanted her he did not love her. He was still witholding part of himself. But so was she. Despite her growing respect and regard, she could not forget the ruthless way he ruined those he had taken in dislike. Nor, despite his having left them behind in London, could she ignore his consorting with all those women others hinted at—in the nicest, most tactful way, of course.

Subsequent to that first morning they rose at their usual early hour and rode about the estate before breakfast, calling in at remote farmhouses to meet Drew's tenants. Hero discovered that he was universally liked and respected. No one hesitated to tell him of necessary repairs and all were willing to discuss the latest methods of farming with him, even if, like the elderly, weatherbeaten Farmer Wellow, they scoffed at them.

Drew cared for the people, as well as the land, and was knowledgeable about both. This fitted ill with his treatment of her father and others, with the bargain he had made to make her his bride. Could it be that he was not as ruthless and without finer feeling as she had thought? He had certainly softened in his attitude to her.

'He were that good last spring when Mr Wellow were took bad,' confided Mrs Wellow, a comfortably built woman, mother of four married daughters and a longed-for son, as the men wandered out into the yard to inspect one of the oxen the farmer used to draw his plough. 'When the apothecary's medicine didn't seem to be doing any good he sent for the doctor and paid the bill. And he came over every day to see that young Alfie, our youngest—he's only sixteen—was managing to get the work done. Not above taking off his coat and doing a bit himself, is the new lord. Not like those that went before him. Mean devils, the lot of 'em. His lordship knows Mr Wellow'll be needing that animal fit before 'tis time to plough after Christmas and he'll see that it is.'

'Where is your son?' asked Hero politely.

'Alfie'll be in the milking shed. They'll be off there after, I don't doubt. Will ye be taking a dish of tea, my lady? I've a mite of fruit cake here if you'd care to sample it.'

'Thank you, Mrs Wellow. The exercise has made me quite hungry.'

'Haven't had breakfast yet, I'll be bound.' The motherly face beamed at Hero as Mrs Wellow placed a large wedge of succulent-looking cake in front of her. 'You look fair bonny, my lady, if I may say so.

Just the kind of wife a nice gentleman like his lordship needed.'

Hero took a large bite of the cake to cover her confusion. Drew had another admirer in Mrs Wellow, for most women found him irresistible, with his athletic build, light brown, sun-bleached hair, clear grey eyes and the smile which banished all trace of harshness from his features. She certainly did, she acknowledged as a wave of warm, weakening emotion swept through her.

'This is delicious,' she pronounced a trifle breathlessly, having swallowed the cake in her mouth. 'Would you allow me to have the receipt?'

After that the two women chatted like old friends until their husbands reappeared, by which time Hero had subdued her wayward thoughts. Drew accepted the refreshment offered by Mrs Wellow, a wedge of her cake and a jug of home-brewed ale.

As they rode back to the house Hero reflected that each day revealed some new facet of her husband's character. The disquiet she felt over his buying up of debts and his subsequent dealings with his debtors began to fade a little. Most of the time she could forget even the way she had been forced into marriage. She supposed he must have his own reasons for such behaviour. One day he would tell her. Until then she would try to trust the man she was coming to know so much better, who, in every other way, was very like the one she had instinctively judged him to be.

To Hero's relief the house party proved a great success. It did not pass without one or two moments of anxiety, however.

Archie Dalmead, faced with the appealing presence of Lady Felicity, at first sought refuge in the company of his friend.

'Devil take it, Drew! Couldn't you prevent your wife from inviting the Beltinge female?'

Drew merely lifted his brows. 'Hero has few friends. She wished to advance the acquaintance. Why should Lady Felicity's presence here concern you?'

Archie, regardless of his careful coiffure, ran agitated fingers through his hair. 'Because, as you are perfectly well aware, that female is out to trap me into wedlock! I won't have it, d'you hear?'

'I hear,' replied Drew, ostentatiously covering his ears against Archie's indignant bellow. 'But, my dear fellow, all you have to do is ignore her. Do not follow her into empty rooms, avoid dark and chilly terraces——'

'Don't play the fool, Drew! You know very well I'm fond of the chit! I believe this is a conspiracy to throw us together.'

'How can it be? You are perfectly free to leave,' observed Drew equably.

'And miss your Christmas party?' Archie flicked open his snuff box and took a large pinch, sniffing deeply and with great deliberation. He snapped the box shut and remarked with studied languor, 'No, I shall not leave, I shall simply treat her with the utmost courtesy when we meet but otherwise ignore her.'

'Lady Calverstock,' began Felicity breathlessly.

'Please call me Hero,' put in her hostess quickly. 'I know we are not well-acquainted yet, but I feel we are to be friends.'

'Thank you! So do I! But. . .' Felicity hesitated and began again with more determination. 'But Hero, had I known his lordship would be here——'

'Which lordship?' enquired Hero innocently.

'Lord Harrington! It is so very difficult. He pays me every courtesy, of course, and I thought he liked me, but he seems to be avoiding me. It is most lowering to be treated with so much indifference when I. . .I admire him so much,' confessed Felicity, colouring. 'I fear I shall find myself much exercised to hide my embarrassment in company.'

'Archie is a perfect gentleman,' observed Hero. 'He will not make his avoidance noticeable, you may depend upon it. Have you considered, Felicity, that it may not be due to indifference at all? That he may simply be running scared? He fears that you may well be able to fix his interest and wear down his resistance to the idea of matrimony.'

'Oh! But then, how much more. . .?' Felicity's breathless words trailed off.

'Just be your charming self, my dear,' smiled Hero. 'Ignore his coolness. Treat him as you would any other young gentleman. In fact, you could concentrate your attention on Lord Edding, could you not? He is a personable young man if a little tied to his mother's leading strings. Make Harrington a little jealous, perhaps?'

Felicity suddenly giggled. 'Hero! I believe you planned this! But how could you know that I cherish a *tendre*. . .?'

'I must confess to eavesdropping at the theatre. You thought our box empty and so did not lower your voice. I do apologise.'

'Oh!' Felicity looked a little confused. 'You mean that evening after the Queen's funeral, before you were taken ill?'

'I do.' Hero firmly repressed her guilty blush and hoped Felicity would not remember the remarks she had made about Calverstock and herself. 'You told your parents you would wed Archie were he to declare himself. We are merely giving him the chance, that is all.'

'No wonder he looked as though he wished to turn and run the instant he saw me here!' A small smile had begun to play about Felicity's mobile lips. 'Poor Harrington! I shall be sweetness itself. But, you know, I do believe I have suddenly discovered that I cherish a *tendre* for a certain young viscount!'

'Well done,' chuckled Hero. 'Archie is struggling against his feelings for you, you know. If that doesn't bring him to the point I cannot imagine what will!'

Presents were exchanged on Christmas Eve. Hero exclaimed over gloves and fans, a lavish writing box from Archie, sundry exquisitely worked handkerchiefs, papier-mâché and enamelled boxes and trays, together with baubles and other offerings from the servants. Members of the staff had all been presented with their Christmas boxes in the form of money, which both Drew and Hero had agreed would be of most use to them. The carefully chosen gifts presented to their guests were received with at least surface pleasure.

Hero had debated the question of what to give Drew for weeks past. While still in London she had decided upon and purchased a leather-bound volume, a first edition, for his library. As the last of the gifts were distributed and opened it became painfully clear that she was to receive nothing from him.

Her disappointment knew no bounds. He had given her Boy, of course, and the new saddle, but had said nothing about those being for Christmas. Surely he would not leave her out, not in front of their guests. It would be too pointed and quite at odds with his more recent behaviour. The omission must be an oversight.

Every parcel had been opened and exclaimed over and Drew had thanked her for an addition to his library that he would always treasure with what she knew to be sincerity. His teasing grey eyes rested upon her with something like real affection as he bowed elaborately before her.

'I fear I could not wrap my gift to you, my lady. If you will call your maid to bring your cloak and bonnet, I will take you outside and present it.'

Hero's eyes began to sparkle. Just the knowledge that he had not passed her over was enough, but to have to go outside—whatever could it be?

Matty had already murmured, 'I'll fetch them,' and left the room. Hero guessed she would bring her own things, too, for she would expect to accompany her mistress.

'May I come with you?' asked Archie, presuming on his friendship with Drew to be the first to speak. Everyone in the room was agog.

'Cannot we all come?' cried an older couple's young daughter, who had been ogling Archie ever since the family's arrival. Hero had not anticipated such a complication and hoped Miss Dickens would not spoil her plans for Archie and Felicity. But Archie seemed disinclined to encourage the chit even to defend himself against Felicity's charms and Hero had only to consider the girl's unfortunate looks and notice her forward manners to understand why.

'Of course,' agreed Drew expansively. 'The more the merrier!'

A rush ensued to fetch or ring for outdoor garments. Drew, in anticipation of the moment, had his caped greatcoat and beaver already waiting in the hall. Matty returned quickly with Hero's things, including gloves and muff. Thereafter Hero's patience was sorely tried as they waited for others to ready themselves to brave the crisp December air.

Eventually all were suitably garbed and the expedition set off, Drew leading the way with Hero on his arm. He conducted them right round the house, quite a long trek, since the building had, over the centuries, tended to sprawl as wings and extensions were added.

'It is a fine afternoon for a stroll, don't you agree?' he murmured, glancing down at Hero, a roguish look in his eyes.

'Where are we going?' she asked. 'Is this some kind of trick?'

'Not at all. Patience, my dear. I am just ensuring that our guests take some exercise.'

He was being mischievous. Perhaps he had not really wanted an audience when he presented his gift, but had felt unable to refuse the escort.

Having almost circled the house, they came at last to the stables. Hero began to tremble with an excitement she could scarcely contain. What could he have for her here? Another mount? A hunter, perhaps?

The others were all talking and laughing, making

jokes and playing a guessing game. As they entered under the stable arch Hero stopped in her tracks, while a concerted cry of astonishment came from those following behind.

Waiting in the yard stood a delightful little open carriage, painted black and gold, with scarlet cushions and a folding hood in case it should rain. Two-wheeled like a cabriolet or curricle, it was neither, for a cabriolet used only a single horse and a curricle had no hood. Harnessed to it, covered by blankets to keep them warm, were two superb black ponies she had never seen in the stables before, their headstalls beribboned and garnished with sprigs of holly. Tribble, his nose pink with cold, stood holding their heads, a wide grin on his face.

Hero looked up at Drew, her eyes enormous. She could hardly speak for the lump in her throat.

'Is that my gift?' she gulped.

He nodded. 'You will need your own conveyance here at Ashworthy. It may not always be convenient for you to ride Boy.' A note in his voice told her he was anticipating a time when she would be increasing. 'In this you may travel to the village or anywhere on the estate in comparative comfort. You can drive? If not, I shall be delighted to teach you.'

She hadn't driven for years, any more than she had ridden a horse. That skill had come back without effort and she supposed that that with the ribbons would too. But did he want to teach her?

'Only a very little,' she answered, moving forward at last to take a closer look at the extravagant gift the others were all admiring.

What must they be thinking? That it was the kind of

gift a rich and noble lord might give to his new and beloved wife? But she knew she was not beloved.

The first shock gave way to excited chatter and cries of congratulation.

Very softly Drew asked, 'Would you like to take a short drive now?'

She looked up and answered the quizzical smile in his eyes. He wanted to shake off their retinue.

'I should like that above everything.'

'Then I'll help you up.'

A groom removed the blankets and Tribble released the ponies' heads. Drew flicked the whip and they left the yard to the sound of a ragged cheer, leaving the others to make a leisurely way back to the house. Sitting close, because the carriage was small, Drew drove at a brisk trot, reminding her of the techniques involved in driving a carriage and pair. With the gates in sight, he handed her the whip and offered the reins.

'Drive to the entrance and then pull up.'

She did as bidden, the thrill of holding the ribbons again showing in the delighted concentration on her striking features. The gatekeeper ran out to open the gates but Drew beckoned him to come to them.

'We are not leaving the grounds,' he explained. 'Lead the ponies round, will you?'

So the carriage was turned and Hero began the drive back. Following Drew's instructions, she diverted into a crossing path which would lead them on a circular route back. Round a further bend, shielded from prying eyes by thick trees and undergrowth, Drew told her to stop again.

With the ponies obediently stationary, Hero looked at him, a question in her smile.

'Was that satisfactory, my lord?'

'Certainly. As in everything else, you are an apt pupil.' He grinned a trifle wryly. 'Is there nothing I can teach you?'

Hero blushed and lowered her eyes. 'You know the answer to that, my husband.'

'Then I shall require proof,' he responded, sending a thrill winging through her. Then, 'You have not properly thanked me,' he complained, injecting a plaintive note into his voice.

Hero, daring to look up again, caught the gleam in his eye but pretended not to notice it.

'I did,' she protested. 'You cannot have forgotten——'

Her words choked off as Drew put an arm round her shoulders, turned her face up and lowered his lips to within an inch of hers.

'Kiss me,' he instructed.

With becoming modesty, Hero complied.

'Mmm. After all my tuition you can do better than that.'

'Will this do, my lord?' she demanded and, abandoning all pretence, gave him the kiss dictated by her heart.

That evening, gathered in the drawing-room, several of the ladies entertained the company at the pianoforte. To Hero's amusement, Lady Felicity, in a pretty manner, persuaded Lord Edding to turn her pages for her. She performed so excellently and looked so delightful with the light of the candles mounted on each side of the instrument playing on her features that Hero felt sure Archie must be captivated. When he strolled across and replaced Edding at her side for an encore, she was convinced of it. Felicity played with greater spirit but less accuracy, which few except Hero noticed.

And then someone, Lord Castlereagh in fact, demanded that Hero should take her place at the pianoforte. She could, of course, have continued to decline, not protesting an inability but by her expression allowing everyone to infer it, as she had in London. But here, in what was now her own home, she thought she would not. She had not dared to practise since leaving Polhembury because Calverstock would surely have found out. She would be rusty, but that could not be helped. The deception had gone on long enough. He had so easily seen through her others that to discover his wife to be a talented musician should scarcely surprise him now.

He did look slightly aghast as she rose to her feet in compliance with the request. Archie and several others who had seen her decline before looked surprised. But Hero, bathed in new assurance of the felicity of her marriage, glided gracefully over to the instrument and settled herself on the stool. She had, surreptitiously, examined the music and knew there were several pieces she could play, as well as those she already knew by heart. As she searched for a suitable sonata by the late Mr Mozart a shadow fell across the music.

'Something else you have no need to learn?' asked a soft voice in her ear.

'I fear so,' murmured Hero.

'Why did you allow me to go on believing you so ignorant of the social graces?'

'Because you assumed it without condescending to ask.'

'Forgive me. I prejudged you, my dear,' Drew admitted. 'Are you able to sing?'

'Not as well as I could wish,' confessed Hero with a laugh. 'My voice is slight, though tuneful, I believe. I will try this.'

She handed him a sheet of music and he placed it on the stand between the candles. Hero flexed her fingers, as she did every day to keep them supple, and began to play the elegant sonata.

The applause when she finished sounded more than merely polite. On being persuaded to play an encore Hero launched into a lively country dance.

Then Drew said, 'Play this.'

He placed a song sheet on the stand. Hero looked up enquiringly and he grinned. 'I, too, have a concealed talent I am at last ready to display,' he teased.

And so he had—a strong, pleasant tenor voice. He had chosen a song with a chorus which Hero joined in, encouraging everyone else to do the same. Afterwards, by request, Hero played Christmas carols and the company raised their voices in joyful harmony.

Soon the village minstrels could be heard outside rendering, rather raggedly and somewhat off-key, the same old tunes. Peering from the windows a group of warmly wrapped figures could be seen, illuminated by the light thrown from the lanterns they carried. However untutored their performance, they had brought with them the spirit of Christmas. Arm in arm, Drew and Hero went to open the door, dispense some largesse and invite the singers in for refreshment.

It was, considered Hero, the best eve of Christmas she had enjoyed since her mother's death.

After church on Christmas Day the tenants followed Lord and Lady Calverstock and their guests back to Ashworthy in gig and cart, some walking their families in procession behind.

With his steward in attendance to keep the records, Drew personally received the rents, wished his tenants prosperity and happiness in the New Year and sent them through to the splendidly festooned dining-room, where preparations for refreshment had been made.

Felicity helped Drew and Hero to entertain their guests while Archie dispensed ale and lemonade with considerable dexterity and charm.

The tenants, subdued by their surroundings, scarcely spoke as they cleared the platters of ham, turkey and salmon, pigeon and lobster patties, fruit tarts and iced plum cake. Even the children, scrubbed and warned not to misbehave, spoke in whispers. Matty, at home in this company, chatted easily with them all, especially the children, encouraging them to eat heartily of the kind of food they seldom enjoyed at home. No one on a Calverstock estate would starve, and some tenants were quite prosperous, but most lived on more simple fare from day to day.

It astonished Hero, changing for their own festive meal, to discover how much she was enjoying the house party. Its success proved that one did not have to remain in London to take pleasure in society. She would enjoy to spend a part of the season in London each year, but much prefer to reside most of the time at Ashworthy. She suspected Drew felt the same, although duty took him to London and to other Calverstock estates from time to time.

And how she would have loathed entertaining if she and Drew had still been at cuffs, if behaving as a happy bride in public had still been all pretence! But the worst of their differences seemed to be over. Memories of their first disastrous weeks together were fading. They had found mutual enjoyment of each other as husband and wife and their attitudes had softened over matters of dissent. Understanding and companionship were growing between them. So, although she was not in fact quite the happy bride others imagined, it took little to maintain the fiction. Perhaps 1819 would bring the child they both desired. That event would give them a common purpose, a small creature they could both love without stint or reservation.

By New Year's Eve the house guests had settled into a routine and, if all had not immediately become bosom friends, no discordant note had so far been struck. The gentlemen spent much of the daylight hours outdoors hunting or shooting or indoors in the billiard-room, while the ladies pursued more decorous occupations, strolling in the gardens when the weather permitted, taking short carriage rides to view the surrounding countryside, or simply sitting before a cheerful fire reading, painting or embroidering.

But the bustle of preparation disturbed the peace and routine on the day of the ball, and not only in household matters. Maids dressed hair, pressed ball-growns, made last-minute alterations and added trimmings for their mistresses' approval, while valets attended to their masters' coiffures, brushed and

pressed evening attire, ironed frilled shirts and prepared snowy cravats.

As the first carriage bringing guests rattled up the
drive, Drew entered the bedroom where Jackson was
putting the last touches to Hero's toilet.

'There, my lady. I think that will do.'

Hero took a last glance in the mirror and smiled
approval.

'Thank you, Jackson. I think the new hairstyle suits
me.' She rose from the dressing-stool and turned to
greet her husband. 'What do you think my lord?'

Drew strolled across the room, took both her hands
in his and spread her arms wide, holding her off to
sweep his eyes down to the satin slippers peeping from
beneath the heavily decorated hem of the shimmering,
daffodil-yellow gown glowing through a mist of chif-
fon, and back up to linger on the swell of her bosom
above the waist, on the creamy texture of the skin of
her shoulders—the contemplation of touching which
sent a remembered thrill through his own body—and
on to study the abundant brown hair piled on top of
her head with curls spilling out to frame her oval face.

'Capital,' he declared. 'I particularly approve of that
ribbon and gauze affair on your head.' Gently, resisting
the temptation to run a finger along the low neckline
of the gown, he touched instead the delicate material
nestling among her curls. 'You look beautiful, my
dear.'

Hero fingered the exquisite heirloom necklace about
her throat, the one he had given her before the lord
mayor's dinner. 'I did not wish to wear the matching
tiara and thought it went well with this.'

'To admiration,' agreed Drew. So saying, he pulled

her close and kissed her lightly upon the mouth, careful not to cause damage to her gown or coiffure. 'It is time to proceed downstairs. I hear our first guests arriving.'

Arm in arm, they descended to the hall to greet them.

Half an hour later, the receiving line having diminished to a trickle, the dancing was about to begin. Drew and Hero hovered by the door of the ballroom for a moment, absorbing the sight of their guests mingling in its restored splendour, the ladies' gowns and jewellery shimmering and glittering under the brilliant yet soft illumination offered by the hundreds of candles flickering amid the scintillating rainbow crystals of the chandeliers. Several long windows and a couple of doors graced the length of the opposite wall. One of the doors led to an orangery and the other directly to the terrace, beyond which lay the formal gardens.

'Ashworthy has come alive at last,' murmured Drew. 'You have worked a miracle, Lady Calverstock.'

His tone rendered the formal title as an endearment. 'I?' demanded Hero, startled. 'I have done very little.'

'Mrs Pilcher would not have managed half so well without your suggestions and encouragement. I could scarcely have entertained such a house party or given a ball alone. Your presence has made it all possible, my dear, and I am grateful.'

Hero, her heart leaping at the compliment, covered her quite inordinate pleasure by fluttering her lashes at her husband. 'I am glad you are satisfied wtih your bargain, my lord,' she responded with a smile half teasing, half sober.

'I am beginning to believe,' murmured Drew seriously, 'that my choice of wife was more admirable than I had ever anticipated.' How, he wondered, could he have guessed that the engaging creature he had met for such a brief moment yet had, on the strength of that slender acquaintance and despite her parentage, decided to wed, would turn out to be an incomparable? His fingers tightened on Hero's arm as he escorted her into the middle of the floor to lead the first dance. If only the marriage had not begun so badly. But he must put from his mind those scathing words he had overheard before the ceremony.

They took their places in the quadrille. As he bowed to acknowledge her curtsy he could not forbear to drink in the sight of her, to acknowledge that the overheard words did not represent the Hero Langage he had come to know. And her present attitude indicated that she might have changed her mind about him as much as he had changed his over her. Which thought gave him, a man who had long since ceased to care for the opinion of any but his dearest family and friends, a quite unwarranted degree of pleasure.

Felicity took to the floor partnered by Lord Edding. Harrington, looking less languid and decidedly less affable than usual, led a simpering Miss Dickens out to take their places in the measure. Hero noted Drew's sardonic eye fixed on Archie.

'Do you think he is suffering from jealousy?' she whispered as the steps of the dance brought them together.

'Lady Felicity has been doing her best to make him so, I believe. She cannot seriously be trying to fix the interest of that milksop Edding.'

It was several moments before Hero was able to answer. 'Of course not,' she maintained stoutly as they came together again. 'I do hope her campaign is successful.'

Drew chuckled. 'So she is mounting a campaign, eh? The designing creature! Poor Archie! But by the way he is glaring across at her, I believe she may be making an advance.'

During the next hour or so Felicity gracefully accepted Harrington's determined efforts to secure her hand and stood up with him on two occasions.

The supper dance ended. The company went through to the room set aside for the purpose to take refreshment. Hero was passing from guest to guest when Lord Edding fussed up to her.

'Lady Calverstock, have you seen Lady Felicity recently? I have been searching for her to take her in to supper, but she is nowhere to be found.'

Hero realised that she had not seen Felicity for some time. 'Had you secured her promise of the supper dance earlier? No? Then she has probably retired to her room to effect some repair to her toilet,' she suggested. 'I should not concern yourself, Lord Edding. I am certain she will return before long. She has a healthy appetite and will not wish to miss the refreshments.'

'I suppose not,' muttered his lordship irritably. 'I cannot search any longer. I must go and wait upon my mother. She will not be pleased at my not securing Lady Felicity's company.'

'You must not neglect Lady Edding,' agreed Hero, noting that his lordship was pursuing the heiress on his mother's instructions and hoping that neither they nor anyone else had noticed the simultaneous disappearance of Archie Dalmead.

She was not much worried. Matty had been given the task of acting as chaperone to any young lady who did not have her mother with her, and to Felicity in particular. Matty had stationed herself on a chair beside the door leading to the orangery. The couple were probably out there enjoying its shadowy privacy. Hero knew Matty would not allow any seriously improper conduct to take place and would do her best to divert anyone who threatened to intrude on the young couple. Though should she fail and the pair be discovered, Felicity would be compromised and Archie in honour bound to do the decent thing. . .

She forgot Felicity as she became absorbed in conversing politely with guests who, until that evening, had been strangers to her. As a good hostess this was demanded of her but she wanted to become acquainted with those who had their homes near by. If she and Drew spent much time at Ashworthy these people would constitute her social circle, and from them would come her closest friends.

Both Felicity and Archie reappeared before the end of supper. For the remainder of the evening it seemed to Hero that, for a man determined not to be caught in parson's mousetrap, Lord Harrington, in paying most particular attention to Lady Felicity Charteris and standing up with her yet again, was behaving in a manner calculated to spring it. He would end the evening heavily compromised.

On the stroke of midnight the year of 1819 was greeted with cheers and toasts. The dancing resumed. Drew had done his duty and danced with almost all their guests and Hero had not lacked for a partner all evening. Drew claimed his wife as the last waltz struck up.

'A most successful evening,' he murmured.

'In more ways than one, I predict,' answered Hero.

Drew did not have to ask what she meant. His hand pressed into her waist, pulling her imperceptibly closer. 'They are admirably suited. It should prove a felicitous union.'

Hero, as was usual when she danced a waltz with Drew, found herself short of breath. 'Archie needs a wife. He is already looking a changed man.'

'Marriage changes most men, whether they like it or not. Which is perhaps why most men try to avoid it.'

'It is as well for us poor females that gentlemen need to wed in order to breed an heir!'

He made no response to this tart observation for the music was speeding to a finish. Hero clung for a moment while she regained her balance and then reluctantly withdrew from Drew's embrace. He tucked her hand under his arm as they moved over to bid their departing guests goodnight.

As the house guests made their various ways upstairs Felicity hung back for a word with Hero.

Her excitement barely suppressed, she gave Hero such a radiant smile that there could be no doubt that Archie had been persuaded to declare himself at last.

'You have won your campaign?' smiled Hero, taking her friend's arm as they mounted the stairs.

Felicity giggled. 'He says it drove him wild to see me hanging out to catch such a poor fish as Edding. I pointed out Edding's pliable nature and his wealth, and Lord Harrington said that if I was going to make

a cake of myself over the viscount he could see he
would have no choice but to rescue me from future
unhappiness by marrying me himself.'

'He didn't!'

'He did! I then confessed that, if he was offering, I
would much rather marry him than Edding. I would
prefer to have his mother as my in-law.'

Hero was laughing outright as they reached her
bedroom door. 'What did he say to that?'

'He caught on that I was roasting him! Said I was a
shocking tease, grabbed me and kissed me.' Felicity
blushed. Her eyes shone softly. 'Then he said he would
travel to London immediately and seek my father's
permission to pay his addresses.'

'Lord Beltinge will not object?' asked Hero
anxiously.

'No. He simply wishes to see me settled. Oh, Hero,
how can I thank you?'

Hero leant forward and kissed Felicity on the cheek.
'By being happy.'

'Like you and Calverstock. I wondered once why he
married you. But anyone can see he is in love with
you. And you with him. You are fortunate, Hero.'

Hero passed no direct comment on Felicity's words.
She hid the sharp pang of regret they brought, for of
course Calverstock did not love her. Instead she
remarked, 'You love Harrington. I think he loves you,
though he may not realise it yet. You suit each other
to admiration.'

Felicity smiled and as they parted threw her arms
about Hero. 'I do hope so! And I must remember to
thank Matty for not pursuing us into the orangery!'

Drew and Archie lingered in the library waiting for

Castlereagh and Bathurst to retire. The two politicians had much of interest to discuss but at length rose to leave.

The door had barely closed behind them before Archie announced that he must take his leave early the following morning. 'Urgent business in London,' he explained.

'You intend to restore Lady Felicity's reputation?' enquired Drew lazily.

'What?' Archie caught the twinkle in his friend's eye and grinned sheepishly.

'I warned you against dancing too often with the lady or taking her into secluded corners.'

'Found I didn't mind bein' caught,' admitted Archie. 'She's a deuced fine female. Throwin' herself away on that ass Edding. Couldn't allow her to do that.'

'Of course not,' agreed Drew. 'So you are off to seek Papa's approval, is that it?' Archie nodded. Drew sighed. 'I may well see you in town in a few days. I have to go up on business myself next week.'

'Does Hero know?'

'Not yet,' admitted Drew and added, 'It's a cursed nuisance. I've no desire at all to leave Ashworthy.'

Or my wife, he might have added.

CHAPTER TWELVE

By Monday afternoon all the guests had departed.

'We could ride again tomorrow morning,' suggested Drew that night, drawing Hero into the curve of his body as they settled down to sleep.

'Oh, yes! Boy will be missing the exercise as much as I am. He must be feeling neglected.'

'Neglected? Why?'

'Since Christmas we have left him in the stables several times while we took the carriage out!'

Drew laughed and tightened his arm. 'Boy will have been exercised, never fear.'

'I suppose so, but I believe he will have missed me.' As his clasp drew her nearer she snuggled her back closer against the solidity of his warmth. 'I shall look forward to our riding out together again in the mornings.'

She felt the touch of his lips against her nape. 'I fear I must make a short visit to London on Wednesday.' He sounded regretful. 'Just a short visit. I should be back on Sunday. Then we may continue our excursions uninterrupted.'

Hero's disappointment was palpable. She shifted slightly in protest. 'So soon in the New Year?'

'Unfortunately, yes. The business will not wait.' His regret seemed genuine. He kissed the nape of her neck again and said lightly, 'I shall look forward to my return rather more than has been usual.'

He was flirting with her, recognised Hero as sleep overcame her. If only she could believe it was love he was expressing and not just affection based on desire. But even affection was better than contempt, was her last conscious thought.

The morning proved damp and rather chilly but, wrapped up in her thickest riding costume, Hero prepared to make the most of the occasion, since she would have to wait several days before it could be repeated. She wondered what his business in London could be; he had not said. A man's affairs were considered to be no concern of his wife, who must be protected from all financial and other worries. Fustian! Had she not largely administered Polhembury for years? She must make him see that she was interested, wished to take her place at his side...

However, he was not visiting one of his estates to solve a problem of administration, but journeying to London. He consulted his lawyer there quite regularly, she knew. Perhaps he had to see him urgently in connection with investments or some legal matter concerning an estate. It was of no use speculating. Just so long as he was not making an excuse to leave in order to visit that woman—or another about whom she knew nothing.

Hero thrust that thought aside as Drew, attentive as a lover, assisted her to mount, waving the groom aside. She could not doubt his recent desire to please her, for whatever reason. His Christmas gift had been nothing short of lavish. A bribe, a sop to stifle her doubts, a gesture to still his bad conscience?

Were that so, she did not know how she could continue as his wife. The hurt would be too great. She recognised the fact but stopped short of asking herself why.

Her spirits rose as the horses cantered and then increased speed to a full gallop in a race around a large field presently lying fallow. Afterwards they rode companionably side by side, walking their mounts, giving them time to recover their winds, before turning to trot for home.

As usual they returned via the thicket by the river, where the horses could rest and drink while they enjoyed a quiet, secluded moment or two before returning to face the day's demands. Tanner, the groom who always followed at a discreet distance in case his services should be required, knew their habit by now and remained well out of sight but within call.

They entered the clearing and prepared to dismount but before they could do so a deafening bang made Hero jump in alarm. For a bewildered moment she did not realise what the explosion meant. Then, as she glimpsed a stocky figure among the trees from whence a flash had come, she gave a great cry of outrage.

She heard a harsh shout of, 'Die, damn you, die!' but by now her attention had flown back to Drew, who had first slumped over and then fallen from his saddle. Panic gripped her as she watched the man she loved crumple to the ground. She knew in that instance that if he died she would not wish to live.

She threw herself from her horse's back and rushed to his side as Tanner, hearing the commotion, galloped up.

She pointed distractedly through the trees. 'A man! He went that way! After him! But be careful, he has a gun!'

'But his lordship——'

'I'll see to his lordship until help arrives.'

The man did as she said without further demur, riding off to circle the copse and cut off the assassin's retreat.

Hero anxiously examined Drew for signs of blood, her heart in her mouth. She had a little knowledge of how to deal with accidents, gleaned during her years as mistress of Polhembury, but if the wound was serious. . .

He could not die! Not now she knew exactly how much she had come to love him.

'Drew,' she whispered, 'oh, my love, please don't die!'

He was insensible yet she could see no blood on his coat, no hole where the bullet had penetrated his clothing. She knelt by his head and gathered it against her breast, murmuring endearments. Only then did she see the shallow furrow parting his hair and the oozing blood matting the strands to a sticky red. A trickle had begun to drip down his brow. Scalp wounds always bled profusely, she reassured herself. There was no need to worry about blood.

Upon closer examination she could see that the shot had done little damage. The bullet must have stunned him as it grazed his scalp. She had heard of that happening to others. Relief washed over her, leaving her shaking. She dug into one of his capacious pockets, found a handkerchief and began to mop up the mess.

In the distance she could hear men crashing about and shouting, the sounds of pursuit. The groom must have found help and be after the intruder. Nearer at hand heavy footsteps pounded along the path towards them and soon two groundsmen burst into the clearing.

By this time Drew had begun to stir. Grey eyes, fogged by pain, gazed up into anxious hazel ones. A ghost of a smile twitched the lips which had taught her how to respond to passion, how to love. 'What happened?' he demanded in a faint tone, content to lie a few moments longer in his wife's embrace. 'Were we attacked?'

Hero kept him pressed to her as he raised a hand to his damaged head. Her voice shook with reaction as she told him.

He struggled to sit up, wincing with pain at the movement, and Hero helped him.

The two groundsmen were making a hurdle, presumably to carry him back to the house, and he called across, his voice much stronger, 'You will not need that, as I am perfectly able to ride.'

'Oh, Drew, are you sure?'

Hero's eyes, huge and glowing with anxiety, met his. For a long moment they stared at each other, seemingly unable to break the contact. Dimly, Drew recalled a soft voice murmuring words of love in his ear. But he had been insensible. He must have been dreaming, imagining words he wanted to hear. At bottom, his wife despised him. He must remember that, or he might become completely entangled in her toils.

Hero watched the bemused expression in Drew's grey eyes harden into resolve as he dragged his gaze away from hers. 'I am perfectly sure. Cannon!' He addressed the groundsman by name, Hero noted. 'Come and help me to my feet.'

Cannon obeyed immediately, taking his master's elbow. Hero refused to relinquish her hold and between them they helped Drew up to stand on shaky legs. He muttered a low-voiced imprecation as he realised his weakness and felt the stab of a twisted knee, then apologised stiffly for speaking so before a lady.

Hero snorted. 'You need have no fear for my sensibilities, my lord! I have heard worse from my father, under stress.' Or the influence of drink. But she did not say that aloud.

Drew swayed as he stood. If only he did not feel so damnably giddy! But Samson had finished quenching his thirst and, sensing something amiss, had come over to nuzzle his master. Drew leant his weight against the bay's flank and felt better. He fished for a clean handkerchief and asked Hero to secure it round his head to stop the blood from running into his eyes. That done, he brushed off some of the leaf mould adhering to his clothing, discovering a few bruises about his person as he did so. Removing the mud and grass stains would require sterner measures. In an apologetic manner, Cannon handed him his hat, which had fallen off and rolled aside. Drew took it, gave it one look and grimaced in disgust. He could hardly put it back on his damaged scalp and in any case it was not fit to be worn again. The bullet had made a mess of it.

'Dispose of it, will you?' he grunted, handing it back. Then, 'Where is Tanner?' he asked, missing the groom for the first time.

Hero, brushing at the skirt of her riding habit, which had collected damp patches and grassy stains where

she had knelt, told him, 'He went after your assailant.
I hope he is all right. Oh! Listen! Is that not another
shot?'

A single, grim word came in response. 'Yes.'

Hero shuddered. 'Pray God none of the servants has
been wounded.'

Drew seemed in no hurry to mount up and make
for the house. He was, Hero guessed, still feeling
extremely shaky, however much he protested the contrary. So they stood listening intently as the distant
commotion gradually died down.

Before long they heard hoofbeats drawing nearer
and Tanner rode into view, his anxious expression
giving way to one of relief and pleasure when he saw
his master standing.

'What news?' demanded Drew.

Tanner dismounted and touched his cap. 'Well, my
lord, I went after the man who attacked you as her
ladyship instructed and soon found Cannon and Ward
and told 'em to come to your lordship's help. I kept
on after that villain, my lord, calling to a couple of
other groundsmen who were working near by to come
with me.'

As he paused to regain his breath, 'Go on, man!'
urged Drew.

'Well, my lord, the knave gave us a good run but
the truth is, my lord, he couldn't escape because of the
high wall. He must've climbed in off the back of his
horse, I'd guess. When we cornered him he turned a
loaded pistol on himself. He had a pair with him, my
lord; he'd used the other on you.'

'He's dead?' demanded Drew. 'Did you
recognise him?'

'Aye, my lord.' Tanner hesitated, as though reluctant to proceed, but, seeing his master's impatient look, he swallowed and went on, 'Lord Blacklock, my lord, dead as a doornail. Begging your pardon, my lady.' He touched his cap in anxious apology.

Drew's already pale face lost all trace of colour. The deeply etched lines stood out on suddenly gaunt features. 'The marquis? The confounded fool! And dead on my land?'

Tanner nodded, his face sombre. 'Just so, my lord.'

'The devil! I am sorry, my dear, but this is bound to cause talk. The scandal-mongers will say I drove him to it.'

Blacklock. A near neighbour. One of the men gossip said had been ruined by Lord Calverstock.

'Perhaps, in a way, you did,' Hero said quietly. It was clear to her that Drew had not envisaged any such result of his actions but even to comfort him she could not deny the obvious. She still did not know why Drew did what he did, but was more than ever convinced that in his own mind he had excellent reasons. And because she loved him that was good enough for her. 'I do not blame you, my lord, but ruined men often take the only honourable course left open to them.' She thought of her father. It could so easily have been him...but he would simply take refuge in the bottle. 'Did you not consider such a possibility?'

'Honourable?' snorted Drew. 'Dastardly and weak, you mean!' He shut his eyes for a moment as though against the pain of his wound. When he went on it was in a calmer tone of voice. 'Perhaps I should have seen the weakness beneath the bluster. But it is done now.

Tanner, help me into the saddle and then see if you can round up that loose horse you spoke of.'

Drew walked Samson steadily back to the house, the jolting to his head causing him obvious pain. An anxious Benbow ran down the steps to assist his master while Matty hovered in the doorway.

'Where have they laid him?' Drew demanded shortly, waving aside Benbow's concern.

'In the gun-room, sir. It seemed. . .'

'Appropriate.' Drew nodded and then looked as though he wished he had not. 'Has the magistrate been sent for? Good. I must see the body.'

No one objected when Hero followed her husband as he headed for the gun-room. At the door, however, Drew seemed to recall the proprieties.

'Stay away, my dear. This will not be a sight fit for your eyes. Why do you not retire to your room with Matty and change?'

Hero did not argue. She had no wish to inspect the body of the dead marquis, only to remain near her husband in case he needed her. So she signalled to Matty to wait and remained by the door as Drew and his henchman entered the room.

Benbow's low voice only just reached her ears. 'You've nothing to reproach yourself with, sir. He deserved to die.'

'I know.' Drew's voice was grim. 'But I would it had not been almost by my hand.'

'He chose his own way out. Not like those poor creatures he condemned——'

'Enough!' Drew cut across Benbow's words, leaving Hero frowning over who Blacklock had condemned and to what. When he continued she could hear the weariness in her husband's voice. He must be operating on sheer will-power. 'I trust Sir John will not be long in coming. This business cannot be cleared up too soon. I must be away tomorrow.'

Benbow, perhaps Drew's closest confidant, whose complete discretion could be relied upon in all circumstances, never wavered in the deference he accorded his master. He murmured, 'Just so, sir. May I suggest you change your clothes and allow me to tend your wound while we await Sir John's arrival?'

'Very well. I must confess to a confoundedly painful headache.'

Hero waited for no more but hurried to join Matty. Together they mounted the nearest stairs. She knew Drew, a man who had survived who knew what privations and injuries during transporation, would resent being fussed over by her, however much she might wish to do just that. His moment of real need, of unconscious weakness, had passed. She had held him in her arms and ministered to him then. That would have to be enough. Benbow was quite able to provide him with all the attention he now required.

Besides, if she sought to nurse him she would be unable to hide her newly discovered love. He might detect her true feelings and, because he could not return them, withdraw some of the warmth from the relationship they had enjoyed since coming to Ashworthy. She might lose him altogether.

The remainder of the day passed in a flurry of official activity which gave Drew little time to recover from the shock and pain of his wound, slight as it had mercifully turned out to be. No one doubted the reason for Blacklock's attempt on Drew's life or that

he had subsequently taken his own. There would have
to be an inquest, but the verdict, said Sir John, was a
foregone conclusion. Drew, who would be required to
give evidence, should be back from London in time to
attend. Some scandal was bound to ensue from the
events of the morning but Sir John assured them that
Lord Calverstock's position in society would not be
threatened.

Drew chose to sleep in his dressing-room that night.
He had the excuse of his scalp wound and a few
bruises from the fall but in truth his decision rested on
deeper motives which he himself could scarcely
explain.

He was on the verge of falling headlong in love with
his wife. To share her bed in his present state might
precipitate matters and he was not ready to acknowledge the inevitability of his capitulation, since he could
not be certain of her regard. For a fleeting moment he
had imagined... But although she had softened her
accusation by protesting that she did not blame him
for Blacklock's death, she had said she believed him
responsible. And once back at the house, while showing the correct degree of concern, his wife had evinced
no sign of the tenderness he had imagined immediately
after the attack. He needed to be sure of her feelings
before he acknowledged his own and allowed them
free rein.

To Hero, caught in the throes of an agonising
unrequited love, his absence from the bed spelt deso-
lation. They had shared it since their second night at
Ashworthy. Now, for no good reason that she could
descry, Drew had chosen to sleep apart from her. Of
course, he was indisposed and had the worry of the

inquest on his mind, but he could have found solace in her embrace had he so desired. It came as a lowering shock to discover that he had not.

Having endured a restless night, she was sitting up in bed drinking her chocolate when he entered her bedchamber early the next morning, dressed ready for his journey.

'You are feeling better? You are certain you are fit to travel?' asked Hero as he leant over to kiss her cheek.

'I am well enough,' he informed her shortly. 'Cuthbert and a groom will drive. I expect to be back in time to dine on Sunday.'

Hero nodded and then, unable to stop herself despite the presence of Jackson, fussing with the washing water, reached up to frame his face with her hands and bring his mouth to hers. For an instant he seemed to stiffen and a deadly coldness began to seep into her being, but then his lips took hers in a hard kiss which told of latent passion fighting to explode into brilliant life. 'Sunday,' he murmured hoarsely as he tore himself from her embrace and strode purposefully from the room.

'Take care, Drew.'

Hero's voice echoed after him as she sank back against the pillows. His kiss had bruised her lip, she realised as she stretched it in a wry smile of satisfaction he might have absented himself from her bed but, however unwillingly, he still desired her.

Since that second night at Ashworthy he had been anything but a reluctant lover. She wondered anxiously what could have caused the change last night.

She had almost five days in which to ponder and

worry over the question. To sit about doing nothing
would drive her to distraction. An idea came to her
while she dressed. Matty had long since found out
where his mother lived—it was no secret among the
servants. She occupied the restored dower-house on
the edge of her small family estate of Hawes, some ten
miles distant. Drew had purchased the estate from its
new owners, offering them a price they could not
refuse, and installed tenants in the main house, a
family he could rely upon to look after the property
and farm the land profitably. Why the Honourable
Mrs Gerald Challoner had chosen not to spend
Christmas at Ashworthy, and why Drew did not wish
Hero to meet her mother-in-law as yet, were mysteries
that teased her mind.

It was a fine day for travelling, crisp and sunny after
yesterday's dampness, and she determined to take a
drive in her carriage to find the place where his mother
lived. That could do no harm. She formed no definite
plan as to what she would do once there. She would
wait to decide whether to call on Mrs Challoner or
not.

Well wrapped up against the cold, with Matty,
smothered in rugs, beside her, Hero set off. Ned
Tribble rode escort, chosen to accompany her because
he could be relied upon to keep her destination secret
and could also find the way, having discovered the
location of the dower-house from other grooms.

The Gloucestershire countryside positively sparkled
under the wintry sun, the ponies responded readily to
her hand on the ribbons, eager but biddable. Despite
the cold Hero had seldom enjoyed a drive more. The
fact that her excursion held a mysterious, almost for-

bidden element lent added excitement. She rested the ponies whenever Ned advised it, and less than two hours after starting out walked them slowly past a pretty, stone-built house surrounded by a large, well-stocked garden with its own gate to the lane, leaving it part of the estate yet independent of it. A little further up, where the road widened slightly, Ned helped her to turn the carriage. As she passed the house again the front door opened and a black-clad woman emerged, flapping a duster.

Hero gasped. Despite the years since she had last seen her, she had no difficulty in recognising Mrs Foster, Ben's and Bessy's mother. She drew the ponies to a halt.

She called across the hedge, 'Mrs Foster! It is you, is it not? I heard you had removed to Gloucestershire, but never expected to run across you here!'

The woman stared, frowning, until recognition brought a glad smile to her worn features. Hero noticed that the hair escaping from her plain cap was plentifully streaked with grey, but she looked better fed and more healthy than she had when living in Polhembury.

'Miss Hero!' she exclaimed, then, flustered, dropped a respectful curtsy. 'I beg pardon, my lady! I did hear that you'd wed the mistress's son.'

'Remember me and Matty, Mrs Foster?' demanded Ned with a grin, presuming on his old relationship with Hero to speak, which she did not in the least mind.

'You are still with Miss Hero!' exclaimed Mrs Foster. 'I didn't know that; I haven't heard from my Bessy since last summer.'

'Who is it, Martha?' demanded a soft, cultured voice

from inside the house, and a slender woman appeared at the door, walking stiffly with the aid of a stick and peering short-sightedly towards the road.

"'Tis Lady Calverstock, ma'am,' explained Mrs Foster eagerly. 'She was passing by and recognised me.'

'Passing, eh?' said Drew's mother sceptically.

Hero coloured with guilt. Mrs Challoner must know that few people passed the house by chance. The lane, Tribble had assured her, led only to some farm buildings.

She put her whip in its holder and motioned for Ned to hold the ponies. 'I had hoped to visit, ma'am,' she called, preparing to descend from the carriage. 'If it would be convenient?'

'By all means,' answered Mrs Challoner. 'Come along in. Your groom and maid may keep company with Martha in the kitchen while we have a comfortable coze. The ponies may safely be tethered in the lane.'

Drew's mother was in her fifties, Hero judged, short to have given birth to so tall a son, but he had inherited her grey eyes and probably her hair, which was now a mixture of gold and grey, pepper and salt, beneath the lacy cap tied beneath her chin.

She wore a neat gown of blue merino wool with a patterned shawl fastened about her shoulders for warmth. As Hero began to tread the path to the door Mrs Challoner turned and disappeared inside. Hero entered the house and Martha Foster, with a quick smile, relieved her of her travelling rug.

'Have you heard from Ben recently?' Hero enquired. 'Is he well?'

'I had a letter at Christmas, my lady. He's well enough, he says, and he's much happier than he was with his first master. Mr Challoner—as was, that is, begging your ladyship's pardon—managed to get him with a good master just afore he came home himself.'

'I see,' said Hero, who did not.

Mrs Foster led her through to a room at the back of the house, comfortably furnished and warmed by the blaze from an ingle-nook fireplace. One of Mrs Foster's younger girls was engaged in piling logs on the glowing coals and bobbed a curtsy as she left the room with her mother.

Mrs Challoner had settled herself into a padded, high-back armchair and, as Hero advanced, waved her to its twin on the other side of the fire. But before she could sit Drew's mother changed her mind and beckoned her visitor nearer.

'Come close so that I can see you properly,' she ordered with a sweet, warming smile. 'My eyes are not very strong these days; I have spent too many hours over close needlework.'

Obediently Hero went to stand before her mother-in-law, enduring her scrutiny with what self-possession she could muster.

'I have been longing to see the young woman my son married——' Mrs Challoner spread her hands helplessly '—but he has been reluctant to bring you to see me. He said there were matters to be settled between you and he wished to wait. I suppose he does not know that you are here?'

'No, ma'am,' admitted Hero. 'I wished to meet you, had hoped you would join us at Ashworthy for Christmas, but he said you preferred to remain here.'

'And so I did; I dislike to travel and am not happy in grand company. I have been too many years on my own. But I would have welcomed you both on a visit to my home.'

The dim grey eyes examined Hero's face beneath the brim of her bonnet, and Mrs Challoner appeared satisfied by what she saw. She gave a little nod and motioned Hero to her chair.

'So,' she said as Hero settled herself, 'you are the young female my son married in such an irregular fashion, without even informing his own mother of his intentions!'

Hero did not avoid her mother-in-law's eyes. The woman deserved nothing less than absolute honesty. 'I fear so, ma'am. It was a sudden business arrangement between Lord Calverstock and my father. I had no say in the matter.'

A frown descended upon Mrs Challoner's brow and her tone sharpened. 'You did not wish to wed my son?'

'No, ma'am. I knew nothing of him apart from the fact that he had inherited the earldom unexpectedly and returned from the penal colony, to which he had been transported, to claim it. My father was in debt to him. He would have lost Polhembury had I not agreed to the match.'

'Polhembury.' Mrs Challoner eyed her shrewdly. 'Ben Foster worked for him, I believe, before he was transported.'

'Yes. Oh!' A dawning comprehension made Hero cry, 'Was that why Drew behaved towards my father as he did?'

'I do not know, my dear. My son does not confide

such things to me. But he did bring Ben's mother here and see his brothers and sisters settled.'

'Yes,' whispered Hero. Everything began to fit together. Those other men he had ruined...was there a Ben Foster in their lives? Her heart lifted. She could not be certain, but believed she had been right to trust in his integrity.

'I wonder why he made you part of the arrangement,' Drew's mother mused. 'He would not have done so had he not wanted you as his wife. Had you met before the bargain was struck?'

Hero, remembering, locked her fingers together in her lap. 'Once, briefly, in Polhembury village. We bumped into each other, literally. Neither of us knew who the other was. I confess it was a great surprise to me to discover that the agreeable gentleman I had met so briefly was the man demanding my hand in marriage on such harsh terms.'

Mrs Challoner nodded. 'That explains it. He must have taken a fancy to you. I cannot say that I blame him, my dear.'

'But afterwards he seemed to despise me!' burst out Hero.

Mrs Challoner gave her another shrewd glance and a small smile appeared on her face. 'Did you not despise him, knowing nothing of him except that he was an ex-convict? And for the way he was persecuting your father, perhaps? You did say that was what he had done, did you not, my dear?' Hero nodded and Mrs Challoner smiled. 'Most women would have felt the same, I dare say, if they did not know my son.'

'Yes, but...'

Hero tried to gather her wits, to remember her

attitude, and realised that his had been a reflection of her own. Or hers had been a reflection of his. They had despised each other. But no longer. On her part at least—and she thought not on Drew's either.

She took a deep breath. 'I am so glad I came to see you, ma'am! I do not know why Drew wants to keep us apart. I shall not tell him I have been here. I beg that you will not either.'

Her mother-in-law shook her head. 'It would be wiser not to mention it. My son has strong reasons for most of his actions and would not like to be thwarted in his plans.'

Hero nodded, comprehending that Drew had not wanted her to meet his mother before the understanding between them was complete. And so far, due to her own censorious attitude, he had felt unable to confide in her. She smiled across at the small woman opposite.

'Drew has gone to London on business. He was injured yesterday—oh, not badly——' she hastened to reassure his mother '—by a man he had ruined, Lord Blacklock. Blacklock killed himself after the attack. There is to be an inquest on Tuesday.' Hero's eyes began to shine. 'I do not fully perceive his motives but I do believe that he is too fine a man to set out to ruin others from carelessness or spite.'

'You had already discovered that, my dear?'

'Yes. And he told me only the other day of the crime for which he was sentenced to transportation. That his grandfather and uncle could be so without pity or mercy...' Hero's words trailed off into a shudder.

'Then he is beginning to trust you, Hero. I may call you Hero?'

'Of course, gladly, ma'am!'

At that moment Mrs Foster knocked and entered with a tea tray loaded with muffins and cakes.

'Thank you, Martha. Martha, of course, came to me on my son's recommendation, and I have never had cause to regret his choice of housekeeper and companion.'

'His lordship saved me and mine from near-starvation, my lady,' Mrs Foster told her. 'He did it for Ben's sake. He saved my boy from ill-treatment while he was a ticket-of-leave man himself. We are all that grateful, my lady.'

'I'm certain you are,' acknowledged Hero, her voice choked.

Mrs Foster left them. Drew's mother busied herself pouring the tea while Hero regained her composure.

'Will you have a muffin, Hero?'

'Thank you.'

Hero was not particularly hungry but the hot, buttery bun proved delicious. The silence between the two women who loved Drew lengthened.

At last, 'Are you estranged from my son?' asked Mrs Challoner softly.

Hero shook her head. 'Not now. Not completely. We have come to an understanding.' She blushed. 'I am hoping to conceive his child.'

Even if Mrs Challoner could not clearly see the softening of Hero's features she could not fail to hear the yearning in her voice. A small sigh of satisfaction escaped her lips. Her voice was gentle as she enquired, 'Have you come to love him?'

Hero swallowed. How could she deny it? 'Yes,' she admitted. 'But I have misjudged him so and he does not love me!'

Again, her voice told Mrs Challoner all she wanted to know.

'Come here, child.'

Hero rose and went to kneel at the older woman's feet. Mrs Challoner put a hand under her chin and lifted her face.

'You are beautiful, loyal and loving. Drew would be a fool not to love you, my daughter. He is not a fool.'

'Pehaps, if I bear him an heir——'

A decisive shake of the head met this tentative hope. 'Long before that. I imagine he does so already but is probably too stiff-necked to admit it because he has been hurt by your attitude. He tries to hide it but he is defensive about his past. Understandable as it might have been, your censure will have hurt him deeply. But, believe me, he would not have asked for your hand in marriage had he'not fallen a little in love with you when you bumped into each other. Keep faith, my dear. He came here just before Christmas and spoke of you with admiration and affection. You will win his love.'

'I do hope so,' muttered Hero, and buried her face in Mrs Challoner's lap to hide her tears.

CHAPTER THIRTEEN

HERO returned to Ashworthy determined to win Drew's complete confidence. She needed him to confide in her fully, an essential step if they were to have a real future together. To know that he trusted her would compensate in some measure for the lack of his love. Sunday could not come soon enough.

When Drew did arrive home late in the evening, having started out at an inconceivably early hour—Cuthbert and his assistant had accomplished the entire journey in an incredible eighteen hours—he looked weary to the bone. Hero welcomed him without reserve, waited while he took a much-needed bath, then, when he descended casually dressed in trousers and frilly shirt topped by a dressing-gown, settled him by the fire and ordered the tray of refreshments to be brought. He leaned his head back and closed his eyes. She regarded the face of the man she loved, the strong, experience-worn features, the shadows about his eyes.

'How is your head? Does it still pain you?'

He stirred slightly but spoke without moving his head or opening his eyes. 'I fear so, from time to time, although not at this precise moment. Unfortunately I found the journey, which normally I take in my stride, excessively trying.'

'I am not surprised, considering how soon you set out after your injury!' Hero tried to keep concern from her voice. 'You should have taken more rest along the way. You could have lain in an inn overnight.'

His eyes opened and his face broke into a smile that set her pulses racing. 'And broken my promise to be back today? Are you not glad to have me home?'

'Husband! You know I am! Has my welcome been lacking? But I would rather delay the pleasure of seeing you than have you tire yourself out and perhaps prejudice your complete recovery. That is the thing I pray for, my dear. You had a narrow escape and my heart fails me every time I think on how close you came to death.'

Drew noticed that, for the first time, she had used an endearment. Unconsciously, he thought. And her voice had shaken slightly on her last words. He watched closely as he asked, 'You would have cared?'

The refreshments arrived at that moment, allowing her time to collect her thoughts. His eyes, for all the tired lines about them, regarded her keenly. Hero met his look with a candour which yet managed to hide the overwhelming love welling from her heart. She must guard her tongue, not give herself away by over-enthusiasm. She had once suffered the unwelcome devotion of a youth she admired but could not love. His unwanted ardour had embarrassed her and she could not subject Drew to such an irritation.

As the servants left them alone again she answered his question. 'Can you doubt it?' she enquired, lifting her brows in smiling query and spreading her hands to indicate the domestic warmth she had organised to greet him.

He grinned wryly. 'I believe a brandy would suit me better than a dish of tea but the food will be welcome.

I was anxious to make haste back to Ashworthy. We barely stopped for refreshment on the journey.'

Rather than call a servant, Hero rose and went over to the side-table, which held glasses and decanters, to pour the drink. She handed the brandy to him, saying, 'Then relax now. Satisfy your appetite and then we may retire.'

Drew swirled the spirit round in the balloon goblet and inhaled appreciatively before drinking with evident enjoyment. Only then did he enquire, with a suggestive lift of one brow, 'To satisfy a different appetite?'

Hero's blush would not be denied. Drew watched his wife's delicious confusion, his confidence growing. He had left the house unsure of her feelings towards him, determined not to fall victim to her growing appeal, which he recognised was composed not simply of physical attraction, which had always been there, but of something deeper, more fundamental and lasting which, was he to allow it, would render him her slave for life.

But her warm welcome, her pleasure at seeing him again, a subtle change in her attitude, gave him reason to hope that one day she might come to feel for him as he did for her. He believed her when she said she would have cared had he died. He could see something in her eyes now which had not been there before. And, despite his undoubted fatigue, he felt stronger mentally to resist her deepest lures for as long as necessary. He could make love to her without the danger of emotional involvement, just as he had to many women over the years.

Hero gathered her wits and managed to answer him

calmly. It would not do for him to believe her abandoned to all modesty. 'I had hoped you would return to our bed,' she told him somewhat stiffly. 'But I would fully understand if you wished to delay the full resumption of marital relations.'

'Very delicately expressed,' he teased, and, lifting his arms, stretched his splendid body from top to toe. 'I feel revitalised already. We shall have to see what the night will bring.'

Hero replaced her empty cup on its saucer. 'Have a muffin or a meat patty,' she suggested. The small table stood between them and she shifted the plates nearer to him. She felt less aware of his powerful attraction when he was occupied in something other than testing her responses. She wondered belatedly whether she would, in the heat of passion, be able to disguise the new tenderness she felt towards her husband. But no matter. It seemed he intended that they should sleep together again and nothing could destroy her anticipation of the night ahead.

Servants removed the refreshment tray. Drew accepted another brandy. It was cosy in the small red drawing-room, warmed by the fire. Hero felt no immediate urgency to move but Drew quickly finished his drink, rose to his feet and held out his hand. 'Come, wife, are you ready? Shall we retire?'

Hero placed her fingers in his warm clasp and smiled up into his face as he drew her up, noting that the lines of weariness had already begun to disperse. Whatever pleasures he may or may not have experienced in London, he did appear content to be home.

'Perfectly ready, husband.'

Upstairs, Drew dismissed both Benbow and Jackson

with an imperious wave of his hand. A small shiver of anticipation ran down Hero's spine. Drew had emerged from the strange mood which had possessed him immediately after his near encounter with death and returned, it seemed, intent on making up for his recent neglect.

The moment they were alone he gathered her in his arms. Their lips fused in a long, rapturous kiss which left Hero with the impression that her limbs had lost all substance. Her eyes closed. Yet through the languorous torpor which invaded her mind she was aware of Drew's fingers working at her back on the row of hooks and eyes fastening the bodice of her gown.

At last he lifted his lips and released her just enough to allow her to slip her arms from the sleeves. The gown fell to form a pool of blue at her feet.

The interruption was enough to restore strength to Hero's muscles and direction to her mind. Boldly, she pushed the dressing-gown from his shoulders, delighting in the feel of the smooth musculature beneath his shirt, and eased his arms from the loose sleeves to drop that garment to the floor as well. Next, her breathing quickening by the moment, her fingers worked at the buttons of his shirt while he untied the strings on her petticoat and chemise. Her undergarments joined the gown at her feet and he gave a rather breathless laugh as, naked apart from stockings and slippers, she pressed a kiss on the gold-tipped fuzz covering his bared chest and set to work, her fingers shaking, on the waist fastenings of his trousers. He had already flung off his shirt and now he removed his slippers and stepped out of his nether garments.

Easing off her own slippers, Hero gazed in fasci-

nated admiration at the roused body of her husband.
She had glimpsed him like this once or twice but he
had never stood before her in all his magnificent glory.
Mesmerised, excited, she forgot what she had been
doing. The blood pounded through her veins, an excru-
ciating throb of desire making her gasp. Before she
could remove her stockings he had swept her up into
his arms and laid her on the bed.

With a growling laugh he came down beside her,
claiming her lips in another enervating encounter
which he followed with a trail of worshipful kisses
down her body until his lips met the tops of her
stockings. These he rolled back in a series of long,
sensuous caresses.

Moaning in protest, Hero sat up, unable to bear
distance between them, and tangled her fingers in his
hair, pulling his head towards hers.

A yelp of pain greeted this impassioned manoeuvre
and Hero let go, crying out in distress.

'My dear love! I'm so sorry! I had quite forgot your
wound!'

'So had I,' he growled, his heart leaping at the
endearment as he finally removed the silk cladding her
legs and pressed his lips to her toes, first one foot and
then the other, while Hero wallowed in exquisite
sensation.

He came back up the bed and lay close beside her.
Trembling, Hero placed a feather-light kiss upon the
still-tender scar which Benbow had left uncovered to
aid scabbing.

'I would not hurt you for the world,' she whispered.

'I know, my dear.'

His lovemaking that night held a different quality

from any that had preceded it. Perhaps because of his impaired condition fierce passion gave way to tender ministrations which forced Hero into articulating meaningless sounds in response. Words of love rose to her lips but she forced them back. He was showing unexpected gentleness, an intensity of feeling she had not noted before, but that did not mean he would welcome a declaration of love.

His long, slow, sure strokes proved so ravishing that her climax broke over her like a tidal wave, washing her to some far shore where even ecstatic sensation seemed lost in sheer, insubstantial delight.

Drew had found his nirvana, too. She knew it because, even as she woke to awareness again, he gave a last convulsive shudder, heaved a great, gasping sigh and buried his face in her neck.

Hero's arms crept round him, holding his shoulders close. For long, long moments they lay, exhausted, all passion spent...yet there had been no fierceness of passion. What they had just shared had been beyond the normal bounds of coupling. She knew it and could not explain it. They might never achieve such wonder again. But they had known it and the experience could never be lost. In some indefinable way it must bind them together. Come what may, it was something she would hold close to her heart for the rest of her life. For, during those moments of union, she had known that Drew had loved her.

February, wet and chilly, did not encourage outdoor exercise and for some days during its third week Hero, feeling unaccountably sluggish, had remained abed rather than join Drew in his regular morning ride. He did not appear unduly upset and returned, exuding the aromas of horse, leather and fresh air superimposed upon his own seductive scents of sweat and sandal-wood, in time to change and join her for breakfast.

Occasionally, if he was late back he would make straight for the breakfast parlour, apologising for eating in all his dirt while knowing that she did not object. That mixture of healthy odours suited him better than the false perfumes and clinging reminders of snuff and tobacco smoke that he picked up in drawing-room or club.

That morning he had not returned in time to change and Hero made her way to breakfast thinking to find him already there. She had heard a light carriage, probably a trap, arrive earlier but had taken little notice, for tenants often called at the house on business. After a few minutes it had driven off again. Because of this she was surprised to hear voices coming from the small reception-room off the hall. Drew's unmistakable tones, followed by those of a woman.

The door remained ajar. A footman stood sentry by the front door and a maid scuttled by carrying duster and mop. Drawn by curiosity, Hero crossed the hall intending to enter the room and greet the caller. Visitors at this time in the morning were rare, so the matter upon which the woman had come must be urgent.

As her hand went out to push the door wider she came to an abrupt halt. Chaotic emotions swamped her, leaving her breathless, her mind in revolt. She swayed as she stood.

The voices had stopped. She could see why. Drew

held a woman in his arms. Her hands rested confidingly against his chest. His head was bent to her upturned face. He lowered it further and Hero knew he was kissing the woman, although she could not precisely see their lips meet.

Something exploded inside Hero's brain. She spun on her heel and ran up the stairs to the sanctuary of her room, leaving a gaping footman staring after her. Jackson was there. She dismissed the maid with a brief word.

It was that woman the duchess had seen him with, Hero was certain. The description fitted. She was not dressed as a lady although respectably attired. She had followed her lover all the way from London to his home and he had welcomed her, kissing her while under the same roof as his wife.

After the last weeks of felicity Hero could not bear it. How could Drew think of another woman when she——?

She had made a fool of herself. That much was obvious. Imagining that on occasion he loved her! Giving herself to him so fully! A dry sob escaped her. She sat on, dazed, feeling sick and shaky.

Sounds below roused her and took her to the window. Peering down, she saw the Calverstock travelling chaise draw up before the door, a pair of Drew's best horses put to, indicating a modest journey ahead.

Someone knocked on her door and a footman entered.

He bowed. 'I am to inform you that his lordship sends his apologies, my lady. He has been called away on urgent business and cannot say precisely when he will return. He hopes to be back in time to change for dinner.'

She managed to thank the man, who left. Hero took up station by the window again and watched as Drew handed the woman into the chaise and Cuthbert, riding postilion, drove off. Benbow had not accompanied his master, a most unusual circumstance.

Drew must wish to be alone with that woman. On a sudden resolution she sent for Benbow, for he enjoyed more of Drew's confidence than she did.

By the time he presented himself she had herself firmly under control. She smiled.

'His lordship did not have time to explain the business on which he was called away. Do you know what it was?' she asked, trying to keep her voice casual, hoping Benbow would not detect her sick despair through the mask of normality she had pasted over it.

Benbow, impassive, shook his head, but Hero saw an evasive look in his eyes. He knew; but he would protect his master with his last breath. She had wasted her time and dignity by asking.

'I am sorry, my lady, I cannot say. But I understand his lordship does not expect to be away above a few hours.'

'So he implied. I did not see him myself; he sent a message by a footman.' She prayed she did not sound as hurt as she felt. 'The matter must have been urgent.'

'So I understand, ma'am.' Hero knew her pain had shown through, for he added, warmly for him, 'Do not concern yourself, ma'am. He will deal with the matter with his usual efficiency and return as promised, of that you may be certain.'

A new attempt to keep the distress from invading her voice failed dismally. 'But what *is* his business?' she asked, almost pleading for an answer.

Benbow shrugged, helpless to allay her fears without betraying his master's confidence. 'He will no doubt inform you upon his return, my lady.'

She doubted that. He had never told her anything in the past. She made an effort and pulled herself together. 'Very well, Benbow. You may go. Ask Miss Bright to come to me, please. She is probably taking breakfast.'

'Very well, my lady.'

Benbow bowed himself out. She liked the man and she thought he liked her but his loyalty to Drew came first. She should have known he would tell her nothing without Drew's express permission. Yet she had learned something from the interview. Benbow was aware of what Drew was about and had not liked having to keep his knowledge from her.

By the time Matty arrived Hero's mind was made up. She could no more sit about all day waiting for Drew to come home than fly. When he did return he would tell her only what he wanted her to believe, not the truth. Where had he taken that woman? To a nest somewhere on the estate? At least he had had the decency not to take her to bed in the house.

'Calverstock has gone off with another woman,' she informed Matty the instant her friend appeared. 'I am returning to Polhembury. Instruct Tribble to harness a team to the travelling coach. He can drive it back afterwards.'

'But Miss Hero, you cannot——'

'Cannot leave an unfaithful husband? Did I not say that he has gone off with some woman?'

'What woman?' demanded Matty suspiciously. 'It might be anyone, and him gone off for any number of reasons. He hasn't left you, my duck.'

She spoke with an absolute assurance which brought a grim laugh from Hero.

'Of course he has not! He will return to his dutiful wife as though his mistress did not exist!'

'His mistress? What makes you so certain the woman is his mistress?'

'She is the one the duchess saw him with in Harley Street.'

'How do you know? You've never seen her——'

'I just know.' She had been obviously pregnant, and perhaps that had been the most painful part. He had taken her to see that doctor because she was carrying his child. 'Stop prattling, Matty, and help me to put a few things into this bag.'

Matty did not move. 'You cannot run away again, my duck. He will not forgive you a second time. And I do not believe a word of it. He is too fine a gentleman to betray you so.'

'Gentlemen,' said Hero bitterly, 'especially noble gentlemen, think nothing to keeping a mistress. You know that.'

'And I also know that if their wives are wise they ignore the fact and make the best they can of their marriage. Not that I think you've any need. He's fond of you, my duck, is growing more fond by the day. Anyone can see it. Why should he trouble himself with a mistress?'

Hero shrugged, but did not stop bundling underwear

into her valise. 'Men are men. He is no different from any other. But I cannot live with him if he is unfaithful.'

Suddenly she was in tears. 'I love him so much, Matty. I cannot stand it!' she wailed.

In the end Matty had comforted her and agreed to their leaving. It was still early and although Hero had not eaten she refused to waste time in partaking of breakfast. She simply wanted to escape.

Thanks to Drew's generosity she had a purse filled with gold sovereigns, enough to meet any expense the journey might entail. She would think about repaying him later. She would think about her whole future later.

Why she should be so upset over Drew's infidelity she did not know. As Matty had pointed out, such peccadilloes were normal. In the first months of the marriage she would not have cared. Even after admitting her love to herself she had been ready to face the possibility of Drew's keeping a mistress. She had not liked it but had not felt compelled to run away.

The change had come after that wonderful night they had experienced together. That and the companionship they had enjoyed since. To discover him to be faithless now was something she could not endure.

It would take two days to reach Polhembury. At the first change of horses she ordered Drew's team to be stabled pending Tribble's return. They spent an uncomfortable night in an inn in Glastonbury, having reluctantly left the prospect of better accommodation behind with Bath. Late on the second day the coach rumbled up the neglected drive to draw up before the familiar, crumbling façade of her old home.

A youth she vaguely recognised ran out to hold the horses' heads. He grinned up at Ned and Ned called a greeting and she realised it was Dick, the stable lad, grown taller and more manly in her absence. An excited maid, a stranger, was dispatched to tell the master that his daughter had arrived.

The emotional upset had affected Hero physically. Her normally strong constitution had quite let her down. Exhausted by the journey, she allowed Tribble to lift her from the coach and Matty to support her indoors, where a beaming Mrs Blackler, looking less smart than when Hero had last seen her, waited to welcome her home, greeting her with a deep curtsy.

'Why, my lady,' she cried, 'I've never seen 'ee looking so fine! His lordship will be that pleased to see 'ee!'

One glance around had told Hero that things at Polhembury had slipped badly since her departure. The old oak lacked its former polish. The carpet had gained several new holes. Remembering the state of the drive and the decrepit appearance of the outside of the house, she deduced that her father had abandoned any pretence of keeping the place up.

'Where is my father?' she demanded, addressing the maid. 'Was he not told of my arrival?'

The girl bobbed a curtsy. 'He'm in the library, my lady. I did tell he but. . .' She trailed off with a shrug.

Without another word Hero strode towards the library door. Her giddiness had gone, banished by the need to discover why her father, since he was at home, had not stirred himself to come to meet her.

Her growing suspicions were confirmed the moment she entered the library. Lord Polhembury sat slouched in his armchair. A hand rested on his knee, an empty glass held loosely in it. On a small table drawn up beside him stood a brandy bottle.

'Papa!'

Hero crossed the room and stood looking down upon her parent. Things were far worse than she had imagined. A wave of anger swept over her, at her father for allowing himself to sink so low and at Calverstock for driving him to such despair. However badly he had treated young Ben Foster, her father scarcely deserved to be made to suffer so harsh a punishment.

'So you've come back to shee how I'm gettin' on, eh?' he slurred. 'Quite the lady now, ain't 'ee? Looksh as though you've done all right for yourshelf, my girl. Kind to you, ish 'e?'

'Papa! Much you would care if he were not! You sold me like one of your prime cattle!' She could not confess that she had left Calverstock. Not yet. However perfidious she thought him, he did not deserve to be denigrated before her father. He was, basically, a fine man, if mistaken in some of his actions and unfaithful, like so many others.

The pain jerked at her heart again but she ignored it.

'Pull yourself together, Papa! How could you allow Polhembury to fall into rack and ruin after you'd sacrificed me to keep it? The least you could have done was to make the best of your bargain!'

'What with?' growled her father and poured the last of the brandy into his glass. His hand shook so much that the liquid slopped on to his breeches. He gulped it down.

'Hard work!' snapped Hero, her patience exhausted.

She turned and left the room. She did not feel strong enough to deal with her father at the moment. She went through to the kitchen, where Matty and Tribble were recounting their experiences since leaving Polhembury.

'Companion, eh, Matty?' Mrs Blackler was saying enviously.

'Have you seen to the horses, Tribble?' Hero asked the groom.

'Aye, my lady, they're in the old stable. But I'd better go and rub 'em down now I've had my refreshment.' He put his empty beer mug on the table. 'Thanks, Mrs B. That was most welcome.'

Hero turned to Matty. 'Will you see that my room is ready? Get that new maid to help you.'

'Very well, my lady,' said Matty respectfully. Gratefully Hero realised that Matty would see that everyone at Polhembury heeded her new status.

With Bessy Fowler, still the kitchen skivvy, dismissed to the scullery, Hero questioned Mrs Blackler over her stewardship of the household.

'Without the money you sends through Mrs Cudlip we wouldn't have managed at all,' she told Hero. 'His lordship is always short, so it seems. On its own, what he do give me for housekeeping wouldn't keep a body and soul together.'

'He's paying the wages?' asked Hero.

Mrs Blackler shook her head. 'We've not had any for weeks now. Everyone has left except those ones you've seen already. Young Dick looks after his lordship as well as the horses and makes hisself generally useful. 'Cepting for the gardener, that is. His wife's got herself a job in the village and he grows his own produce on his plot; that's how they manages.'

'I see. So there are just you and two maids to keep the house in order?'

'That's right, my lady. And I'm nearly always busy cooking. So Joan does most of the housework, with a bit of help with the grates from Bessy, and Dick does the heavy work.'

'No wonder the place looks neglected. Something must be done. I'll see to it while I'm here.'

'Will his lordship be coming, my lady? Only I'll have to make a special effort with the meals if he is.'

'I'm not sure, Mrs Blackler. He may follow me here if he has no urgent business to keep him elsewhere. We left the question open.'

'He'll not be here tonight, then. You'll want supper, no doubt, my lady. Will Matty eat with you?'

'Yes, and my father if I can rouse him sufficiently. No doubt Tribble has told you that he will be taking the coach back tomorrow. His lordship may need it.'

'Aye, ma'am. You'll be staying a few days, then.'

Hero nodded, unwilling to commit herself in words. 'Supper in half an hour?' she enquired.

'I'll do me best, my lady. It won't be anything fussy.'

'I am not feeling like anything fussy. Hot soup would be welcome.'

'I've plenty of rabbit stew, that's no trouble.'

'Half an hour, then.'

Rabbit stew reminded her of Drew's nightmare experiences. Would he follow her? She had made no secret of her destination this time. A visit to her father could easily be explained away should their differences be resolved.

Matty had said he would not follow her a second time. But then, Matty was not wholly aware of the more recent relationship which had sprung up between them.

Perhaps she had been rash. Perhaps there was an innocent explanation for Drew's conduct. If so, would he ever forgive her for doubting him?

CHAPTER FOURTEEN

DREW did not arrive the following day as Hero had been dreading—and hoping—that he would.

'I warned you he wouldn't follow you a second time,' said Matty grimly. 'Mark my words, a proud man like his lordship does not run after his wife more than once.'

'I am glad he has not come after me. It is he who needs forgiving,' asserted Hero defiantly.

'Huh,' grunted Matty as she swept a final stroke of the brush through Hero's brown waves. 'Well, there you are, my chick,' she went on after a moment, letting the topic drop as she laid down the brush, picked up a nightcap and gathered the hair into it. 'You've only to tie the strings and you're ready for bed. Sleep well, my chick.'

'Goodnight, Matty. And thank you. It is like old times to have you to tend my needs again.'

'You'll be missing Jackson,' said Matty dourly. 'I haven't half her skill.'

'But you have a hundred times more feeling, dear Matty. Whatever should I do without you?'

'Go your own foolish way as usual,' muttered her old nurse, turning away.

Hero grasped her hand, holding her back as she prepared to leave for her own bed.

'Am I so foolish, Matty? Did I not have reason to be upset?'

'Maybe,' conceded Matty, 'but you should've given his lordship a chance to explain. I still can't believe he's acting wrong.'

Hero sighed. 'You always did favour Lord Calverstock. I remember the day we were wed. He bamboozled you with his charm from the start.'

'If you say so, my chick. But I thought you'd given up your foolish notions about his character and been won over yourself. Especially after meeting Mrs Challoner. Martha Foster couldn't speak highly enough of her or his lordship.'

Hero closed her eyes, squeezed Matty's hand and let it go. 'I don't know any more, Matty. But I mustn't keep you up any longer. I'll decide what to do tomorrow.'

Alone in her old bed, Hero could not sleep. The previous night exhaustion had overtaken her and she had quickly dropped into welcome oblivion. During the day she had kept herself busy trying to restore order to the chaos into which Polhembury had fallen. Mrs Cudlip, word having reached her of Hero's visit, had arrived in her husband's trap to give an account of her stewardship of Hero's remittances, after which the two women had caught up on their gossip. Hero had given a lively account of life in London and the pleasures of Ashworthy, hiding her distress at being forced to leave it all.

Mrs Cudlip, ten years Hero's senior yet youthful, amiable and romantic enough to interest herself in her young friend's affairs with enthusiasm, exclaimed as she was leaving, 'I am so glad the marriage has turned out well!'

Hero had given her no reason to suppose otherwise.

Time enough to confess her unhappiness when all hope had finally gone. She merely smiled in acknowledgement of the remark.

'When the little one arrives your happiness will be complete.'

Jerked from her morbid reflections by these words, Hero allowed the smile to fade from her lips and stared at her friend, a conscious blush and frown taking its place. 'We are hoping——' she began, only to be cut off by the other's surprised laugh.

'But my dear, surely you realise you are breeding? The signs are all there.'

'They are?' murmured Hero, bemused.

Mrs Cudlip, used to confinements, her own and those of her parishioners, had been right, Hero realised. The lethargy, the nausea, even the dizziness. Counting back, Hero wondered how she could have missed the absence of her monthly flow. Except that, since that wonderful night, she had been living in a euphoric haze disturbed only slightly by the necessity for Drew to attend the inquest on Blacklock. But that hurdle had been passed without trouble, no blame had been imputed and no question had arisen over the cause of death. A verdict of suicide had been returned as expected and Hero had been able to relax again.

As she thought of the baby growing inside her tears blurred her eyes, making a star of the flame of the candle left burning by her bed. She could not be absolutely certain yet, but it did seem likely that she was to bear Drew a child. The knowledge brought both joy and pain.

And she wondered whether, perhaps, her condition had been responsible for her shattering reaction to seeing Drew with another woman. Females could become very emotional in such circumstances.

Had she over-reacted? Matty thought she had. Confused thoughts jumbled about Hero's brain as she tried to work out what to do. Only one thing seemed certain: although she had thought she could not bear to remain with Drew, the thought of living without him now seemed infinitely more distressing.

The prospect of residing permanently at Polhembury filled her with apprehension. Until her marriage she had known nothing else. Now she realised how unsatisfactory existing as she had before—isolated, the victim of her father's temper—had been. Her horizons had widened. Living here, even with Drew's child to care for. . .

But she could not imagine Drew allowing a child of his, particularly his heir, to be brought up anywhere but at Ashworthy. She would not wish it, either. The child would deserve the best she could provide. And that meant a return to her husband; but he must not think she had returned simply because of the child. If only he had come after her, given her an excuse to change her mind and allow him to take her back. . .

The indubitable fact was, he had not come. Tribble had already left and must be halfway to Ashworthy by now. Perhaps when the groom arrived back without her and he knew for certain that she intended to stay at Polhembury, Drew would come. . .

Should she wait? Three more days, possibly——

But no! That would be the coward's way out. She had made a mistake and must face the consequences. It only remained to plan how her return could be accomplished.

Her father's hack was still in the stables, a poor beast sadly lacking in exercise. At the earliest moment tomorrow she would send Dick to the nearest post house to hire a chaise. The only vehicle for hire in the village was an old trap drawn by a lazy pony and Dick would have to travel further afield to find a suitable conveyance.

Having settled on her course of action, Hero settled down to sleep, hoping that, once back at Ashworthy, she could pretend that her flight had always been intended as no more than a filial duty visit.

In the morning she woke retching and feeling like death. She could eat nothing and refused her normal cocoa but drank several cups of coffee and felt slightly more human. Not to be deterred from her purpose, she sent Dick off on his errand. It would take an hour or so for the post chaise to arrive.

Matty dealt with their few possessions with rather more alacrity than she had shown when packing to leave Ashworthy.

'So you've come to your senses, my duck,' she commented when Hero told her of her decision. 'His lordship will welcome you back, I dare swear.'

'He might not realise I ran away,' suggested Hero hopefully.

'Benbow knew.'

'You told him?' cried Hero, outraged.

'Of course I didn't, ninny. But he knew. And Tribble knows.'

'Tribble would not say anything——'

'Not if you could get to him before his lordship does.'

Deflated, Hero sighed. 'In that case I shall simply

have to bow my head and apologise. I cannot allow pride to ruin our lives.'

'That's the spirit, my chick.'

While Matty packed, Hero went to see Mrs Blackler and leave instructions for the future. 'I shall make a point of visiting every few months,' she told her. 'I will see what can be done about the back wages meanwhile. Lord Polhembury has promised to pay you regularly in future.'

'Huh.' Mrs Blackler, fists planted on her ample hips, looked doubtful. 'Maybe he will, maybe he won't. Depends on whether he goes off on one of his sprees or not.'

Hero pictured the scene with her father the previous evening after supper. He had been truculent but also, she thought, a little ashamed. 'He has promised——'

'Aye, my lady. But promises don't buy food and such.'

'You have managed well, Mrs Blackler, and things will improve in future, you may depend upon it. Just stand by my father and try to ensure that he does not go completely to pieces. I will see that you do not lose by it.'

'I'll do me best, my lady, seeing as how it be for you, and besides, this is the only home I've got.'

With that promise Hero had to be satisfied. Now to say farewell to her father if she could rouse him from his bed.

She wore her travelling gown but had not yet donned her pelisse and bonnet. Time enough for that when the chaise arrived. She came up from the semi-basement kitchen to cross the hall to the stairs, the handrail of which, on her instructions, Joan was polishing. The sound of hooves pounding up the neglected drive brought her up short.

It was too soon for the hired chaise to arrive and in any case she could detect no crunch of iron wheels on gravel. It sounded like a single horseman. Dick, perhaps? No, too soon and he would accompany the chaise. And neither he nor tenants, except in an emergency, would push their horses as this animal was being pushed.

Joan hurried to open the door. Hero glimpsed an unmistakable figure swinging from his saddle and her heart jumped into her throat.

Drew *had* come after her! Alone and on horseback.

He strode into the hall and she could see by the state of his boots, by the damp clinging to his capes and beaver, but above all by the tired lines etched about his eyes that he had not just mounted up and come from some nearby hostelry. He had been travelling all night.

She did not quite know how to greet him but willed her legs to carry her forward. 'My lord,' she murmured, since they were not alone, 'I had not expected you.'

'Had you not, ma'am? I debated whether to come.'

Her heart sank a little. But he could mean several things by that remark. 'Come into the library. The fire is laid—it only needs a light. Joan, bring brandy and ask Mrs Blackler to supply a tray. His lordship needs refreshment.'

'The master keeps all the spirits locked away in a cupboard in the library, my lady.'

'You know where he keeps the key?'

Joan nodded. ''Tes in his room.'

'Then go and fetch that and a glass.'

Joan hurried off on her errand and Hero led Drew through to the threadbare library. Being here, in the house where they had been married, must evoke memories for him as well as for her, she thought, and wondered whether they were kind or otherwise.

He laid his gloves and stock on the desk then placed his beaver alongside. Apart from the weariness he could not hide, he appeared quite unmoved. Hero took a tinderbox from the mantelshelf, bent to strike a spark and watched as the paper and kindling caught and flames began to lick up the chimney.

She turned to find that he had discarded his heavily caped riding coat and was standing watching her, his expression unreadable.

'Drew,' she began, but he shook his head.

'Wait until we are served. What we have to say to each other should be said in private.'

'Then sit,' she invited. 'You look weary. How long have you been in the saddle?'

He took the chair she indicated, her father's, drawn up before the fire. She sat on a stool on the other side of the hearth.

'Fourteen hours,' he said. 'It was no hardship, I worked harder for longer periods in the penal colony.'

She was saved having to reply to that—and what could she have said anyway?—by the arrival of Joan with two glasses on a tray and the key.

'His lordship still sleeps?' asked Hero.

Joan nodded. 'Yes, my lady. Dick had told me where he hid the key. That's the cupboard, my lady.'

'Thank you, Joan. You can help Mrs Blackler with the refreshments now.'

'Right 'ee are, my lady.'

Drew rose, took the key and unlocked the cupboard. Several stone bottles stood on a shelf.

'Contraband, I'd hazard,' he murmured as he took one out. 'Will you have some?'

Hero nodded. She felt in need of a stimulant. Drew was behaving with perfect courtesy but impersonally, as though they were almost strangers. She hoped it was because they might be interrupted at any moment.

She took the glass he handed her and took a sip of the stinging liquid. It passed down her throat like fire, warming her chilled insides. Her hands were icy, where a few moments ago they had been warm enough, coming as she had from the kitchen. One thing Polhembury did not lack was fuel for its stoves and fires. The estate abounded in old trees and it was all too easy to find a fallen branch, or even a trunk, to saw or chop up and burn.

They sat with their drinks in strained silence until Joan brought in the tray of refreshments. Mrs Blackler had been baking and the aroma of hot bread made even Hero's mouth water. She accepted a thick, fragrant slice, spread it with butter, and nibbled as Drew consumed his, together with slices of cold chicken and a wedge of fruit pie.

'Well, wife,' he said as he swallowed the last bite and wiped his fingers on a napkin, 'here I am, come after you again, as you can see.' Suddenly the strain showed itself on his face. Desperation laced his tone as he asked, 'Why did you leave me, Hero? What did I do to make you run away this time? Do you still trust me so little that you could imagine for one moment that I had taken Elizabeth Warner as my mistress and was off to some place with her?'

'Is that what Benbow said?' whispered Hero, shivering despite the flames now leaping up the chimney.

'It is what he deduced from your questions and your attitude. I could not believe. . .after all we have been to each other——'

'I saw you kissing her,' gulped Hero. 'She is breeding, is she not? I thought she was bearing your child.'

The sight of Drew's ravaged face made her catch her breath. 'What a confounded fool I have been!' he groaned. 'If only I had confided in you earlier! My darling, do you not realise that I love you?'

'Love me?' croaked Hero. What was this he was saying? Could she truly believe her ears?

He was on his knees before her, clasping her cold hands in his warm grasp. 'My dearest girl, you must have known! You have me completely in your toils. I cannot imagine life without you as part of it.'

'I did not know. How could I? You despised me from the first.'

'Not from the first, my love. I fell in love, I think, when we met so fortuitously in Polhembury. Your maid addressed you as Miss Hero and I knew you must be Polhembury's daughter. Him I did and do despise, and I had already determined to take my revenge on Ben Foster's behalf, but you, I thought, were different. For your sake I would let Polhembury off the hook to the tune of ten thousand pounds, more than the estate was worth.'

'Then why. . .?'

'Did I treat you so harshly?' His fingers tightened. 'I heard you talking with someone, Matty, I afterwards discovered. You condemned me unseen. Talked scathingly of me as a convict, someone obviously beneath contempt. And called my mother a common woman. That, in particular, I found it difficult to forget or forgive.'

Hero closed her eyes. Then, resolutely, opened them again, meeting his grey gaze without evasion. 'What a pity you overheard that nonsense. Matty put me right immediately. But Drew, how would you have felt had you just been informed by your father that you had no choice but to wed a man you had never met and whose reputation, even you must admit, was not of the best?'

A faint glimmer of a smile touched his lips but his eyes remained intent. 'Indignant, despairing and aggressive, I dare say.'

'Exactly so. Especially as I had so recently met the gentleman of my dreams in Polhembury——'

His hands now gripped hers so hard that she winced with pain. 'You cannot mean. . .'

'The attraction was mutual, Drew. But I heard my prospective bridegroom dealing brutally with my father and entered the room furious and disgusted for, although Papa had brought his troubles upon his own head, he did not deserve to be dealt with so severely. And I quickly discovered that the person I must marry to save my father from complete ruin was both the heartless creditor I held in contempt and the gentleman I had so briefly met in the village. Imagine my confusion!'

'And mine, when I heard you talking. . . My dear, have we truly wasted all these months despising each other over nothing?'

'Not over nothing,' asserted Hero bravely. 'I could

not understand why you chose to ruin certain gentlemen.'

'Have you not guessed, my dear? They have all been instrumental in condemning comparatively innocent people to the terrible trials of transportation. I met all their victims out there and tried to ease their lot if I could. That became easier once I obtained my ticket of leave. But none of them deserved such harsh measures to be taken against them, any more than I did. Or than you did,' he added with his first real smile, a roguish one that caused a jolt in Hero's heart. 'In the view of many a landowner, magistrate and judge, you would have deserved transporation for stealing my plums!'

'Your plums?' choked Hero, gazing at him in guilty astonishment. 'You own Wanleat now?'

He grinned openly. 'I must plead guilty as charged, my dear. But although I recognised my plums I did not have the heart to prosecute such an attractive thief!'

'Oh!' Hero's breath quite deserted her and for a moment, as colour flooded her cheeks, she was nonplussed. Then she decided to ignore his teasing and press on with what she had been about to say.

'I admit my father merited punishment for his intransigence over Ben,' she went on earnestly. 'I pleaded with him at the time to have mercy, but to no purpose. But Drew, did he deserve to be ruined? And Blacklock? Did he deserve to be driven to the point of murdering you in revenge, and finally to suicide?'

'That incident gave me pause for thought,' admitted Drew soberly. 'I shall review my methods for the future.'

Hero's eyes sheened with tears. 'I am glad of that. No man should think himself worthy to be both judge and jury of the actions of others.'

Drew nodded. 'I realise that you have a point.'

Hero went on with her explanation, speaking gently. 'Also, the rumours of your involvement with other women persisted. You seemed to be two different men.'

He let go of her hands and stood up. Now she had offended him. Hero yearned to have him close to her again. But he stood apart, looking down on her with a strange glow in his eyes.

'You thought I had betrayed you with Elizabeth Warner. Dare I believe that you were jealous?'

'As the very devil!' declared Hero with unladylike forthrightness. 'What was your business with her?'

'You noticed that she is pregnant. I was not kissing her, merely offering comfort. Her husband was arrested before she realised her condition and was finally transported last week. She was distraught and came to me for help once again. You see, I seek out those left behind to starve, and do what I can for them. I have opened a home in Kent to house some of the families who would otherwise be begging on the streets.'

'Oh, Drew! Why did I not trust you? My love, can you forgive me?'

He pulled her to her feet and encircled her with his arms. Secure in his embrace, Hero lifted starry eyes to his, her mouth soft and vulnerable, expecting his kiss. His lips curved into a mischievous smile.

'I can forgive you anything as long as you call me

your love. Am I truly so, my dearest girl? Do you feel for me as I feel for you?'

'Oh, yes,' breathed Hero. 'I believed it was just a desire to have you again in my bed. I despised myself for my weakness. I did not want to love the kind of man I thought you were.'

Drew groaned. 'You, too? What fools we have been!'

'But I just could not help myself,' confessed Hero.

'Nor I,' admitted Drew, just as a knock at the door disturbed them. Reluctantly he allowed Hero to leave his arms.

'Come!' she called.

Dick peered in, his face rosy from fresh air and exercise. He bobbed his head in a respectful greeting. 'The chaise be here, my lady.'

'Oh, the chaise!' she glanced uncertainly at Drew. 'Thank you, Dick. I won't keep it waiting long.'

Drew eyed her somewhat warily. 'You were intending to travel?'

Hero blushed. 'I intended to return to Ashworthy. I left in a fit of anger and despair. I had already decided that, whatever you had done, life with you would be more agreeable than without. Shall I retain the chaise? We could return at once.'

'Now I am here I would prefer to stay for at least one night. I have, as you deduced, missed my sleep. And there must be estate matters which need my attention. Shall I pay off the post boy and send him away?'

'Yes. You could arrange for him to return tomorrow.'

'No need, my love. I crossed paths with Ned Tribble

on the way here. He has turned round and is following me back. Between them, he and Benbow persuaded me that I might hope for your return.' He took her hand and told her softly, 'They both informed me, though in different words, that my lack of thought, my failure to repose confidence in you, had caused you great unhappiness. Tribble said it had made you ill.' He touched the shadows under her eyes. 'He did not exaggerate.'

'Why did you not confide in me, Drew?'

He shook his head. 'I will explain. First I must dismiss the post chaise.'

Hero sank into the chair by the desk as he left the room and, elbows on its surface, rested her face in her hands. The relief was almost overwhelming but it was the knowledge that Drew loved her that brought joy bubbling to the surface. And renewed her strength. She could face anything, any further revelations he might have to make, confident in his love.

He was not absent for long. When he returned he sat in the baron's armchair and held out his hand.

'Come here.'

Hero obligingly went over to him and was immediately drawn down on his knees. Wrapped once again in his arms, she sighed contentedly. He kissed her and she almost forgot that she had asked him a question. But the answer seemed important and so, when she was able, she repeated it.

'How could I confide in you?' he murmured. 'You are your father's daughter. And what I had heard. . .'

'You thought I was like him.'

'Not for long.' He kissed her again. 'But speaking about my past, explaining my attempts to mete out retribution and confessing my other activities are things I find it difficult to do. Benbow knows everything, of course—he has been with me throughout—and so does Archie Dalmead. We struck up one of those friendships which seem predestined and he divined my true purposes almost at once. He helps where he can, but I exacted his promise not to reveal his knowledge to anyone. Anyone at all.'

'And as a man of honour he could not ease my mind! Neither could Benbow! Really, Drew——'

'Do not berate me! Even my mother does not know!'

'Well, I will berate you! For laying yourself open to a vindictive attack like that of Blacklock's. Do you not think, my lord, that to take up your seat in the House of Lords and to mount a campaign against transportation from there might be a safer and better way forward than to continue to take individual revenge on people? You could be another Wilberforce. He is winning his battle against the slave trade—it is already illegal here and will soon be banned throughout all our possessions. You could expose all the horrors of transportation and no one could accuse you of not knowing what you were talking about!'

Drew looked quite struck. 'No, though they might think me prejudiced! And the stigma might rub off on you, Hero. Would you not mind?'

She shook her head. 'I would join your campaign.'

'My darling!'

'And you should tell your mother, Drew.'

He grimaced. 'I suppose I should. And speaking of her, I did not wish you to meet her until I had assured myself that when you did you would not despise her.'

'Drew! Did you really think me such a snob?'

'After what I overheard I found it difficult to believe otherwise. I know better now. I think you will like each other and I will take you to see her very soon, I promise. I have told her all about you.'

Hero almost confessed to her visit then, but decided to keep to her original decision. Nothing would be gained by admitting to the acquaintance and she would deprive Drew of the pleasure of bringing his wife and his mother together.

So she merely said, 'I am certain I shall love her, as you do.' She grinned impishly. 'I do not imagine she is like Lady Edding. Felicity told Archie that she would rather marry him than Lord Edding because she would prefer his mother as an in-law!'

'And brought him to the point, the devious chit!'

Hero chuckled, her happiness overflowing to embrace their friends. 'I quite look forward to seeing Archie leg-shackled in June!'

'The wedding will be a large one. Not like ours. Would you have preferred a society affair, my love?'

'No. Just one in which I had some choice! But truly, as long as I am married to you I do not now care how it happened.'

He smothered a yawn but his declaration was none the less heartfelt. 'Nor I.'

'You must go to bed!' exclaimed Hero, all concern. 'We can talk of the future later. I would like to think Polhembury will receive better management than my father seems capable of giving. He has not paid the wages for weeks.'

'Do not concern yourself, my dear. Polhembury shall have a steward and will be restored to its former glory.

It is your inheritance, and must be protected as such. I had thought it necesssary to take matters into my own hands long ere this. I receive reports and they have not been good. Without your financial support——'

'You knew!'

'Little escapes me where you are concerned, my love. Only my stubborn blindness prevented me from acknowledging the truth about you months ago. When you went to your aunt's I realised just how much your presence meant to me. I tried to make things up to you. I thought you were happy, although you did not love me.'

'I was happy, until I saw you with Mrs Warner. And because I loved you so much I could not bear to see her in your arms!'

'Yes, that. And, since I was all innocence, I could not imagine why you had left me again! I determined not to follow you, to let you go if you must, but Benbow's disapproval and twenty-four hours of missing you were enough to send me galloping *ventre à terre* to win you back.'

'I am glad you came after me. I was returning to you, but it would not have been quite the same if you had not.' She stopped to kiss his tired eyes. 'You really must sleep, my love. But one more thing before you do. Mrs Cudlip, the vicar's wife, thinks I may be breeding. It would explain how dreadful I have been feeling recently.'

'My dearest love! That is the best news you could have given me! After news of your return to me, of course!' He looked at her, suddenly anxious. 'Did her revelation have anything to do with your decision to return?'

Hero stroked his rough, unshaven cheek. 'Only to confirm what I already knew. Child or not, I could not live without you.'

With every breath he became more certain of her love. He had only to look into the depths of her lovely hazel eyes to see his own emotions reflected there. Content, he kissed her again, a ravishing kiss, the effects of which went with him as he sought a bed in which to catch up on his lost sleep.

Hero had no doubts left, either. 'You may unpack again, Matty,' she informed her companion as she skipped into her bedroom. 'You were wrong for once! His lordship did come after me again and we have finally come to a complete understanding. He is resting now and we will be staying for at least one more night.' Despite all her experience, all the confidences she and Matty had shared, she could not stop the blush which suffused her features. 'He will, of course, sleep here with me.' Oh, how she longed for the night to come! 'Ned,' she went on, 'is on his way back and we will all return to Ashworthy together in the Calverstock coach.'

'Humph,' muttered Matty dourly, though her face was wreathed in smiles. 'I thought it was about time you two realised you were meant for each other.'

MILLS & BOON

Don't miss our great new series within the Romance line...

Landon's Legacy

One book a month focusing on each of the four members of the Landon family—three brothers and one sister—and the effect the death of their father has on their lives.

You won't want to miss any of these involving, passionate stories all written by Sandra Marton.

Look out for:

An Indecent Proposal in January '96
Guardian Groom in February '96
Hollywood Wedding in March '96
Spring Bride in April '96

Cade, Grant, Zach and Kyra Landon—four people who find love and marriage as a result of their legacy.

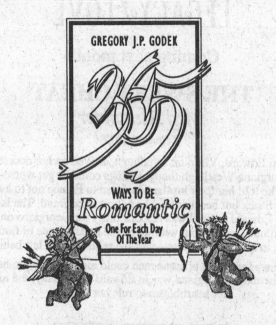

LEGACY of LOVE

Coming next month

THE SWEET CHEAT
Meg Alexander
Regency 1817

When Edward, Viscount Lyndhurst, arrived on her doorstep, Georgiana Westleigh thought things couldn't get worse—until he told her their brothers had fled to France not to avoid creditors, but because they had committed fraud. The last thing Edward wanted was responsibility for Georgiana on the hazardous journey, but without her he had no hope of finding them to sort out the mess—and she refused to be left behind.

She was sure this brusque man could mean nothing to her, but the more Georgiana was in Edward's company, the more her heart began to rule her head…

BELOVED WIFE
Lynda Trent
Texas 1887

She was a surprise package, this mail-order bride. Feisty, practical, caring, even pretty…and Clay Morgan caught himself wishing he could be a *real* husband to her. But that would never be, for his heart was married to a memory…

What Amity Becker needed was an escape. A safe haven from the scandal that haunted her. And someone who cared about her. What she got was a brooding Texas widower—with five daughters! A man whose heart was under lock and key. How could she convince Clay that she could be more than a wife in name only?

A year's supply of Mills & Boon Romances—absolutely FREE!

Would you like to win a year's supply of heartwarming and passionate romances? Well, you can and they're FREE! Simply complete the wordsearch puzzle below and send it to us by 30th June 1996. The first 5 correct entries picked after the closing date will win a years supply of Mills & Boon Romances (six books every month—worth over £100). What could be easier?

READER SERVICE
ROMANCE
RESIST
HEART
MEMORIES
PAGES
KISS
SPINE
TEMPTATION
LOVE
COLLECTION
ROSES
PACK
PARCEL
TITLES
DREAMS
COUPLE
SPECIAL EDITION
EMOTION
DESIRE
SILHOUETTE
MOODS
PASSION

M	E	R	O	W	A	L	R	L	M	S	P	C	O	S
O		E	C	I	V	R	E	S	R	E	D	A	E	R
R	O					E		O	S	M	A	E	R	D	S
O	D	H	E	A	R	T		S		S		S	E	L	T	I	T
M	S			S		E		M	E	M	O	R	I	E	S	S
A	E			C	G			S	A		C				E
N	P	T		A		E	K		W		O	I			W
C		T	P	K	I	S	S	C			L	T	T		O
E			E		H		A	E	V	O	L		E	N	N
	A	E		U		M		P	R		T	E	I	M	O	E
	E	N		L	O			L	I		S	C		P	I	O
	S	L	I			H	A		S		I	T		T	S	A
	P	P	A	R	C	E	L	N	E		S	I		A	S	Z
	U	S	D	B			I	D		E	O		T	A	I
O	O		O		N			B	S		R	N		I	P	S
	C		E	N	N	A	M	T	R	R	L	G	N	O	L	T
	O		E	M	O	T	I	O	N			O		N		I
N	O	I	T	I	D	E	L	A	I	C	E	P	S	K

Please turn over for details of how to enter...

How to enter

Hidden in the grid are words which relate to our books and romance. You'll find the list overleaf and they can be read backwards, forwards, up, down or diagonally. As you find each word, circle it or put a line through it.

When you have found all the words, don't forget to fill in your name and address in the space provided below and pop this page into an envelope (you don't need a stamp) and post it today. Hurry—competition ends 30th June 1996.

Mills & Boon Wordsearch
FREEPOST
Croydon
Surrey
CR9 3WZ

Are you a Reader Service Subscriber?　　Yes ❑　　No ❑

Ms/Mrs/Miss/Mr _____

Address _____

_____

_____ Postcode _____

One application per household.

You may be mailed with other offers from other reputable companies as a result of this application. If you would prefer not to receive such offers, please tick box. ❑

COMP295
F